DEADLY NIGHT

A DETECTIVE JANE PHILLIPS NOVEL

OMJ RYAN

INKUBATOR
BOOKS

Published by Inkubator Books
www.inkubatorbooks.com

ISBN (eBook): 978-1-915275-46-2
ISBN (Paperback): 978-1-915275-47-9

PROLOGUE

FRIDAY 5TH NOVEMBER 1993. 7 P.M.

As he watched, the number of people gathered around the unlit bonfire grew. Constructed over the past week by the residents of The Crescents from discarded pallets, broken chairs, old doors, and anything else flammable that could be found, the large pile towered fifteen feet into the air. It sat in the middle of the grassed area that surrounded The Crescents, a rundown council estate on the outskirts of Manchester city centre, to honour the British tradition dating back to the seventeenth century – the failed Gunpowder Plot by Guy Fawkes and his fellow conspirators. In the year 1605, they had attempted to blow up the Houses of Parliament. It was indeed a murderous plan, but at the eleventh hour it had been thwarted, resulting in the gang being hung, drawn and quartered for their treachery to the king, suffering unspeakable agony in the process. How fitting then, he thought, that tonight he would deliver his own brand of justice as the effigy of Guy Fawkes burned brightly on the inferno.

The time for him to make his move approached.

The sky was black and foreboding, with low-hanging

clouds. Excited chatter filled the chilly autumnal air as people made their way towards the scene of the upcoming celebration.

Pulling up the hood of his thick winter coat, he lowered his head slightly to hide his face, then slipped out of the shadows and made his way along the path towards the next block of dilapidated apartments. With people everywhere, he was just another person in the crowd: anonymous and unremarkable. Exactly what he wanted.

A few minutes later, he heard the unmistakeable whoosh of the petrol-soaked pallets being set alight. The flames spread across the bonfire in a matter of seconds. Checking his watch, he was pleased to see the organisers were sticking to their published schedule.

As he reached the bottom of a concrete stairwell that led up to the first- and second-floor apartments, he took a moment to survey the area for any unwanted eyes that may be watching him. But none of the people walking alongside him seemed to have the slightest interest in anything other than the raging bonfire. Confident of his anonymity, he turned away from the procession and took the stairs, slowly and deliberately.

Archie Boothroyd's apartment was on the second floor, on the opposite side of the building to the crowd gathered around the fire. It was one of the main reasons he'd chosen tonight to make his move. Everyone's attention would be else-where. The second reason – the fireworks display – was due to start at 7.30 p.m.

As he took up his position in the shadows at the end of the concrete landing – just opposite Boothroyd's apartment – he checked his watch; the time approached 7.15 p.m.

Boothroyd's front door had been broken down during a recent police raid, and a flimsy-looking makeshift repair had been attempted. It seemed the slightest bit of force applied would open it easily.

Everything was in place. All he had to do now was wait.

Wrapping his gloved fingers tightly around the handle of the pistol in his coat pocket, he imagined the look on Boothroyd's face as he stared down its barrel. It caused his spine to tingle. Archie Boothroyd was finally going to get what was coming to him, the treacherous prick. With his other hand, he tapped the industrial pliers in his left pocket, and smirked. He closed his eyes and waited.

Sometime later, the digital watch on his left wrist began to beep. It was 7.30 p.m. and time to go to work.

Releasing the pistol in his pocket, he pulled the black ski mask down over his face. A moment later, the first firework of the organised display soared, whistling, into the night sky before exploding with a loud bang. A second firework followed shortly after. Then the display erupted into life, sounding, to his ears, like machine gun fire.

There was no time to waste.

Stepping forward, he pulled the pistol from his pocket and kicked the makeshift front door. As expected, it offered no resistance.

Rushing inside, he spotted Archie at the end of the small hall, barefoot and dressed in shorts and T-shirt. Shock etched his face. 'Who the fuck are you?' he shouted, eyes wide. Archie had the physique of a man who spent a lot of time in the boxing gym. In any other circumstances, he would have been no match for Archie, but tonight he'd come prepared.

Archie raised his hands and began stepping backwards into the small lounge room, his eyes on the pistol. 'Whatever they're paying you, I'll double it,' he said as the fireworks continued to explode across the night sky outside.

'On your knees!' he shouted, and trained the gun on Archie's forehead. 'Do it! Do it, now!'

Archie appeared reluctant to follow the order at first, then slowly dropped to the floor, hands still raised.

'Not such a big man now, are you?' His pulse quickened as he clutched the pistol and stared down at his nemesis.

'Show me your face,' Archie demanded.

'Shut the fuck up. I'm giving the orders now,' he spat back, and slammed the pistol's muzzle onto the bridge of Archie's nose. Archie cried out as blood began to pour from his nostrils.

He glanced at his watch; it was 7.36 p.m. He had only a few minutes left before the fireworks ended. The gun in his hand shook as the enormity of what he was about to do finally hit him.

Archie winced in pain as he wiped blood from his nose with his left hand. 'What do you want?' he growled.

'Revenge. That's what I want.'

Boothroyd straightened and stared at him. 'I know you, don't I?'

He ignored the question and, as the fireworks came to a crescendo outside, thrust the pistol into Archie's eye socket. 'An eye for an eye, Archie!' he shouted, then pulled the trigger.

Boothroyd's head recoiled as fragments of skull and brain splattered on the wall opposite. A split second later, his lifeless body slumped to the ground in a heap. Blood soon pooled onto the grubby grey carpet, around the remains of his head. The room fell silent. The fireworks display came to an end, then the crowd began to applaud.

His heart pounded. He struggled to control his breathing as he took a moment to survey the macabre scene at his feet. He wasn't sure if it was adrenaline or hysteria, but he couldn't stop the smile of satisfaction that spread across his face. He felt giddy and lightheaded. Giggling to himself, he reached for the pliers in his coat pocket before kneeling down and locking them onto one of Archie's front teeth. 'A tooth for a tooth, you bastard,' he whispered, then yanked and pulled with all his might until the tooth finally came free.

Holding it up to the light, he examined the bloody roots before allowing it to drop into the palm of his gloved hand. A second later, he slipped it into the pocket of his jacket, along with the pistol and pliers.

Pulling off the ski mask, he took one last look at Archie Boothroyd's crumpled body. He resisted the temptation to spit on the corpse. *Leave nothing behind,* he reminded himself as he retraced his steps back to the front door. Closing it softly behind him, he checked left and right. No one had seen him. He moved gingerly along the concrete landing and back down to the stairs. A moment later, with little fuss, he joined the bustling crowd of spectators making their way home.

With his hood pulled up over his head, he weaved through the sea of people, careful to maintain a steady pace despite the adrenaline rushing through his veins. As he glanced at the faces around him, he wondered how long it would be before anyone realised what had happened. Who would be the first person to discover Boothroyd's body? In truth, it didn't matter. The job was done.

In time, there would be ramifications, but no one would ever come looking for *him*. Why would they?

The adrenaline started to wane, causing his mouth to dry. He found himself craving an ice-cold beer. *Why not?* he thought. The plan had worked like a charm. Boothroyd was dead, and revenge was indeed *sweet.*

1

DCI Jane Phillips took a seat next to Adam on the L-shaped grey sofa in the lounge. It was a balmy Sunday night, and she would have loved a glass of wine with dinner, but it wasn't possible due to her being the on-call senior investigating officer for the Major Crimes Unit of the Greater Manchester Police. Working weekends hadn't bothered her before Adam came into her life less than a year earlier. Nowadays, though, she hated waiting for the phone to ring, and resenting having to leave Adam at home when it did. As luck would have it, there had been no calls so far, no fresh crime scenes to view. Still, being the ultimate professional she was, she had remained on high alert since leaving the office on Friday night.

Cradling her hot cup of tea, she bent her legs back beside her on the sofa and settled down to watch the local news programme that always followed the national bulletin. It was only ten minutes long and focused predominantly on Greater Manchester events. Each time she watched it, she couldn't help but feel sorry for the local news anchors, squashed onto their flimsy-looking sets compared to the lavish surroundings enjoyed by their national counterparts.

Adam, wearing shorts and a T-shirt, moved to lie down on the seat, stretching his bare legs out so they rested on Phillips's knees. Instinctively, she dropped one of her hands onto his perfectly formed ankles and gently rubbed his soft, tanned skin.

'That's nice,' he murmured as he closed his eyes. 'Being on my feet all day every day is taking its toll on my trotters.'

Phillips chuckled at his description of his feet as she looked at his handsome face, filled with contentment. 'At least you get to wear trainers to work, babe. Not something I can see happening in my world.'

Adam was a senior emergency room doctor in the A&E department of the Royal Liverpool University Hospital, just under an hour's drive from Manchester. As he worked shifts, often through the night, and on weekends, whatever time they got to spend together was all the more precious.

'Watch this,' said Phillips.

Adam opened his eyes and looked at the TV. The news reporter stood with her back to a large fireworks display in full flow. The text banner placed her in Alexandra Park, a mile from the city centre in the suburb of Moss Side.

'I don't get it. Since when did we start celebrating the fourth of July in England?' asked Phillips.

'Since people realised they could make money from it,' Adam replied.

'But it's utter nonsense. Why would we, the English, celebrate having our arses kicked in the War of Independence?'

Adam smirked. 'Because we Brits have a morbid fascination with all things American. Plus, we have selective memories. If celebrating losing a war a couple hundred years ago gives us an excuse to dress up, get drunk and eat loads of rich food, then we'll gladly do it. Not to mention the fireworks; everyone *loves* fireworks,' he added playfully.

'I don't,' Phillips took a sip of her tea. 'They sound far too much like gun shots to me, and I've had enough of guns to last me a lifetime.'

'To be fair, I'm glad I'm not on shift tonight. The fourth of July is always crazy busy with people covered in burns from cheap or badly managed firework displays. In fact, I take it back. *No one* in A&E departments likes fireworks.'

The local news done, Phillips switched off the TV and dropped the remote onto the sofa, only just missing Floss, her blonde Ragdoll cat, who had suddenly appeared from nowhere in search of some attention. Drawing the animal into her arms, Phillips began to stroke her. Soon, the rhythmic sound of purring filled the air. Phillips yawned suddenly. 'I don't want to tempt fate, but I think I might go to bed.'

Adam checked his watch. 'Well, it's just over an hour till midnight. I'm sure you won't be called out before then.'

Phillips nodded, without conviction, and turned her attention back to Floss, stroking her thick blonde coat with relish.

'Janey?' said Adam, his tone unusually hesitant.

Phillips turned her head to face him.

'Have you thought anymore about us moving in together?'

Before she could check herself, she let out a frustrated sigh and closed her eyes.

'Obviously not,' said Adam sharply, pulling his legs away and sitting upright.

'Please, Adam, let's not have this conversation now. It's late and I'm tired.'

'You're not the only one,' Adam shot back. 'I'm tired of living out of a suitcase when I'm here, and tired of wasting money on a flat I hardly ever use. With our shift patterns, it's hard enough to see each other as it is. At least if we moved in together, we'd be able see each other every day.'

'Yeah. In passing, maybe,' Phillips replied.

Adam shook his head. 'I just don't get it, Jane. Why are you *so* against us living together?'

'I'm not. I just don't want to talk about it *right now*. Is that such a big deal?'

Just then, Phillips's mobile began to vibrate on the chair next to her. She picked it up. 'It's Jonesy. I have to take it.'

Adam stared at her without saying a word, then stood and headed for the kitchen.

Phillips watched him leave as she accepted the call. 'Jonesy. What's up?'

'Sorry, Guv. I know we're due off shift at midnight, but I think you'll want to see this one.' DS Jones was her second in command at Major Crimes.

'Go on.'

'I'm out in Alderley Edge. Two men broke in and murdered the homeowner, Paul Bradley.'

'As in *the gangster*, Paul Bradley?'

'Theoretically that's never proven, boss, but yeah, that Paul Bradley.'

Phillips got up off the sofa in a flash. 'I'm on my way.'

'And be prepared, Guv. It looks like shit got a bit weird.'

'How do you mean?'

'I'll explain it all when you get here.'

Phillips ended the call and made her way upstairs. Five minutes later, having swapped her jogging bottoms and T-shirt for her customary black pants, white shirt and charcoal suit jacket, she slipped on black boots, then pulled her dark hair into a ponytail and headed downstairs in search of Adam. She found him in the kitchen watching the smaller

TV, drinking a bottle of beer. 'Looks like I spoke too soon. A case has come in and I've got to get over to Alderley Edge.'

Adam nodded without taking his eyes off the screen.

'Look. I *will* talk about the moving in stuff soon. I promise.'

Adam didn't acknowledge her.

Phillips opened her mouth to try and explain, but thought better of it. She didn't have the energy for the fight, and she needed to get to the crime scene ASAP. 'I've gotta go,' she said, picked up her car keys from the bench, and headed for the front door. A moment later, she stepped outside and pulled the door firmly behind her till it locked. 'Why can't things stay the way they are?' she mumbled under her breath as she walked down the path towards her car.

2

_____

The journey from Phillips's home in the bohemian suburb of Chorlton to the affluent Cheshire village of Alderley Edge took just over half an hour thanks to the lack of traffic. It also helped that she drove her father's classic British racing green Mini Cooper, on loan due to his recent bout of seizures, which had him banned from driving for the next twelve months. She loved it because it was very low to the ground and incredibly powerful for such a small car. Her dad, once a high-ranking officer in the Hong Kong Police, had bought the car when she was a little girl. Being in it now conjured up memories of her childhood, with the smell of the old leather seats mixed with the faded aroma of the Chinese cigarettes her dad used to smoke. Happy memories from simpler times.

Following the Sat Nav on her phone, she took a left onto Swiss Hill and soon spotted the flashing lights from the ambulance and the patrol car. Parked next to them, she recognised the unmarked MCU squad car Jones used, and in front of that, the 4x4 that belonged to Andy Evans, the senior crime scene investigator. Pulling in behind the vehicles, she performed her normal ritual of cleaning her glasses and tightening her ponytail before opening the passenger door.

Jones appeared as she stepped out. 'So, finally I get to see the infamous Mini Cooper,' he said, taking in the little car. His accent was pure South London, his wiry frame accentuated by his slim-fitting suit.

'Thought I'd give it a spin,' Phillips said proudly as she closed the driver's door.

Jones placed his hand on the roof and bent forward to scan the interior through the window. 'I've wanted one of these ever since I saw Michael Caine and his gang chucking them around an Italian sewer.'

He was, of course, referring to the classic 70s movie, *The Italian Job*.

'"You're only supposed to blow the bloody doors off,"' he said, imitating Caine's infamous line from the film – and sounding just like him.

'You do that too well,' said Phillips. 'You've practiced, haven't you?'

Jones straightened up and grinned. 'Maybe once or twice.'

Phillips glanced towards the open door of the impressive-looking house in front of them, now sealed with blue and white police tape with a uniformed officer standing guard. 'So, what's the deal with this one? You said on the phone that shit got weird. In what way?'

'You'll see for yourself inside, but the headlines are: Evans reckons the victim was shot at close range through his eye socket...'

Phillips frowned.

'...and one of his front teeth has been pulled out.'

'Jesus. Not what you'd call a normal Sunday night in Alderley Edge, is it?'

'No. It's not.'

'So what the hell happened in there?'

'Well, like I mentioned on the phone. The victim has been identified as Paul Bradley, and from what I can gather from his wife, Melissa, two masked men entered the house a few hours ago, tied her up, then shot her husband.'

'How did they get in?'

'The French doors in the lounge had been left open.'

Phillips closed her eyes for a moment. 'Jesus. Why do people do that? This is Manchester, for God's sake.'

'Hot summer night, I guess. And like you said, people don't expect this kind of stuff in a leafy suburb like this, do they?'

'Any signs of a robbery? Anything taken?'

Jones shook his head. 'Nothing.'

'So we could be looking at a professional hit, then?'

'Potentially. I mean, there's been rumours about Bradley being involved in the drugs trade for years, but so far nothing's ever been proven.'

Phillips glanced towards the house once again. 'Just because we couldn't prove it doesn't mean it didn't happen. Come on. We'd better get in there and have a look.'

'I'll take you in, Guv.' said Jones, and led the way up the gravel drive.

As they reached the front steps, they stopped to put on protective shoe coverings and latex gloves left in place by the crime scene investigators, then headed up to the front door.

The uniformed officer lifted the police tape and nodded. 'Ma'am.'

Phillips nodded silently in return as she followed Jones underneath the tape and through into the expansive double-height hallway. A grand, split staircase ran from the centre of the space up to the curved balcony above. Two large doors were positioned ahead of them on the ground floor, one to the left and the other to the right, leading to each side of the house.

'Very posh,' she said softly, gazing around the opulent space.

Jones gestured in the direction of the left-hand door. 'The wife and son are in the kitchen with the paramedics. She doesn't appear to have any injuries, but they're giving her the once-over just to be sure. I explained you were coming and that you'd have some questions, but I figured you'd want to see the body first.'

'You know me too well.'

Jones thumbed to the right. 'Over this side of the house. In his office.'

This time, Phillips led the way. She found Evans and his team at the murder scene. As ever, each of the CSIs sported the prerequisite forensic suits with hoods pulled up, along with face masks, gloves and shoe coverings. They were busy collecting samples of what looked like blood and brains from the far wall, as well as looking for any less obvious trace evidence left around the room.

Bradley's corpse, in a crumpled heap on the floor, legs partly buckled under the torso, looked untouched. What remained of the head lay at an angle, facing the carpet. One of the eyes was gone, thanks to the killer's bullet, while the other stared straight ahead at death. Phillips took a careful step forward and squatted for a moment, taking a closer look at the victim's mouth and the large gap at the front where a tooth was missing. She stood again, taking mental pictures of the scene as she did. 'Has the house been swept? Are we sure this is the only body?'

'Provisionally,' Evans chimed in as he turned to face them. 'So far, everything suggests he was killed in here. We'll check each of the rooms in due course.'

'Ok, thanks Andy.' Phillips turned her attention back to Jones. 'Well, I think I've seen enough in here for now. Let's go and talk to the wife and son, shall we?'

They were met by one of the uniformed paramedics as they stepped back into the entrance hall. He had finished his examination and was heading back outside to the ambulance. 'She's fine, as far as I can tell. I've suggested she come with us to the hospital to get a full check-up, but she said she doesn't want to come. The reality is, I can't force her. So she's all yours.'

'Thanks,' said Jones, before leading the way into the gargantuan open-plan kitchen.

Inside, a dark-haired woman with an expensive-looking haircut – Phillips placed her in her early fifties – was perched on a high stool next to the large granite-topped island, staring into a brandy glass cradled in her hands. A man, who appeared to be in his late twenties, sat next to her, an arm around her shoulders. Both looked up as Jones and Phillips walked in.

'This is DCI Phillips, the senior investigating officer on the case,' said Jones. 'Guv, this is Paul's wife, Melissa, and his son, Freddie.'

Phillips offered a faint smile. 'I'm very sorry for your loss.'

'Well, what the fuck are you gonna do about it?' Freddie snapped.

Phillips didn't bite. She'd been here before and knew shock could cause outbursts and anger. Instead, she focused her gaze on Melissa. 'My sergeant has briefed me already, but it'd be really helpful if you could you tell me, in your own words, what happened here tonight.'

Melissa pulled a tissue from a box on the countertop and wiped her nose briefly as she took a deep breath. 'I was upstairs in the bedroom when it happened. Earlier tonight, I thought I could feel a migraine coming on, so decided to have a bit of a lie down on the bed.'

'What time was that?' asked Phillips.

Melissa took a moment to think. 'It must have been about

8 o'clock or so, because the fireworks in the village had just started. Paul and I had planned to go along to the display, but I didn't feel up to it, so we stayed in.'

Phillips glanced at Freddie. 'Were you here as well?'

'No,' he said, shaking his head. 'I was at my mate's place in the city, with a girlfriend of mine. I came over as soon as Mum called me.'

'I see,' replied Phillips. 'OK. So, what happened next?'

'I was lying there with my eyes closed when I could have sworn I heard raised voices downstairs. I didn't know if I was imagining it or if it was the fireworks. Anyway, I got up off the bed and shouted down to Paul to see what was going on. When he didn't answer, I went out onto the landing and shouted down again. That's when I saw him walking out of Paul's office...'

'Who did you see?' asked Phillips gently.

'A masked man.'

'Where was Paul?'

'I don't know. In his office, I guess. I couldn't see him at that point. Just the man in the mask.'

Phillips nodded.

'He started up the stairs towards me, so I panicked and ran for my phone to call the police, but by the time I'd unlocked the handset, he was already in the bedroom.' Melissa closed her eyes and a tear rolled down her cheek.

'You're doing really well,' said Phillips. 'What happened then?'

'He grabbed the phone off me and threw it across the room. Then he pushed me face down onto the bed and wrapped his hand over mouth and put gaffer tape over it so I couldn't scream. I was terrified he was going to rape me and I tried to fight him off, but he was too strong. He climbed on top of me to hold me down as he taped up my wrists and ankles. When he was done, he left me lying on the bed and left the room. A few minutes later, I heard more raised voices; Paul's, and at least two other people I didn't recognise.'

'Are you saying more than one person broke in?'

Melissa's brow furrowed. 'I think so. I couldn't hear all that clearly from up there, but it sounded like it to me.'

'Ok. So then what happened?'

'I heard Paul shouting, telling them to get the fuck out of the house. Then, not long after, there was a really loud bang that sounded like a firework going off inside. Again, I wasn't sure if I'd imagined it or if it was the fireworks from the village, but then I couldn't hear anything.'

'Who raised the alarm?' asked Phillips.

'Me. The tape on my wrists wasn't all that tight, so I managed to get a hand free and pulled the rest off. I crept onto the landing again and listened out for them, but the house was totally silent. I waited there for ages before I plucked up the courage to come downstairs. That's when...' Melissa's words tailed off as her shoulders began to shake and tears welled in her eyes.

'Does she really need to talk about this right now?' Freddie cut in.

Phillips locked eyes with him. 'I know this is very difficult, but it's vital we understand as much as possible about what happened while it's still fresh in your mother's memory.'

'I'll tell you what happened,' said Freddie. 'Adders Bahmani and his crew broke in here and murdered my dad.'

Phillips recoiled slightly. 'Bahmani? What makes you think Bahmani was involved?'

'Because he's been threatening my dad for months and telling everyone and anyone that will listen that he's taking over his business. Plus, Mum said she thought the guy that tied her up was Asian.'

Phillips glanced at Melissa again. 'Is that right, Mrs Bradley?'

'Yes. The skin on his wrists was brown. I saw it when he put it over my mouth.'

'Did he speak to you at all when he was tying you up?'

'Briefly. He told me to be quiet if I wanted to live.'

'And did you detect an accent of any kind?'

'To be honest, it sounded mixed.'

Phillips's brow furrowed. 'How do you mean *mixed*?'

Melissa took a moment to find the right description. 'You know. Manchester, but there was a trace of something else underneath, another accent. Maybe Indian or Pakistani.'

'I see,' said Phillips, glancing at Jones, who was scribbling in his notepad.

'I'm telling you, it was Bahmani,' said Freddie. His agitation showed no sign of dissipating. 'And if *you* don't get him for what he did to my dad, *I* bloody will.'

Melissa slammed her hand down on the countertop. 'Shut up, Freddie. Don't be so stupid.'

Phillips observed as the young man stared at his mother with wide eyes, then attempted to stifle his anger. It was evident he had a temper and didn't like being told what to do.

Phillips locked eyes with Freddie. 'You can rest assured, we'll do everything we can to catch the people who did this. Right now, the best thing *you* can do is take care of your mum. We don't need anyone taking matters into their own hands, ok?'

Freddie said nothing.

'*Ok?*' Phillips repeated.

'He's just angry,' said Melissa. 'He didn't mean it.'

Freddie stared at Phillips for a long moment, his eyes filled with rage, before looking away.

'Do you have anywhere you can stay tonight?' asked Phillips. 'The forensic team will be here most of the night, and until the house has been swept clean, I'm afraid you can't be here.'

'We can go to my sister's,' said Melissa wearily.

Phillips pulled a business card from her pocket and passed it over. 'I'm sure we'll talk again, but in the meantime, if you think of anything that might be relevant or you may have forgotten, please call me, day or night.'

Melissa took the card and placed it on the countertop before taking a gulp from the brandy.

'Well, we'll be going,' said Phillips, and signalled to Jones to lead the way out.

'Quite a temper the son has,' said Phillips as they walked down the long drive.

'Yeah. A proper hothead.'

'Let's keep an eye on him. The last thing we need is him stirring up trouble.'

'Will do, Guv.'

'So, what do you think about his claims it was Bahmani?'

Jones blew his lips. 'I wouldn't put many things past that slimy bugger, but murder? I'm not so sure that's his style.'

Phillips stopped as they reached her car. 'Me neither. Plus, there's something familiar about this crime scene.'

'In what way?'

Phillips shook her head. 'I'm not sure, but I felt like I was having déjà vu in there. Almost as if I'd seen it before.'

'Really?'

'Yeah. Don't ask me why.'

'You been working on your psychic powers again?' said Jones.

'Something like that.'

'Maybe you should start doing the lottery.'

Phillips laughed. 'Yeah, maybe. Well, there's nothing more we can do tonight. Come on. Let's get some sleep.'

Jones nodded.

'Can you pick me up in the morning?' Phillips asked. 'I

think we should go and say hi to Mr Bahmani. His yard is as good a place as any to start the investigation.'

'Eight o'clock?'

'Perfect.' Phillips opened the door to the Mini.

Jones placed his hand on the roof of the tiny car. 'Any chance I could drive us over there in this?'

Phillips jumped in behind the wheel. 'What? And take my dad's pride and joy to Bahmani's scrap yard? You need your head checking, Jonesy.'

'Well, it was worth a shot,' chuckled Jones.

'See you tomorrow,' said Phillips with a smile, then closed the door and fired the engine.

3

MONDAY 5TH JULY

Adders Scrap Metal Merchants, located in the industrial suburb of Ancoats just north of Manchester city centre, was surrounded on all sides by chain-link fencing topped with rings of razor wire. Signs attached to the perimeter warned of guard dogs on patrol 24 hours a day, and the yard was piled high with vehicles in varying states of dismemberment. The whole place emanated a sense of foreboding to the uninitiated. However, Adders Bahmani was well known to Phillips and Jones, and this was not the first time they'd visited the headquarters of his various business enterprises.

On the journey over, Phillips made a call to the office and briefed Entwistle on the night's events. An early riser, he could always be counted on to be at his desk before anyone else. It was one of the many things she liked about working with him.

As the time approached 9 a.m., Jones guided the unmarked MCU squad car onto the grubby lot and parked up next to Bahmani's gleaming white Range Rover Sport. He eyed the expensive SUV as he switched off the engine. 'As my old dad used to say, "There's money in scrap."'

'And drugs and prostitution,' Phillips shot back sarcastically.

'If only we could prove it, Guv.'

'Yeah. *If only.*'

It was set to be another baking hot summer's day. The sun shone brightly in a clear blue sky as they stepped out of the car and made their way towards the door of the Portakabin that acted as Bahmani's office. Phillips stopped just outside. Bahmani's cousin, Tahir, was already at the wheel of a large fork-lift truck, carrying what looked like the shell of an old Ford Mondeo towards the compactor.

'Busy boy,' said Jones, following her gaze. 'Doing Bahmani's dirty work.'

'I wonder what other dirty work he does for him,' Phillips mused before climbing the steep metal steps and entering the office.

Bahmani sat at far end of the space in a black leather office chair, behind a large oak desk and hunched over his laptop. He glanced up as they walked in, and immediately closed the screen. 'You never heard of knocking?' he said curtly, his accent thick Mancunian with a hint of Urdu.

Phillips flashed her ID. 'I don't need to knock when I've got one of these.'

Bahmani, sporting a heavy gold chain around his neck and wearing a navy blue Lacoste polo shirt, reclined in his chair and folded his thick arms across his chest. 'So, what do you want *this time*?'

There were no other chairs on offer, so Phillips and Jones remained standing. 'Where were you around 8 o'clock last night?' she asked.

'At home,' Bahmani said, without missing a beat.

'Anybody vouch for that?'

'My wife.'

Phillips forced a thin smile. 'Ah, the ever-faithful alibi of Mrs Bahmani.'

Bahmani matched her smile. 'What can I say? We like spending time together.'

'So you weren't in Alderley Edge last night, then?'

'Why would I be all the way out there?'

Phillips stared him straight in the eye. 'Murdering Paul Bradley so you could take over his business empire.'

Bahmani's eyes widened. 'Paul Bradley's *dead*?'

'Yes he is, and we have good reason to believe you were involved in his murder.'

'Me?' Bahmani guffawed, rocking back in his chair. 'I think you must be mistaken Chief Inspector. I'm a scrap metal merchant. Nothing worth killing for in this game. Besides, Bradley's into clubs and restaurants. Not my thing.'

'Really? Because his son reckons you've been trying to buy him out for months.'

'Young Freddie?' Bahmani shook his head. 'I think the boy's getting ahead of himself. His dad and I *did* have a conversation a while back about him selling me a few of his business interests, but we couldn't agree a price, so it never went any further.'

Phillips eyed him suspiciously. 'Which businesses in particular?'

'Why do you wanna know?'

'Because I'm investigating Paul Bradley's murder and it might be relevant.'

Bahmani sat forward now and linked his fingers together on the desk. 'Do I need to call my lawyer?'

'You tell me.'

Bahmani remained silent for a moment as his gaze dropped to his hands on the desk, then sighed loudly as he looked up again. 'Is it because I'm Asian, Chief Inspector?'

Phillips recoiled. 'I'm sorry?'

'This harassment. Is it because I'm Asian? I mean, you've got form for it, haven't you? It wasn't that long ago you were accusing me of murdering all those prostitutes in the canal. And that turned out to be one of *your* lot.'

Phillips's brow furrowed. 'That's a ridiculous thing to say. I'm not harassing you.'

'Oh yes you are. Some white guy from a posh part of town gets murdered and what's the first thing you do? Come and knock on my door, all the way over here in north Manchester. Why aren't you speaking to his neighbours, asking what they were up to?'

'We're simply following a line of enquiry.'

'Based on what evidence?'

'Like I said, we have a witness who believes you could have been involved.'

Bahmani scoffed. 'So why haven't you arrested me, then? If you had anything concrete, you'd have kicked my front door in last night. But you didn't, which means you *don't*.'

Phillips said nothing for a moment as she held his gaze.

Bahmani nodded as he reached into his pocket for his phone. 'I think maybe I will call my lawyer and see whether she thinks this is harassment or not.' He unlocked the screen. 'Unless, of course, this conversation is over, Chief Inspector?'

He was right, of course. As it was, they had nothing on him other than the word of a hot-headed grieving son. That said, it still took all her strength not to reach across the desk and drag his arrogant arse over it. Deep down, she believed he was dirty, but there was nothing to be gained by pressing him further at this moment in time.

'We're done,' she said. 'For now, at least.'

Bahmani grinned. 'Close the door on your way out, will you?' he said. Without looking at them, he opened the laptop once more and began typing.

4

Phillips decided she needed a coffee to help improve her mood, so headed to the canteen as soon as they arrived back at HQ, while Jones went straight upstairs.

As she queued for drinks for the team, her mind wandered back to the scene of Paul Bradley's murder. She couldn't shake the sense of familiarity. Where had she seen something similar before?

Ten minutes later, and armed with a cardboard tray containing four steaming cups, she wandered into the Major Crimes office on the third floor.

The man-mountain that was DC Bovalino sat at his desk staring at his ancient PC monitor, a scowl of concentration on his thick brow, his huge fist clenched and propping up his chin as his elbow rested on the desk.

'He looks like he's got wind, doesn't he, Guv?' teased Jones as Phillips placed a coffee cup in front of the big man.

'Piss off,' replied Bovalino with a grin.

'It's all those meatballs he eats,' added DC Entwistle, who sat opposite the big Italian.

Entwistle was the odd one out on the team. Of mixed race, tall and athletic, he carried himself with the grace and poise of a fashion model, and had the chiselled features to match.

Phillips handed him his usual Earl Grey tea and took a seat next to him at the spare desk on the bank of four. 'There you go, Whistler,' she said, using his nickname.

'How did it go with Bahmani?' Entwistle asked, removing the lid before taking a tentative sip of the steaming liquid.

'It didn't. Claims he has an alibi for last night, and that we're only asking questions because of his ethnicity.'

Entwistle's face crumpled slightly. 'He what?'

'Thinks we're harassing him cos he's Asian,' Jones cut in.

'Pah,' scoffed Bovalino. 'Bahmani's a total rat-bag, Guv, plain and simple.'

'You know that, and I know that, but true to form, we've got nothing we can pin on him.'

'The Teflon Man,' muttered Bovalino.

'Exactly,' replied Phillips. 'But I don't care what he claims. I want him checked out from top to bottom. Let's look at his phone records, any ANPR or traffic cameras near his house – or the Bradleys', for that matter – and see if you can find any CCTV around the crime scene.'

'I can do that, Guv,' said Bovalino, making a note in his pad.

'Good.' Phillips placed her cup down on the desk. 'There's something else that's bothering me about this case.'

'What you thinking?' asked Jones.

'Just what I mentioned last night at the Bradleys'. That the crime scene looked somehow familiar.' She turned to Entwistle. 'How far back do the GMP's digital records go?'

Entwistle shrugged. 'I wouldn't know specifically, but I can quickly check.' He began typing into his laptop.

As he did, the rest of the team sat in silence, nursing their hot drinks.

A few minutes later, he found what he was looking for. 'Depending on the type of information you want, the oldest case files were logged as far back as 1986. However, it seems the early digital logs recorded just the top-line information.'

'Which was what?' asked Phillips.

'Looks like the case number, type of crime – with a brief description such as murder, knife attack, etc. – the victim's name, the lead detective's name and rank, and a filing location for the physical evidence in the records room. If you click on it, it also gives you a short paragraph of detail.'

'Is it possible to do a search on the type of crime committed?'

Entwistle's eyes narrowed as he navigated the system on screen. 'I'm pretty sure you can, yeah.'

Phillips sat forward now. 'Try typing in murder, shot through the eye.'

He followed the instructions. 'Nothing coming up.'

'Try shot in the face instead.'

Once again Entwistle did as instructed. A moment later, his eyes widened. 'Wow, looks like there's loads on here.'

'You're joking?' Jones cut in.

Entwistle shook his head. 'I'm not. There's got to be at least fifty cases containing the description "shot in the face" since 1986.'

'What a lovely city we live in,' Jones said sarcastically.

'Better than that southern shithole you come from,' Bovalino quipped.

Jones opened his mouth to respond, but appeared to think better of it when he spotted Phillips glaring at him.

'Are you two quite finished?' she asked through a half smile.

Jones nodded.

Phillips turned back to Entwistle. 'Can you read the victims' names out to me?'

'Sure, boss. Daniel Ambrose, Stuart Barrie, Lennox Thomas, John Farrar...'

Entwistle continued for another minute, when Phillips interrupted him. 'Say that one again?'

'Archie Boothroyd?'

'That name rings a bell for some reason. Can you open his file?'

Entwistle obliged, and began reading from the screen. 'Archie Boothroyd, murdered. Shot in the face in his flat in The Crescents in Hulme, November fifth, 1993.'

Phillips stood and moved to his shoulder so she could see the screen.

'And look at this, Guv.' Entwistle tapped the screen with his pen. 'It says one of Boothroyd's teeth had also been removed.'

'That's it!' cried Phillips. 'That's why Bradley's murder looked so familiar. It's because it was the same as *Archie Boothroyd's*.'

Jones frowned. 'Who's Archie Boothroyd?'

Phillips continued to stare at the information on screen. 'God, it's totally coming back to me now.' She patted Entwistle on the shoulder as she turned her attention to Jones. 'We studied Archie Boothroyd's murder when I was training at the academy.'

'Wow, that's going back a long time, boss,' Jones joked.

'Hey!' said Phillips with a chuckle. 'Anyway, listen. Boothroyd was shot through the eye on Bonfire Night, at the exact same time a fireworks display was taking place outside his flat. And like Entwistle just said, the killer pulled out one of his teeth.'

'Exactly the same as Paul Bradley last night,' muttered Jones.

'Bloody hell,' Bovalino said. 'Well, that can't be a coincidence, can it?'

'No, because there's no such thing as coincidence in our world, Bov.' Phillips never tired of reminding the team of this fact.

'So, what? We could be looking for a copycat killer almost thirty years in the making?' asked Entwistle.

'Or the same killer,' replied Phillips. 'Boothroyd's case was never solved.'

Jones ran his hand through his thinning hair and let out an exasperated sigh. 'Just when I think I've seen it all in this job.'

Phillips stood up straighter. 'I know. It gets weirder by the week, doesn't it? So we have to wonder, if it was a copycat killer – or even the *same* killer from the Boothroyd case – why now? Why wait almost three decades to kill in this way again?'

The team fell silent for a long moment.

'Ok,' said Phillips. 'The first thing we need to do is get a hold of the hard copy of Archie Boothroyd's case file and go over every detail of how he was killed back in '93.'

'I'll get right onto it, boss,' Entwistle said.

'As quick as you can, Whistler,' said Phillips. 'These murders are so similar I'm sure these two cases have to be linked in some way. Now all we have to do is found out how.'

5

TUESDAY 6TH JULY

Phillips was running late, so decided to skip breakfast. When she made her way into the kitchen to say goodbye to Adam, he was stood next to the kettle, waiting for it to boil.

'Seeing as you're obviously not having breakfast, I'm making you a coffee to take with you,' he said, and grabbed a travel mug.

'Don't worry. I'll get one on the way.'

'It's almost ready,' he replied as the kettle finally boiled.

As he poured the water into the cup, she headed into the hall in search of the keys for the Mini, returning a moment later with them in her grasp.

Adam handed her the mug before leaning forward to kiss her on the forehead.

'Thanks,' said Phillips. 'I'd better go. I promised Tan I'd be with her at 8.30 at the latest.'

Adam offered a cheeky grin. 'How is Doctor Death?'

'She's fine, and don't let her catch you calling her that.'

'I won't. Let her catch me, that is.'

Phillips punched him playfully on the arm. 'Will I see you tonight?'

'Yeah. In fact, I was hoping we could have that chat about us moving in together.'

Phillips felt her jaw tighten.

'For once, could you at least try and look like you don't hate the idea?' Adam had obviously noticed.

'I don't hate it.'

'So what's the problem?'

Phillips glanced up at the large clock on the wall of the kitchen. 'Look. I don't have time to get into this now. Can we talk about it later?'

Adam shook his head and exhaled loudly. 'Look, just forget I even brought it up.'

Phillips grabbed his hand. 'Hey, don't be like that. We will talk about this, I promise, but I've really got to go.' She kissed him on the cheek. 'Have a good day.' With that, she marched down the hall and out through the front door, into another warm summer's day.

Since being asked to look after her dad's Mini Cooper for an extended period, she'd decided not to bring squad cars home unless absolutely necessary. Driving the Mini was much more fun, and a lot easier in rush hour traffic. Plus, parking the tiny car was a breeze. Now considered a classic, it had been built long before central locking, which meant she had to use the key to open the door. It had also been designed without the now-ubiquitous cupholders of modern vehicles, so as she jumped in the driver's seat, she took a moment to carefully place her steaming coffee in the special holder Adam had installed for her a few weeks ago. Next, she pulled on her prescription sunglasses in an attempt to block out the glare of the early morning sunshine, and with everything finally in place, she set off on her journey to Manchester

Royal Infirmary and her first appointment of the day – Paul Bradley's post mortem.

The journey into the city took Phillips through the suburbs of Chorlton and Whalley Range, then along the border of Hulme – the location of Archie Boothroyd's murder almost three decades ago. It looked very different now, of course. The Crescents – a vast concrete jungle that had covered the area and became a breeding ground for violent crime, drug use and gang warfare – had been demolished, flattened and regenerated at the turn of the century. A brand-new Hulme for a brand-new millennium. Casting her gaze across the myriad redbrick townhouses, large blocks of flats and overspill university campus buildings, it was difficult to imagine how close it had once come to being a war zone.

Zooming past the Heineken Brewery as she intersected the Princess Parkway, she headed for the MRI at speed. She *hated* being late.

Mercifully, she spotted the unusual sight of a parking space on the ground floor as she pulled the Mini into the multi-storey car park that annexed the hospital. It soon became evident why no one had taken it: juxtaposed to a huge 4x4, it was way too small to fit most modern cars. But the Mini slipped in easily. Switching off the engine, she took a moment to straighten her ponytail and switch her sunglasses for spectacles, then stepped out of the car, locked it and headed at pace for the main building.

Phillips reached the reception area and took the stairs down to the basement, where the morgue was located. Standing outside the locked doors, she pressed the intercom and waited for the loud buzz signalling the electric lock's release, then stepped inside. The smell of chemicals was instant and pervasive.

The chief pathologist, Doctor Tanvi Chakrabortty, waited for her in reception, dressed in her usual blue scrubs and

Crocs on her feet. In spite of her attire, she appeared as tall and elegant as ever as she moved with quiet grace across the polished floor. 'Morning Jane,' she said, handing Phillips an orange apron and a face mask.

'Morning, Tan. Sorry I'm a bit late.'

Chakrabortty flashed a smile of perfect white teeth, accentuated by her prominent cheekbones. 'I'll let you off, just this once.'

Phillips returned her smile.

'Mr Bradley is ready and waiting. Shall we go through?'

'I'm all yours.'

A few minutes later, Phillips stood opposite Chakrabortty at the mortuary table. 'Good job I skipped breakfast,' she said playfully.

'Don't make a habit of it, Jane. The most important meal of the day,' replied Chakrabortty as she pulled back the green sheet that covered Bradley's torso. 'Right. Let's see what happened to him, shall we?'

The post mortem took the usual ninety or so minutes. Phillips watched on as Chakrabortty worked methodically, and with great deference for Bradley's corpse. The sound of the small circular saw cutting through his skull made Phillips's toes curl. It was something she'd witnessed many times before but never quite come to terms with, and she was relieved, to say the least, when that part of the examination was complete.

As the examination drew to a close, Chakrabortty summed up her conclusions. 'Without any other wounds to the body, we can say for sure that the bullet through the eye killed him. The damage to the brain stem would have been catastrophic, and life would have been extinct almost instantly. To be honest, I'd say he was probably dead by the time he hit the floor.'

Phillips nodded and pulled down her face mask. 'And you said the tooth was pulled post mortem?'

'Yep.'

'That's what so odd. Why pull it after he was dead?'

Chakrabortty shrugged. 'That's your department, Jane, but my best guess would be as some kind of a trophy.'

'Yeah, it would make sense, wouldn't it? Did you manage to get a look at the records for the Archie Boothroyd post mortem?'

'I did. I have to say, they do look pretty much identical. The shot to the right eye, the tooth pulled post mortem. It's uncanny.'

'So it's more than possible they're connected?' asked Phillips.

'I'd certainly say it's a *possibility*, yes. But equally, it's a well-known historical case and you can find loads of information about it online now. Anyone with a smartphone could have read up on the details of how Boothroyd died and copied them.'

Phillips said nothing for a moment. As useful as the confirmation of cause of death was, it really didn't move the case forward in any meaningful way. 'Thanks, Tan,' she said eventually, feeling more than a little deflated.

'Sorry I can't give you anything more concrete.'

Phillips checked her watch. It was approaching 10.30 a.m. 'I'd better be going. See what else the team have managed to dig up on this one while I've been out.'

Chakrabortty removed her latex gloves and dropped them into the peddle bin, leaving it open for Phillips, who quickly pulled off her own apron and mask and threw them in.

'One of the team will email over the full report, either this afternoon or first thing in the morning,' said Chakrabortty.

'Great. Much appreciated.' Phillips made to leave.

'By the way, Jane, are you still seeing that dishy doctor from Liverpool?'

Phillips stopped in her tracks for a moment, their morning's disagreement flooding into her mind. 'Adam? Yeah. Why do you ask?'

'No reason,' replied Chakrabortty. 'I was just wondering if you were finally managing to have some kind a personal life outside of all this craziness.'

Phillips forced a thin smile. 'In this job, is there really such a thing, Tan?' she asked, and headed for the door.

6

Phillips made it back to the office within the hour. Once in the MCU, she took up her usual position at the spare desk and briefed the guys on Chakraborty's somewhat frustrating findings.

'So, what have you got for me?' she asked once she was done.

Entwistle lifted a large cardboard box onto his desk. 'This arrived from archives about twenty minutes ago. It contains photocopied duplicates of every piece of evidence gathered in the original Boothroyd murder.'

'Wow,' said Phillips. 'Looking at that box takes me back.'

Jones chuckled. 'To a land before shared drives and data clouds, you mean?'

Entwistle lifted the lid off and rested it against the side of his desk. 'I don't know how you kept track of everything with so much paper.'

'Looks like you've got a lot of reading to catch up on, Whistler,' quipped Bovalino.

Entwistle sighed. 'Doesn't it?' He fished out a thick Manila folder and passed it to Phillips.

As she scanned the first page, she spotted a name she recognised. 'DCI Stuart Monaghan was the SIO. I'd forgotten that. Long since retired, I'm guessing.'

'Almost thirty years on? I'd say so,' Jones cut in.

Phillips continued flicking through the pages, though she had no idea what she was looking for.

'I'll dig into the files over the next few days and see if I can trace the original investigators.' Entwistle retook his seat. 'Hopefully they'll be up for talking to us about it.'

'They will. I'm sure of it. If there's one thing detectives hate, it's unsolved cases. Thirty years is a long time to sit and wonder who did it.'

'Alternatively,' said Jones, folding his arms across his chest, 'they may want to distance themselves from what is still seen as one of the great failures in GMP policing.'

He had a point. She turned her attention to Bovalino. 'What did you find on our friend Bahmani?'

The big Italian glanced down at his notepad and shook his head. 'As ever, he's clean as a whistle, Guv. The phone company placed his phone at his address from 6 p.m. Sunday all the way through to 8 a.m. Monday, when he headed to the yard.'

'And what about ANPR and CCTV?'

'I'm still working on the CCTV in the area. The council are dragging their feet on the footage from their cameras, but after he arrived home, there's no sign of his car anywhere on ANPR that night.'

'Well, he was never going to make it easy, was he?' replied Phillips. 'As we've seen many times before, just because his phone was home doesn't mean *he* was. The same goes for his car. If Bahmani *was* going to commit murder, he's smart enough to know we could trace his movements through both. So, as far as I'm concerned, he's still in the frame. Chase down that CCTV, Bov, and if you need someone to stick a boot up the council's arse, just shout. I'm sure Carter will be more than happy to wade in.'

Bovalino made a note in his pad.

'You're looking for anything, no matter how small, that suggests he was in or near Alderley Edge when Bradley was murdered.'

'On it, Guv.'

Just then, Phillips's phone began to ring in her office, which usually meant either Chief Superintendent Carter or, heaven forbid, the chief constable was trying to reach her. She moved quickly back to her desk to answer it. 'Phillips.'

'*Good morning, Ma'am. I have a call for you.*' It was from reception.

'Who is it?'

'*I'm afraid he wouldn't give his name.*'

'Well, did he at least say what he wanted?'

'*No, Ma'am. Just that it was about the Bradley case and he would only speak to you.*'

'Put him through,' said Phillips.

There was an audible click on the line, followed by a moment of silence. '*Is that Phillips?*' The voice sounded distorted, as if it was being filtered electronically.

'Yes, Chief Inspector Phillips. Who am I speaking to?'

'*That's not important right now.*'

'Well, it'd help if I knew what to call you.'

'*No names.*' The voice was measured.

'Ok. So, what can I do for you? The receptionist said you had information relating to Paul Bradley.'

'*I know where you can find the gun that was used to shoot him.*'

Phillips felt a rush of excitement, but kept it in check. After all, this wouldn't be the first time she'd received a crank call. 'Really? So where is it?'

'*Adders Scrap Metal Merchants. It's in the boot of a silver*

BMW 3 series at the very back of the yard.' Despite the distortion, the accent was undeniably Mancunian.

'How do you know that?'

The man ignored her question and continued. *'The car will be crushed in the next couple of days. If you want to find out who killed Paul Bradley, you'd better get down there and find it before that happens.'*

'Why are you telling—'

The phone went dead. She dialled 1471 in the hopes she could trace the number, but it came up as unregistered.

Jones appeared at the door. 'Everything ok, Guv?'

She turned to face him. 'I've just had a tip off that the gun used on Bradley is in Bahmani's scrap yard.'

Jones's brow furrowed. 'Do you think it was credible?'

Phillips shrugged. 'I don't know. Maybe? I mean, they went to great lengths to disguise their voice. Plus, it's not general knowledge that Bahmani may be involved.'

'What do you wanna do?'

'Whoever it was said the gun is being stored in a silver BMW that's due to be crushed in the next few days. If that's true, then we need a warrant ASAP.' Jones stepped back as Phillips marched passed him and out into the office. 'Bov.'

The big man looked up from his PC. 'Yes, Guv?'

'Have you still got that mate at the Magistrates' Court?'

'Yeah. What do you need?'

'A search warrant for Bahmani's yard.'

Bovalino's eyes widened. 'What we looking for?'

'Suspected possession of a firearm.'

'When do you need it?'

'Yesterday!' said Phillips.

Bovalino picked up his iPhone from the desk. 'You got it.'

7

Thanks to Bov's connections at the Magistrates' Court, the warrant was approved and sent via email by 4.30 p.m. Under blues and twos, and with Bovalino at the wheel, they swept into Bahmani's yard at 5.20, ten minutes before it was due to close.

As they jumped out of the squad car, the door to the Portakabin opened. Bahmani appeared and stepped down onto the dusty ground. 'Twice in one day? This really is harassment.'

Phillips didn't respond as she marched towards him and held up her iPhone. 'This is a warrant to search these premises for a firearm we believe may have been used in the murder of Paul Bradley.'

'This is fucking bullshit,' said Bahmani. 'You're not doing anything until I've read through that warrant.'

Phillips offered him her handset. 'Read away, mate. It won't change anything, and as you'll see, if you attempt to delay or prevent the search, I can arrest you for obstructing a police investigation.'

Bahmani refused to take the phone and instead glared at Phillips, hatred fixed on his face.

Phillips turned to Jones and Bovalino, and handed them a pair of purple latex gloves each. 'Right, guys. The information states we're looking for a silver 3 series BMW, somewhere to the rear of the yard. I'll wait here with Mr Bahmani while you undertake the search.'

'I'm not having this,' said Bahmani, and fished his own iPhone from the pocket of his jeans as the two men set off across the yard. 'I'm calling my lawyer.'

Phillips made a point of looking at her watch and forced a thin smile. 'Let's hope she's not finished for the day, hey?'

As soon as Bahmani's call connected, he walked away from Phillips and began pacing around in circles, gesticulating with his arms as he relayed his current situation to the person on the other end of the phone. A few minutes passed before he stepped back towards Phillips.

'All sorted?' asked Phillips.

He glared back at her. 'By the time my lawyer's finished with you, you're gonna wish you'd never laid eyes on bloody Adders Bahmani.'

Phillips nodded silently. She'd heard it all before from criminals just like him, many of whom were now serving long sentences in Hawk Green, Manchester's maximum-security prison.

A few minutes passed before Jones and Bovalino came back into view, Jones carrying a large clear evidence bag in his right hand that appeared to contain something heavy.

'That doesn't look good for you, does it?' said Phillips.

'Whatever that is, it's not mine,' Bahmani protested as the two men drew closer.

As Jones reached them, he raised the bag to chest height. 'One Glock G17, found in a 3 series BMW exactly as described, Guv.'

'Bingo,' said Phillips.

Bahmani shook his head. 'This is a bloody stitch up, man.'

'The serial number's been filed off, too,' continued Jones, 'so I'm guessing it's not legal.'

Phillips sucked air through her teeth. 'An unregistered firearm? That's a mandatory five-year sentence, Adders.'

'Pah!' Bahmani scoffed. 'I've never seen that gun before in my life.'

'Really? So how did it get here?'

'You lot must have planted it!'

'Of course we did,' Phillips said sarcastically. She turned to Bovalino. 'Get a uniform team down here pronto.'

'Guv,' said the big Italian, and headed to the car to make the request through the police radio.

Pulling a pair of cuffs from her pocket, she stepped next to Bahmani, grabbed his right wrist and spun him round so his back was to her. 'Adders Bahmani, I'm arresting you for the possession of an unregistered firearm. You do not have to say anything, but it may harm your defence if you do not mention, when questioned, something which you later rely on in court. Anything you do say may be given in evidence.'

'This is fucking harassment!' spat Bahmani over his shoulder as Phillips locked his left hand into the cuffs.

'Well, I'm sure we'll be hearing all about that from your lawyer, won't we?' replied Phillips facetiously.

'Damn right you will!'

Bahmani was placed in the back seat of the squad car. While they waited for uniform to arrive, Phillips used the time to go through the details of the search. 'It didn't take long to find, so I'm guessing it wasn't very well hidden?'

'Under the driver's seat, Guv,' said Jones.

'Seems a bit slack for Mr Teflon, doesn't it? I mean, why

not stick it in the compactor and get rid of it? Why keep it?' she mused.

'Maybe he's not finished?' said Jones.

Bovalino nodded. 'Yeah. He could have been planning on using it again?'

Phillips glanced over at the back of Bahmani's head, visible through the rear window of the squad car. 'Maybe,' she said, without conviction.

Ten minutes later, the unformed team arrived in a large police van fitted with a holding cell at the rear.

'Hand him over, will you, Bov?'

'Sure thing, Guv,'

As soon as Bovalino pulled him out of the MCU squad car, Bahmani began shouting at the top of his voice. 'This is harassment because of my race. Because the bigoted police don't like an Asian man like me making money. It makes you lot sick, doesn't it, Me being successful and you lot earning sod-all? You won't get away with this. I'm telling you now, you're all in big fucking trouble!'

Phillips watched in silence as Bovalino handed him over to the uniformed team, who quickly deposited him in the back of the van. A moment later, the double doors closed with a thud, silencing his protests. She turned her gaze to Jones and Bovalino. 'Right. Let's get back to Ashton House and see how "The Teflon Man" explains this one away.'

8

Phillips gathered the team in the observation suite, a small space located at the far end of the corridor in Ashton House that housed the six interview rooms. Entwistle sat before three monitors that displayed the feeds from the three cameras in Interview Room Two. The rest of the team stood behind him, watching Adders Bahmani, who sat at the small table alongside his lawyer, Nicolette Johnson. As ever, she was immaculate in her designer suit, flawless makeup and perfectly maintained black bob. The MCU team were very familiar with Johnson, a formidable defence attorney with an unrivalled track record of getting her clients out of incredibly difficult situations. Her list of clients included millionaire business leaders, celebrities, sports stars and now, it seemed, scrap metal merchants.

'Your dad was right, Jonesy,' said Phillips. 'There really is "money in scrap".'

Entwistle glanced over his shoulder, eyebrows raised, a quizzical look on his face. 'What do you mean by that, Guv?'

Phillips pointed at the screen. 'Nicolette Johnson is one of the most expensive lawyers in town, if not *the* most expensive.

If – as he's always at great pains to tell us – Bahmani is just a humble scrap merchant, how come he has Johnson on speed dial? If that doesn't suggest he's involved in nefarious dealings, then I don't know what does.'

'We all know he's as bent as they come, boss, but proving it's another matter.' Jones held up the evidence bag containing the Glock. 'Although this might help, for once.'

Phillips stared at the gun in silence for a long moment. She had an uneasy feeling she just couldn't shake. Had this all been a little too easy? The tip-off, the gun being exactly where they'd been told to look? It was very unlike Bahmani to be so sloppy.

Glancing at her watch, Phillips let out a long, audible breath as she cast her gaze back to the screen.

'You ok, Guv?' asked Jones.

'Yeah. Just trying to figure out the best strategy for this one,' Phillips replied. 'Do you fancy it?'

'Damn right. I'm looking forward to seeing him try and talk his way out of this one.'

Phillips offered a faint smile. She had a funny feeling that was exactly what Bahmani and Johnson were about to do.

She turned to Bovalino and Entwistle. 'You guys watch the monitors like hawks. You're looking for any gestures or reactions that might indicate guilt. Timestamp them and we'll review when we're done.'

'On it,' said Bovalino, then rolled a chair across the floor before taking a seat next to Entwistle.

A minute later, with Jones at her back, Phillips took a long silent breath before opening the door to Interview Room Two. Bahmani's eyes jerked towards them, but Johnson didn't look up from her yellow legal pad. Instead, she continued making notes with an expensive-looking pen that matched her outfit.

After taking their seats, Jones placed the bag containing

the gun on the table, whilst Phillips explained the protocols in place: the fact the Digital Interview Recorder and the three video cameras would capture everything said during the interview. All standard procedure in modern policing. With the formalities taken care of, Phillips activated the DIR, waited for the long activation tone to finish, then got straight to it. She touched the gun through the bag. 'Can you tell us where this gun came from?'

'No,' said Bahmani, his voice flat.

'Really? After all, we found it hidden in a car in your yard. I thought you'd have some idea of how it got there.'

Bahmani shrugged.

Johnson took the bait. 'Officers. Just because something was located on my client's property does not mean it belongs to him.'

'I beg to differ,' Phillips shot back.

Johnson flashed a thin smile, but her eyes appeared almost black. 'I'm sure you do, but may I remind you that you've been here before, Chief Inspector, only a few short years ago.'

Phillips frowned. 'I'm not following you.'

'Really? I find that hard to believe. After all, it's fair to say you have a history of accusing my client of being involved in crimes he did not commit.'

Phillips opened her mouth to reply.

Johnson was too quick for her. 'Two years ago, you tried to connect Mr Bahmani to a series of murders because the person who actually committed the crimes used licence plates stolen from his salvage yard.'

'That case was entirely different to this situation.'

'Was it?' Johnson tapped her pen against the evidence bag. 'My client has denied having any connection to that gun, yet you still claim it belongs to him because it was found on his yard. The same thing happened before. You accused him of being involved in the murders because the plates came from his place of business. Yet it was proven, without a doubt, that he was not involved in those crimes. In fact, as you're well aware, Mr Bahmani was completely exonerated in that case.'

Phillips took a moment to think before she responded. 'Here are the facts.' She placed her hand on the gun. 'This weapon is unregistered and was found in a car belonging to Mr Bahmani. That means *he* is responsible for it. It also means we can charge him under Section One of the Firearms Act, 1968.'

'*If* you can prove it belongs to my client, Chief Inspector.'

'Which I'm confident we will.'

Johnson let out a sardonic chuckle. 'Confident is not the same as *certain,* is it?'

Phillips's gaze was unflinching.

'So, when can we expect the fingerprint analysis on the gun?' asked Johnson.

'Tomorrow afternoon.'

'And the DNA?'

'A couple of days.'

Johnson made a note in her pad, then checked her very expensive-looking watch. 'My client was arrested at 5.40 p.m. The time is now approaching 8, which means you have approximately twenty-two hours to find evidence connecting him to the handgun, or you must let him go.'

'I know how the law works, Ms Johnson,' said Phillips doing her level best to hide her contempt for the woman.

'My client maintains he knows nothing about the gun or how it happened to make its way onto his yard. He is supremely confident that you will find no evidence whatsoever connecting him to that handgun.'

'And as you rightly pointed out, Ms Johnson,' said Phillips, '*confident* isn't the same as *certain*, is it?'

Johnson flashed her perfectly white teeth. 'Look, Chief Inspector. I don't want to do this, but I feel like you're giving me no choice.'

'Do what, exactly?'

'This is the second time you've accused my client of being involved in crimes he didn't commit. It could be argued that you are singling him out because of prejudice within your team.'

'Prejudice? What exactly are you implying?'

'Do I really have to spell it out for you?'

Phillips leaned back in her chair and folded her arms across her chest. 'I think you do.'

'Very well.' Johnson locked eyes with Phillips. 'My client believes you and your team are targeting him based on his race, because the GMP is endemically racist.'

'That's absurd.'

'Is it, Chief Inspector?'

'Absolutely. He's not been targeted, as you put it. He's been arrested because we found an unregistered gun at his place of work. How is that prejudiced or racist?'

'So who found the weapon?' asked Johnson.

'I did,' said Jones, 'along with Detective Constable Bovalino.'

'And no other witnesses? Body cams, for example.'

'Detectives don't wear body cams,' replied Jones, his tone calm.

'Where are you going with this?' Phillips asked.

It was Johnson's turn to fold her arms. 'Well. If no-one else was there, who's to say your team didn't plant the gun in Mr Bahmani's yard?'

Phillips sensed Jones's body tensing next to her. The small red patch of skin that had suddenly appeared on the side of his neck confirmed he was as angry as hell. She jumped in before he could react. 'DS Jones and DC Bovalino conducted the search by the book. Their integrity has never been in question.'

'Maybe not, but *yours* has, hasn't it, Chief Inspector?'

Johnson was, of course, referring to the time Phillips had stepped outside the law in a previous murder case to prove a suspect's innocence. A suspect who had actually been one of Johnson's clients at the time, which meant she knew all the details of what Phillips had done. '*I* am not under investigation here.'

Johnson stared at Phillips in silence. 'Maybe not.' She looked deliberately at her watch again. 'Look, to show goodwill on your part, I'm proposing you allow my client to go home. If you do find any evidence that the gun belongs to him – which, of course, you won't – I will ensure he surrenders himself to you at an agreed time.'

'Not a chance,' said Phillips, shaking her head. 'He's in custody and he'll remain so until we either charge him or we pass the twenty-four-hour custody limit.'

Johnson pursed her lips. 'Very well, but don't say I didn't warn you, Chief Inspector. You certainly haven't heard the last of this. You might want to let Chief Constable Fox know she'll be hearing from me.'

Phillips, ignoring the threat, glanced at the clock on the wall for a moment before turning to face the DIR. 'Chief Inspector Phillips, terminating this interview at 7.59 p.m.' Stopping the recording, she stepped up from the chair and locked eyes on Bahmani. 'DS Jones will escort you back to the custody suite.'

Ten minutes later, after handing Bahmani over to the custody sergeant, Jones rejoined the team in the observation suite. 'That Nic Johnson's got a nerve.' His voice brimmed with anger.

'We saw,' said Bovalino. 'What a bloody liberty claiming we planted the gun.'

'She was just trying to get under your skin,' said Phillips. 'That's how she operates. But she was right about one thing: unless we find any fingerprints or DNA connecting Bahmani to that firearm, he'll walk right out of here tomorrow afternoon.'

'Teflon Man strikes again,' said Bov.

Phillips nodded, deep in thought. 'On that, I have to say it seems very unlike Bahmani to leave a murder weapon lying around.'

'What are you saying. Do *you* think he was set up?' asked Jones.

'Maybe. Or maybe he finally screwed up.'

The team fell silent for a moment.

'When are we expecting the results back from ballistics?' said Phillips.

'The next couple of days,' replied Jones.

'Ok. See if you can get them any quicker. And who's on fingerprint analysis tomorrow?'

'I think it's Becky, Guv,' said Bovalino.

'Hasn't she got a crush on Whistler?'

'Hasn't everyone?' joked Jones.

Entwistle grinned. 'What can I say? She's only human, Jonesy.'

Phillips patted Entwistle on the shoulder. 'Well, Romeo. That's your first job in the morning: turn on the charm and expedite the fingerprints on that gun.'

'I'll try my best, but I can't promise anything.' Entwistle appeared more serious now.

'Promise *everything*, Whistler. Whatever it takes,' said Phillips, before turning to face the door. 'There's nothing else we can do tonight, so let's go home and get some rest. We can start afresh first thing in the morning.'

9

WEDNESDAY 7TH JULY

Phillips made the short trip down to the second floor to visit the Serious Crimes Unit, the team tasked with tackling all gang-related crime in Manchester. The inspector in charge of the department, DCI Steve Cleverly, was well known to Phillips, as they'd come up through the ranks together. He was a good copper who cared about his team almost as much as she did. In fact, there was more than a little professional rivalry between the two elite units.

The SCU office was empty, making it easy to note that the layout was almost identical to that of Major Crimes on the floor above. Wandering past the empty workspaces, she found Cleverly sitting behind his desk in his office. He was a slightly awkward-looking man – probably around six foot three, she guessed – with long limbs, and a narrow face sitting under what could best be described as a conservative hairstyle that receded at the temples.

He looked up as she walked in. 'Jane? This is a pleasant surprise.'

'Morning, Steve.'

'Good to see I'm not the only early bird. To what do I owe the pleasure?'

Phillips took a seat opposite him. 'I need your expertise.'

Cleverly picked up a steaming cup from the desk. 'Can I get you one?'

'Not for me, thanks.'

Cleverly took a sip. 'I heard you landed the Paul Bradley murder.'

'I did, yeah, and that's one of the reasons I'm here. What can you tell me about him?'

Cleverly placed the cup back down on the desk. 'Nothing of interest, I'm afraid. I mean, there've been rumours circulating for years that he was involved in money laundering, drugs and racketeering, etc., but no one could ever make it stick. He was either too clever or actually clean, although my money was always on *clever*.'

'And what about Adders Bahmani.'

Cleverly blew his lips. 'That bugger? There's a reason they call him "The Teflon Man".'

Phillips nodded. '*Nothing sticks*. I know.'

'He's another one we've been after for years now, but again haven't been able to catch him in the act.'

'Well. I'm hoping that might be about to change.'

'Really? How so?'

'He's in a holding cell downstairs as we speak,' said Phillips.

'No way.' Cleverly's eyes widened. 'What did you get him on?'

'Possession of an unregistered firearm that we believe could have been used to kill Paul Bradley. We received an anonymous tip-off about it yesterday, and found it stashed in a car on his lot last night.'

Cleverly frowned. 'That's not like Bahmani to be so careless.'

'The same thought occurred to me. Maybe we finally got lucky?'

'Maybe,' said Cleverly. He crossed his arms and chewed his bottom lip.

Phillips continued. 'He claims to know nothing about it, of course.'

'Naturally. And no doubt he's peddling all that "humble scrap merchant" bollocks.'

'Oh yeah. Took him about thirty seconds before he got that into the conversation.'

Cleverly chortled. 'He's nothing if not predictable, our Adders.'

'His lawyer's also threatening to kick up a stink with Fox. She claims she's going to put in an official complaint against MCU based on the fact we're targeting him because of his race.'

'Who's the lawyer?'

'Nic Johnson.'

Cleverly whistled. 'He must have moved up in the world. Ms Johnson's certainly not cheap.'

'That's what I said to my guys. If he *is* just a scrap merchant, how come he can afford her extortionate fees?'

'Scrap merchant my arse – Bahmani is crooked!' spat Cleverly. 'I'm sure of it, but – like Bradley – he's way too clever to get caught with his hands in the cookie jar. That's why I'm so surprised you found a gun where you did.'

'He reckons he's being set up.'

'Of course he does.'

'I've tasked my guys with getting the fingerprint analysis back today. Hopefully that'll tie the gun to him, which would at least mean a mandatory five-stretch in Hawk Green. And if the ballistics team can prove it was the gun that killed Bradley, then he's well and truly in the shit.'

Cleverly pursed his lips.

'Are you familiar with Bradley's son, Freddie?' said Phillips.

'Yeah. The so-called heir to the throne. Bit of a hot-head by all accounts.'

'That was certainly my experience of him. Well, he's also claiming that Bahmani's behind his dad's murder.'

'Based on what?' Cleverly asked.

'Apparently Bahmani had been going round telling anyone who'd listen that he was taking over Bradley's businesses.'

'Well, if he was, we didn't know anything about it. We'd usually hear at least a whisper or two from one of our informants.'

'Look, Steve, you know these guys better than most. Do you *really* think Bahmani could be Bradley's killer?'

Cleverly took another mouthful of his coffee. 'Well, anything's possible, I suppose, but two questions immediately spring to mind: why? And why now?'

'Gang rivalry, perhaps?'

Cleverly's face twisted momentarily. 'Possibly. I mean, it's well known they were both gangbangers from rival territories back in the nineties. But since all that nonsense stopped, they've played nice with each other – or at least stayed out of each other's way. I've certainly never heard of any major beef between them, and nothing that would suggest murder was on the cards.'

Phillips folded her arms across her chest. 'When I first spoke to Bahmani after Bradley was killed, he admitted that he'd tried to buy some of his businesses, but that they couldn't agree a price.'

'Again, that's news to me,' said Cleverly, his eyes narrowing.

'Do you know if Bahmani had any connections to a guy called Archie Boothroyd back in the nineties?'

Cleverly shrugged. 'Never heard of him, so I really couldn't say.'

'It's so frustrating, Steve. Like you, I'm sure he's as dirty as hell, but I can't shake the feeling that the tip-off – and then us finding the gun – was all a bit too easy.'

'What? So you think Bahmani really is being set up?'

Phillips exhaled sharply and shook her head. 'I don't know. I just don't know. I guess we'll have to wait and see if the fingerprint and DNA teams come up with anything.'

At that moment, the main door to the SCU office opened and chatter filled the air as several plain clothes officers filed in holding takeaway cups.

Phillips glanced in their direction, then checked her watch. It was 9 a.m. 'Right, well. I'd better get back upstairs and see where the team are at. Time's ticking on Bahmani, after all.'

'Keep me posted, won't you, Jane.'

'Sure,' she said, and stood.

'And good luck. It's about time someone put that slippery bugger in Hawk Green.'

Phillips flashed him a faint smile, then turned and headed for the door.

10

L ater that day, as the door to Adders Bahmani's cell opened, he sat upright on the blue plastic mattress that had been his bed overnight.

'Looks like you're free to go, Adders,' said the custody officer.

Bahmani smiled to himself as he stood and left the cell. Detective Jones stood next to the custody sergeant's elevated desk. 'Is your gaffer not coming to say goodbye?' Adders asked, a glint in his eye as he fastened the thick gold Rolex watch to his wrist.

'She's busy,' said Jones.

Bahmani clipped his thick gold chain around his neck. 'So she sent her lackey instead, did she?'

Jones took a step closer. 'Careful now, Adders. You don't want to get too cocky too quickly. Just cos your fingerprints weren't on that gun doesn't mean it's not yours. The DNA analysis will be back in a few days, and we could well be seeing you again.'

'I very much doubt that,' replied Bahmani as he slipped his wallet into his pocket.

'Do you need a ride home?' asked the custody sergeant.

Bahmani turned to face him. 'Are you joking?' He chuckled. There was no way he would be seen dead arriving home in a bloody police car. 'I've got someone waiting outside.'

Jones stared at him in silence.

Picking up the last of his things, Bahmani produced a wide grin. 'Right. I'll be off, then.' He strolled casually towards the exit. 'Ta ta, ladies.'

Out in the main car park at the front of Ashton House, he spotted Tahir behind the wheel of the white Range Rover parked up on the kerb, engine running. A moment later, Bahmani pulled open the passenger door and jumped up into the comfort of the cool air-conditioned cabin.

'You ok?' asked Tahir slowly. His English had been getting steadily better since he arrived from Pakistan three years back, but still needed work.

'I will be when I find out which bastard is trying to set me up.'

Tahir remained silent, his English not up to the task of continuing the conversation any further.

For simplicity, Bahmani switched to Urdu. 'Let's go see that slippery grass, Dillon Wilton, and find out who's trying to screw me over. But first we need to change vehicles.'

Tahir nodded, then slipped the big SUV into drive and gunned the accelerator. The massive five-litre V8 engine growled like a wild animal as they shot out of the car park and onto the main road.

Bahmani allowed himself a smile. No matter how hard they tried, the police just couldn't catch him.

———

BECAUSE OF HIS fondness for taking money from the police in exchange for coughing up underworld intel, Dillon Wilton was widely regarded amongst the criminal fraternity as someone not to be trusted. His very demeanour appeared to support that fact. His hair was as thin as his bony body, his face gaunt with dark rings under bloodshot eyes, and when he answered the door to his small, terraced house in east Manchester, he carried himself apologetically, peering out from behind the chain.

'Not inviting us in?' asked Bahmani jovially.

'I'm a bit busy just now,' said Wilton, his voice weak and low.

Bahmani scanned up and down the street. 'Too busy to talk to *me*, Dillon?'

'Look, it's nothing personal. I'm just trying to keep a low profile at the moment. You know how it is.'

Bahmani pointed his thumb at Tahir. 'Have you met my cousin Tahir before, Dillon?'

Wilton eyed the huge, heavy-set man standing to Bahmani's left.

'He was brought up in Islamabad in Pakistan, and where he comes from, it's considered very disrespectful to leave your guests standing out on the street. Now, *I'm* a reasonable man, as you know, but see, Tahir, he has a bit of a temper. If he thinks you're being disrespectful to us by not inviting us in, then I can't be responsible for his actions. You know what I'm saying?'

Wilton looked Tahir up and down again, then forced a weak smile. 'Well, I don't want to be rude.' He closed the door for a moment as he released the chain.

As soon as the door was untethered, Bahmani pushed it open and stepped across the threshold to tower over Wilton. Wilton backed down the narrow hallway. 'How about you put the kettle on, hey?'

Wilton nodded, then moved quickly through the lounge and out into the small kitchen at the rear of the property.

'Two teas, black, with no sugar.' Bahmani followed him through. 'We're sweet enough.'

Behind him, Tahir closed the front door and locked it quietly.

By the time Wilton came back into the lounge carrying two steaming cups, Bahmani had taken a seat in the armchair opposite the massive flatscreen TV. Taking one of the cups on offer, he stared over at the large appliance. 'That must have cost a few quid, mate. You been talking to the feds for money again?'

Wilton let out a nervous laugh. 'I don't know what you mean, Mr Bahmani.' He passed the second cup to Tahir, who remained standing by the entrance to the hallway.

Bahmani produced a wide grin and pointed to the thread-bare sofa to his right, positioned against the wall. 'Why don't you sit down, Dillon.'

Wilton swallowed hard and took a seat, his eyes darting between the two men.

Bahmani noted the fact he hadn't made himself a drink. 'You not having one?'

'I'm not thirsty.'

'Suit yourself.' Bahmani took a sip of his scalding hot tea. 'Now then, Dillon. You're a man who hears things, aren't you, mate? On the street, I mean. If it's happening in Manchester, *you* know about it.'

Wilton opened his mouth to speak, but seemed to think better of it.

'Which is why I'm here. You see, someone is trying to fuck up my business, giving the law excuses to come down to the yard. I need to know who that person is.'

'I haven't heard anything about that,' Wilton replied – too quickly. 'If I had, I'd have told you about it, wouldn't I?'

Bahmani stared at him in silence for a long moment. 'You see. Here's the thing, Dillon. I'm not sure I believe you.'

'I'm telling you the truth, honestly I am.'

'Did you hear what happened to Paul Bradley at the weekend?' asked Bahmani.

'Yeah. Bad business, that.'

'Any rumours about who killed him?'

Wilton shifted in his seat. 'Nothing I've heard.'

'You sure about that?'

'Honest,' said Wilton, nodding vigorously.

'Because someone's trying to pin it on *me*.'

Wilton swallowed hard again. 'You, Mr Bahmani?'

'You look nervous, Dillon.'

'Me? No. Why would I be nervous?'

'Maybe because you're not telling me the truth. Maybe you do know who's trying to set me up, and you're protecting them.'

'I wouldn't do that.' Wilton produced another nervous laugh. 'If I knew anything, I'd tell you. Straight up I would.'

Bahmani locked eyes with Wilton but said nothing, allowing an awkward silence to fill the room for the next ten seconds. He'd known the man was a police informant for a long time, and so far – because he'd stayed out of Bahmani's business affairs – he'd let it slide. But things were different now. Someone was trying to take him down, and if anyone knew who that person was, it was Wilton. It was time to find out exactly what he knew.

Bahmani stepped up from the armchair and headed into the kitchen, out of sight of Wilton and Tahir. It didn't take him long to find what he was looking for: a large metal-bottomed saucepan. Pulling a pair of leather gloves from the pocket of his hoodie, he switched the gas hob on to maximum heat and placed the empty pan directly onto the flame. Next, he wandered over to the small breakfast table next to the back door. Dragging out a battered wooden chair from under it, he placed it close to the gas hob, which was heating up nicely. With everything set up as he wanted it, he walked back into the tiny lounge.

Wilton had obviously heard him moving the furniture around, because there was genuine fear in his wide, expectant eyes. 'Everything all right?'

Bahmani stared down at him. When he spoke, his voice was calm and measured. 'Who's trying to fuck me, Dillon?'

'Like I said, I don't know.'

'You wouldn't lie to me, would you, mate?'

'Of course not, Mr Bahmani.'

'Because that would be a very stupid thing to do.'

Wilton chortled nervously. 'I know that. *Everyone knows that.*'

Bahmani nodded, then turned to Tahir and barked at him in Urdu.

The big man threw his mug of tea to the floor and stepped forward. He grabbed Wilton by the scruff of the neck and dragged him off the sofa, much like a rag doll, and in the direction of the kitchen.

'What the fuck's going on?' Wilton shouted.

'Just making sure you're telling me the truth, Dillon.' Bahmani watched as Tahir deposited him on the kitchen chair, then removed Wilton's belt and used it to tie Wilton's hands behind his back and tether him to the chair.

'I don't know anything! I swear on my mother's life!' Wilton's voice was shrill now, brimming with fear.

With his hands securely in place, Tahir pulled Wilton's grubby tracksuit bottoms down around his ankles, revealing pale, bony, almost hairless legs.

'Seriously, you've got to believe me. I haven't heard anything!'

'We'll soon see if that's the case,' said Bahmani. He slipped his hands in the pockets of his jeans and leaned casually against the door frame to the kitchen as he spoke to Tahir in Urdu again.

The big man moved across the room to the metal pan, which smoked slightly from the intense heat. Picking it up, he held it so that the red-hot underside faced downwards.

'Last chance, Dillon,' said Bahmani, almost playfully. 'Who's trying to fuck me?'

Wilton writhed against his restraints. 'Please. I'm telling you the truth. I don't know anything!'

'Have it your way.'

A moment later, Tahir slammed the red-hot pan down onto Wilton's bare thighs.

The screams that followed were like nothing Bahmani had ever heard.

11

Phillips was at her desk when Jones wandered in. Despite the fact it was approaching 8 p.m., the sun still shone through her office windows.

'How you getting on, Guv?' he asked, fatigue etched into his face.

'I'm not,' she replied with a heavy sigh as she leaned back in her chair.

Jones took a seat opposite her. 'I still can't believe we had to let Bahmani walk.'

'I know. Sometimes it's as if the law works *against* coppers rather than *for* us.'

Jones rubbed his hands down his face, making his skin redden. 'Honestly, Guv. You should have seen his face, the smug prick.'

'I can imagine.'

'Well, hopefully the DNA will finally connect him to the gun.'

'I wouldn't bet on it,' said Phillips. 'Look at what Cleverly said. Bahmani's not the type of guy to leave a gun lying around covered in fingerprints. I doubt we'll get a match on the DNA either.'

Just then, there was a knock at her door.

'Speak of the devil.' Phillips smiled as she waved DCI Cleverly into her office. 'We were just talking about you.'

'I thought I could feel my ears burning.'

'Did you hear we had to let Bahmani go?'

'I did, and actually, he's the reason for my visit,' he said, taking a seat.

'Oh?' said Phillips.

'Yeah. Look, this is strictly confidential, ok?'

'Of course,' replied Phillips.

'A couple of my lads attended a house in east Manchester this afternoon. The guy who lives there, Dillon Wilton, is one of our informants. Very well connected and pretty reliable with his intel, to be fair.'

'Right.'

'Well, it seems that someone decided to attach a red-hot frying pan to his knees this afternoon.'

Jones winced, and Phillips grimaced. 'Holy shit. Why?'

'We don't know, I'm afraid. For once, he's not talking. Insists it was an accident, and that he did it to himself. However, the neighbour who heard him screaming and called it in said she saw two well-built men getting into a transit van and speeding off before the police arrived.'

'Did the neighbour get a proper look at them?' asked Jones.

Cleverly shook his head. 'Apparently not. She said they were wearing tracksuit tops with their hoods pulled up as they walked away, so she couldn't see their faces. She did, however, get the registration of the van.'

Phillips sat forward. 'And?'

'It was carrying clone plates that came off a 2005 Golf GTI.'

'Of course it was,' said Phillips.

'I thought you might like to know that the plates belonged to a car that was registered as off-road by Adders Scrap Metal Merchants.'

Phillips raised an eyebrow. 'Go figure.'

'Yeah, but we've been here before with him though, haven't we?' Jones chipped in. 'Is Bahmani really going to use plates registered to his own yard? He'd know we'll connect them.'

'True,' Phillips replied. 'But maybe that's what he's counting on: our previous issues with the canal murders and the plates stolen from his yard. His lawyer can dismiss the plates' connection all day long thanks to that case, which provides him with the perfect cover.'

'Sounds like Bahmani,' added Cleverly.

'So where is the victim now?' asked Phillips.

'The MRI, Burns Unit. He's in a pretty bad way.'

Phillips glanced at Jones. 'We should go and see him.'

Jones shrugged his shoulders. 'Why not? I'm already late. Another couple of hours won't make Sarah any *less* pissed off at me.'

'I honestly wouldn't bother,' said Cleverly. 'I think you'll have a wasted trip. We tried earlier, and he's refusing to say anything about who did it to him or why.'

Phillips produced a wry grin. 'Well, maybe he'll fall for my womanly charms.'

Cleverly guffawed. 'Womanly charms? Yeah right.'

Phillips caught Jones trying to stifle a smirk. 'Oi!' she said, half joking. 'It's not that funny.'

Cleverly got up to leave. 'Look, guys. If you want to waste time visiting Wilton, that's up to you, but remember, this case belongs to SCU. I don't have an issue with you talking to one of my witnesses, but I also don't want you trampling all over my investigation. Plus, he's a very valuable CI. I don't want anything scaring him off.'

'We'll be the ultimate professionals, Steve.' Phillips stood up from her chair. 'I promise.'

Cleverly's eyes narrowed for a moment. 'Why do I get the feeling you're just saying what I want to hear?'

Phillips forced a thin smile. 'Maybe you're just falling for my womanly charms.'

Cleverly produced a wry grin. 'Maybe. Well, you two can do what you like, but I'm going home.' He walked out.

PHILLIPS AND JONES presented their credentials to the senior sister in charge of Wilton's care, an Afro-Caribbean called Sheila Morris, according to her name badge. 'I'm afraid he's not up to having visitors. He's very poorly,' she said, sounding like a school mistress.

'We only need a couple of minutes with him.' Phillips offered a soft smile in an attempt to get on Morris's good side. 'It's very important. Mr Wilton may have vital information that could help us catch a killer.'

Morris exhaled sharply. 'Mr Wilton has sustained life changing injuries. He's on a lot of medication and needs to rest. I really don't think it's a good idea, and besides, he's already spoken to the police this afternoon.'

'That was a different team.'

'Don't you lot *share* information?' she spat back.

'Yes we do, and we already have, but there are a few questions we need to ask Mr Wilton directly.'

Morris appeared unimpressed. 'Like I said, he needs rest. Maybe you can come back tomorrow.'

Phillips wasn't giving up. 'Please, Sheila, the people who did this to Mr Wilton are still out there on the streets, free to hurt and maim someone else. *He* can help us find them and make sure that doesn't happen.'

Morris's expression began to soften.

Phillips continued to press her. 'We'll only be a few minutes, and I promise that at the first sign of any distress from Mr Wilton, we'll leave.'

Morris said nothing for a moment, then nodded. 'Ok. You can have *five minutes*, but no longer.'

'That's all we need,' said Phillips, grateful.

Morris handed them a disposable plastic apron each, along with surgical face masks and a pair of latex gloves each. 'His injuries mean he's at high risk of infection, so you'll need to put these on before you go in.'

Phillips and Jones took the protective gear and spent the next few minutes making sure it was put on correctly before turning to Morris for final approval.

'He's in Room 4, this way,' she said, and led them down the corridor.

As they stepped inside Wilton's single room, Phillips was struck by the total silence save for several machines that emitted the occasional beep or bing. She recognised the patient-controlled analgesia pump used by patients to administer their own morphine. She had used one herself after she'd been shot several years back.

Wilton lay in the bed, his torso propped up at a forty-five-degree angle. He appeared to be asleep. His injuries remained hidden under the sheets, which had been raised up on a special frame to avoid any contact with his burnt skin. Phillips could only imagine the damage.

She padded softly to the farthest side of his bed as Jones took up a position closest to the door. 'Mr Wilton,' she said softly. 'Mr Wilton?'

There was no response.

'Maybe we *should* come back tomorrow, Guv. He's spark out.'

Phillips leaned in closer and tried again. 'Dillon,' she said, louder this time.

Wilton's eyes opened, and he blinked rapidly as he took in Phillips and Jones.

'I'm DCI Phillips and this is DS Jones,' she said, and flashed her ID. 'We'd like to talk to you about what happened today.'

Wilton shook his head and shifted in the bed slightly, groaning with the pain.

'It's very important, Dillon.'

Jones shook his head. 'This doesn't feel right. He's off his tits on medication. Whatever he tells us will never stand up in court.'

She knew Jones was right, but even the slightest clue now could help accelerate their investigation. Plus, once Wilton was well enough to talk properly, Serious Crimes would swallow him up and she'd never get access to him. Her gut told her it was now or never, so she pressed on. 'Dillon, who did this to you?'

Wilton closed his eyes and clenched his jaw.

'Dillon?' Phillips's voice said more loudly.

'Piss off,' Wilton mumbled, his eyes opening to glare at her.

'*Who* tortured you, Dillon?'

Wilton swallowed hard, his dry throat cracking. 'It was an accident.'

'I don't believe that,' Phillips said, leaning in closer.

'I did it,' he repeated.

Phillips glanced across at Jones. His stony expression betrayed his concerns.

Avoiding his gaze, she turned back to Wilton. Their five minutes would soon be up. She had one last throw of the dice before Morris reappeared. 'Dillon, we know Adders Bahmani came to your house today. We know *he* was the one who tortured you.'

Wilton's eyes suddenly widened, oozing fear.

'It was him, wasn't it? Tell us what happened, and we can protect you.'

Wilton shook his head. 'Leave me alone,' he said. He scrabbled for the PCA with his right hand.

Phillips knew what was coming next, but was powerless to stop it from happening. 'Come on, Dillon, tell us the truth.'

Wilton's finger pushed the button on the PCA. A shot of morphine left the machine and rushed into his system.

'Who did this to you, Dillon? Who tortured you? Dillon, was it Bahmani?' She was almost shouting now.

Wilton's eyes began to close. A few seconds later, his head rolled sideways on the pillow.

'Damn it!' Phillips growled.

Morris opened the door at that moment, a scowl fixed on her face. 'Please leave.'

Phillips's frustration was like a living thing writhing inside her. Bahmani was going to get away with yet another heinous crime and, it seemed, no matter what she tried, she couldn't pin a single thing on him. Moving round the bed, she passed Morris without speaking, then followed Jones out of the room and back along the corridor. As they reached the nurses' station, they stopped to remove their protective gear, throwing it into a nearby bin before heading to summon the elevator. Neither said anything for the next few minutes until they stepped inside and the lift doors had finally closed behind them before descending to the ground floor.

Phillips was first to speak. 'You saw his face in there when I mentioned Bahmani, didn't you? Tell me it wasn't just me.'

'I saw it, Guv.'

'It has to be Bahmani who tortured Wilton. Has to be. Otherwise, why react like that?'

'I agree. But if he won't tell us who did it, what can we do?' said Jones. 'Nic Johnson will destroy any attempt to arrest Bahmani without hard evidence.'

'What about the plates on the van? They were registered to his yard after all.'

'Johnson will kick that into touch in a heartbeat. You know that.'

'No, you're right.' Phillips sighed. 'Which means we're back to square one.'

'Seems that way,' said Jones, before checking his watch. 'Look, it's after nine. I don't know about you, but I'm knackered. Why don't we call it a day and see what the morning brings?'

'Yeah. Hopefully the DNA or ballistic report might come in tomorrow and give us something to go on.'

At that moment, the elevator came to a stop and the doors opened onto an empty lobby. The night air was warm as they stepped outside a few moments later and headed for the multi-storey car park.

'Seriously, Guv,' said Jones, 'try not to put too much pressure on yourself. We *will* find out who killed Bradley in time. I'm sure of that.'

'I hope you're right, I really do. Still, I can't help thinking that's what DCI Monaghan said in 1993 about the Boothroyd case, and here we are, thirty years later, still with no clue who killed him.

12

THURSDAY 8TH JULY

DCI Cleverly was good enough to share the witness statement from Wilton's neighbour with Major Crimes, and after a couple of hours with her head in her laptop studying it, Phillips began to develop a headache. She knew better than to ignore the pain or it could easily turn into a migraine. With that in mind, she pushed her chair back, stood, and moved to look out the window. The view outside was of nothing more glamorous than the Ashton House car park, but there were at least a few plants and trees visible. Plus, the sun was out, which made everything brighter. Sadly, the weather could do nothing for her mood, which was dark with frustration at the team's lack of progress. Admittedly, it was less than a week since Paul Bradley had been shot, but she couldn't help feeling the investigation was stagnating, with their only suspect impervious to the law. Still, she'd been a detective long enough to know that could change. All they needed was one lucky break, or a sharp piece of detective work, to change the landscape in a heartbeat. She prayed that moment would come soon.

Turning from the window, she focused on the main office,

which was unusually quiet. Everyone had their heads down, working hard. It had been that way all morning. Like her, they wanted a result as quickly possible, and were doing everything they could to get it.

Just then, the relative silence was broken as Jones's landline began to ring. As she watched, he picked it up.

'DS Jones.' He listened intently for a long moment. 'And you're absolutely sure of that?' A while later, Jones thanked the caller and replaced the handset.

Phillips wandered out into the main office as Bovalino and Entwistle looked up from their respective computers.

'That was ballistics, Guv.'

She felt her pulse quicken. 'And?'

'They've matched the gun we found at Bahmani's yard to the bullet that killed Bradley.'

Phillips let out a sigh of relief.

'We've got the bastard,' Bov chimed in.

Phillips tried her best to contain her excitement. She knew only too well that a ballistics match wasn't enough to connect Bahmani to the murder weapon. All it really proved was that that particular gun had killed Bradley. On its own, that would never deliver a conviction. Nic Johnson's impressive court room record suggested she could easily see to that. 'Where are we at with the DNA on it?'

'Still waiting,' said Jones.

'Give them a call and tell them to get a bloody move on, will you?' Phillips rubbed her temples. Her headache was getting worse. She needed a change of scenery to hopefully stave off the potential migraine. 'I'll be back shortly,' she said. She grabbed a packet of painkillers from her desk and set off to the canteen to get some water.

It was just after 11 a.m., which meant the lunch rush was yet to arrive. With the space mercifully quiet, she took a seat at one of the empty tables and sipped the water slowly while she waited for the meds to kick in.

When she returned to the office twenty minutes later, Jones was on the phone. He beckoned her over as he wrapped up the conversation.

'Tell me it's good news,' she said.

Jones's expression was grave. 'Sorry, Guv. The only DNA they found belonged to Bradley. Blood splatter. Nothing else.'

'Shit,' said Phillips. 'There's no way the CPS will charge Bahmani on the ballistics alone.'

'He's got more lives than a bloody cat, that one,' said Bovalino.

'Yeah, he does,' said Phillips. Frustration gnawed at her gut. She felt deflated, but she couldn't afford for the team to lose focus. She needed to keep them motivated. 'Look. It's not ideal, but equally, it's not over. Bahmani may be crafty, but then, so are we. Keep at it, guys. The breakthrough could be just around the corner. In fact, I know it is. We *will* get him.'

Each of the team nodded. She turned and walked back into her office, unsure who she was trying to convince the most, them, or herself.

About an hour later, Phillips's landline rang. It was Sonia on reception.

'Another caller who won't give their name, DCI Phillips. I've tried to find out who he is, but he's not having it.'

Phillips's pulse quickened. Could this be the informant again? 'Put him through.' A moment later, the call connected. 'This is Phillips.'

'Is this line secure?' The voice was unaffected this time, the accent thick Mancunian.

'Yes,' said Phillips. The truth was, she had no clue.

'I was a close friend of Paul Bradley.'

'I see,' Phillips said without conviction. She'd been

expecting the odd crank call since the story was released to the press, an occupational hazard in high-profile cases.

'I know who killed him.'

Phillips sat to attention. 'Say that again.'

'I know who killed Paul Bradley.'

A surge of adrenaline shot through her body. 'Can you tell me their name?'

'Not over the phone. It has to be face to face.'

'Like I said, this is a secure line,' she lied. 'Nobody will know that we've spoken.'

'I don't think you heard me. Either we meet face to face or I'm telling you nothing.'

'Ok, ok. I hear you. Let's do it your way. Where do you want to meet?'

'The car park at Alderley Edge Country Park. Tonight, at 10 o'clock.'

Phillips frowned. 'Why so late?'

'Because it'll be empty by then, and that's when it gets dark. I can't risk being seen.'

'How will I know who you are?'

'You won't, but I'll know you.'

The phone went dead.

There was little point trying to trace the call. Instead, she shouted for Jones.

He arrived at her door a moment later. 'What's up?'

'What are you doing tonight?'

'Why? You fallen out with Adam?' he joked.

Phillips was too focused on the call to notice the banter. 'I've just had another anonymous call from someone claiming they know who killed Bradley.'

Jones's brow furrowed. 'Same as last time?'

'No. This was a real voice, no tricks or distortion.'

'And did it sound kosher?'

Phillips shrugged. 'Hard to tell. He didn't really give me

anything other than he claimed to be a friend of Bradley's and he wants to meet face to face. The Alderley Edge Country Park car park, tonight, at 10.'

'That's late.'

'Apparently he won't be seen that way.'

Jones's eyes narrowed. 'Sounds a bit cloak and dagger to me, boss. Are you gonna go?'

Phillips sighed. 'I don't think I have much choice. We're hitting dead end after dead end. This guy could be telling us a load of crap, but then again, if he *is* legit, it could be the breakthrough we've been waiting for.'

'In that case, I'm coming with you. It's not safe on your own.'

'Are you sure? Like you say, it is late, and I don't want you getting into Sarah's bad books.'

Jones laughed. 'Bit too late for that, Guv.'

13

Nothing was sacred in the criminal underworld. He was starting to realise that. When people like Hodgey turned against you, swift action had to be taken to stop others following suit. And that's what he was doing.

Standing in the shadows of the quiet tree-lined street in Prestbury, he watched as the front door to the modest house opened and Mitchell Hodge stepped out. Closing the door behind him, Hodgey locked it, then turned and made his way down the short path to the street. After glancing left and right, he appeared satisfied and crossed the street towards his car, parked on the opposite side the road.

Before he could deal with Hodge, he needed to ensure there was no one about; no witnesses. He'd already checked for any CCTV cameras fitted to the surrounding homes, and was pleased to see that only a couple of the residents had bothered to install them – and that those locations had no sight of his current position.

As Hodge reached his car, a loud beep and a flash of

lights indicated the central locking had been deactivated. It was time to move.

Pulling his balaclava over his face, he raced out of the shadows. As he went, he drew the Glock G17 from his pocket. In a flash he was on Hodge, and pressed the muzzle of the pistol into the base of his spine. 'Don't you fucking move, cunt!' he growled in his ear.

Hodge instinctively raised his arms in surrender.

'Off to have a nice chat with the police, are we?'

'I-I-I...' Hodge stuttered. 'I don't know what you're talking about. I'm just going to pick up a curry from the village.'

'Don't lie to me.'

'I'm not lying. It's a Lamb Madras,' Hodge replied with forced joviality.

'Move!' he said, voice low, as he pressed the gun harder into Hodge's back to force him forward.

Hodge walked slowly forward, hands raised.

Holding the gun tight against Hodge's spine, he pushed Hodge up onto the pavement and along the street until they reached his own car, parked a few meters along the road. 'Open the boot,' he said, his voice cool.

'Look, there's no need for this.' Hodge's voice was laced with panic.

'Do it now.'

Hodge reluctantly obliged, and the large boot opened softly.

He stepped in closer, and put his mouth next to Hodge's right ear. 'Nobody likes a rat, Hodgey.'

'I'm not a rat.'

'Yes you fucking are.' He took a step backwards now.

Hodge's head began turning towards him. 'Look. I swear on my mother's life, I'm not a gra—'

He slammed the base of the pistol grip into the base of Hodge's skull, knocking him out cold. The top half of Hodge's body slumped forwards into the boot of the car. Bending down, he quickly grabbed the man's legs with both arms and bundled the rest of him into the small space and out of sight.

He checked the street one more time and was relieved to see it remained empty, with no sign of any front doors opening. Satisfied no one was watching, he pulled the cable ties from the pocket of his hoodie and set about tying Hodge's hands and feet together before placing duct tape over his mouth. Standing up straight, he stared down at Mitchell Hodge, unconscious and hog-tied. A grin spread across his face. 'You know what they say, mate – "snitches get stitches".' He slammed the boot closed with a satisfying thud.

14

Jones pulled into the Alderley Edge Car Park just before ten. As the caller had suggested, it was completely empty, dog walkers and day trippers long since gone for the day. The summer sunshine had begun to fade and the sky was alive with colour, the orange and pink hues indicating another fine day was on the way.

Jones switched off the engine, and silence filled the car as they both said nothing for a long moment. He checked his watch. 'Well, whoever this guy is, I hope he's on time.'

'Me too,' replied Phillips.

'Have you heard about Josh Castillo?' Jones asked, and turned to face her.

Phillips frowned. 'No. Should I have?' Josh Castillo was serving ten years in Hawk Green for the manslaughter of his wife, and *she* had put him there.

'He's getting out.'

'Since when?'

'Since last week. The parole board approved his licence, so he'll be a free man in the morning.'

Phillips was incredulous. 'He's getting out *already*? How

long's he actually served?'

'Five and a half of the ten-stretch.'

'So what? That's it? He'll be back on the streets?'

'Yep, but under licence, Guv.'

'What?' Phillips scoffed. 'You mean the watchful eye of an overworked probation officer? How bloody reassuring.'

'I know, I know. I'm not happy about it either, and I'm not telling you to upset you. I just thought you'd want to know.'

Phillips blew her lips. 'Look, I'm sorry. Of course I want to know. It just feels like we break our necks trying to get bloody killers off the street, and before we know it, the parole board is chucking them right back at us!'

'Apparently he finally admitted to killing her.'

'Really? That does surprise me.'

'Me too. I mean, he was adamant he was innocent.'

'Aren't they all?' replied Phillips, before checking the time on the car's central console. It was 10.06 p.m. 'Our man's late.'

'Maybe it was a prank after all?'

Phillips hoped beyond hope that wasn't the case. 'Let's give him until 10.15, then take a look around.'

Jones nodded, and cast his gaze out the window.

As soon as the in-car clock display changed to 10.15, Phillips opened the passenger door. 'Right. Time to go look for him.' She stepped out into the warm evening air.

Jones followed suit, then headed for the boot and pulled out a heavy-duty torch.

Leading away from the car park, several numbered walking paths ran in various directions into the surrounding woodland. Each offered an alternate route towards *the edge*, a collection of rocks with stunning views across the Cheshire countryside, and gave the nearby village its name, Alderley Edge. Phillips was certain the mystery caller had named the car park as the meeting point, but figured, with a growing sense of impatience, that it was worth checking the edge itself. 'You wait here in case he turns up,' she said, and took the torch from Jones.

'Where are you going?'

'Out to the edge.'

'On your own? At this time of night?'

'I am capable of looking after myself, you know.' she replied curtly.

'I'm not saying you aren't, but it's getting dark and we have no idea who this guy is – or what he really wants.'

Phillips waved the torch. 'Which is why I've got this.'

'A torch won't be much good if he comes at you from the bushes. No, I'm coming with you.'

'Don't be daft, I'll be fine.'

'Sorry, boss. I'm coming with you and that's final.'

Phillips raised her arms in surrender. 'All right, all right,' she said, and set off down the darkened path.

The heavy-duty torch illuminated the world around them as they moved through the forest, taking care to avoid the odd fallen branch or large rock. The silence that surrounded them was broken only by their laboured breathing as they crested the brow of a hill, and the sound of their boots crunching against the hard ground as they moved along the path. Ten minutes later, they reached the edge just as the sun was setting on the horizon. It would be pitch black soon.

Phillips stood motionless for a moment, taking in the vista of the rolling hills beneath her feet, now shrouded in near darkness. Allowing her eyes to close, she could hear the gentle summer breeze susurrating through the trees at her back, accompanied by the hoot of an owl somewhere in the distance. For the first time in a long time, a sense of peace washed over her. An unexpected moment of respite from the chaos of her life.

'You ok, Guv?' asked Jones.

Phillips opened her eyes. 'Yes, just having a moment.'

A loud crack behind them sliced through the serenity.

Phillips heard movement, and heavy footsteps nearby. Her adrenaline spiked as she spun round on her heels and cast the torchlight into the trees. But there was nothing and no one to see. 'What the hell was that?' she whispered.

'Fucked if I know,' Jones whispered back.

With Jones at her side, Phillips stepped forward slowly, her heart pounding. 'Who's there?' she shouted, doing her best to keep her voice even.

No response.

Stepping farther forward now, she shouted again. 'I am DCI Phillips and this is DS Jones from the Major Crimes Unit. Who's there?'

Footsteps shuffled nearby, to their left. On instinct, Phillips turned towards them, casting the torch beam in their direction. The eyes that looked back at her now seemed to glow in the dark. 'Holy shit!' she said loudly.

'Jesus!' Jones said.

Staring back at them from the darkness was a large adult deer.

Phillips exhaled loudly, and an involuntary chuckle fell from her lips. She watched in awe as the magnificent beast gave them one last cursory look before turning and bolting deeper into the forest.

Jones giggled. 'God. I think I've just shit my pants.'

'Me too,' Phillips replied giddily before checking her watch. It was after 10.45. 'Well, it doesn't look like we're going to find our man out here, does it?'

'No, boss. Shall we head back to the car?'

'Good idea,' said Phillip as she arced the torchlight over the trees surrounding them. 'I think we've had more than enough wildlife for one night, don't you?'

'Yeah. And I really need to change my undies,' joked Jones.

15

FRIDAY 9TH JULY

Phillips had slept badly, the no-show at Alderley Edge playing on her mind. Had it been a crank caller, or had the informant been spooked by something? Had she and Jones unwittingly made a mistake regarding the location of the meeting point? The questions had rolled round and round in her mind all night, mixed in with wild, frenetic dreams as brief moments of sleep came and went. Eventually, just after 5 a.m., she gave up trying and left Adam snoring lightly in the king-sized bed.

She arrived at the office just after 7 and got straight to work, only looking up from her laptop when Entwistle arrived with a coffee for her at 8.30.

'Another early start, Guv?' He passed her the takeaway cup and took a seat opposite.

'Yeah. I couldn't sleep,' she said, and brought him up to speed on the events of the previous evening.

'So do you think it was just a crank caller?'

'The no-show would suggest that, but I can't help thinking, what if the person was legit and got spooked?'

'Want me to check the ANPR cameras around that area last night? See if anything of note shows up?'

Phillips took a sip of her coffee. 'Yeah. Do that. You never know, we might *finally* get lucky on this case.'

Entwistle drained his cup and dropped it in the waste bin. 'By the way, I've managed to track down a number of detectives who worked on the Boothroyd case back in ninety-three.'

'Anyone we can speak to?'

'Most of them are retired now and a couple of them have passed away, but there is one who was a young DC when Boothroyd was murdered, who is now an inspector. I've got her details on my desk.' Entwistle got up from the chair and headed out to his desk, returning a moment later with a leather-bound pad in his hands. 'Inspector Lia Hayley. She's based over in Sheffield with the South Yorkshire Police.'

Phillips took a moment to process the name, but it didn't ring any bells.

'She's been a uniformed inspector for close to ten years now,' said Entwistle, retaking his seat.

'Don't get comfy,' Phillips said, looking at her watch. 'If we leave now, we can be in Sheffield by ten.'

Entwistle recoiled slightly. 'You want *me* to come with you?'

'Yeah, Whistler. It'll do you good. Plus, if you have any plans of making detective sergeant anytime soon, you need to get out from behind that desk of yours. That ok with you?'

A broad, perfect smile flashed across his chiselled features. 'Yeah, great.'

Phillips threw a set of car keys at him. 'We'll take the squad car. I don't think a growing lad like you will fit in my Mini.'

WITH ENTWISTLE AT THE WHEEL, they left Ashton House and headed clockwise around the M60, Manchester's gargantuan outer ring-road. After taking the Sheffield exit, they passed through the villages of Hyde, Mottram and Glossop before finding themselves in the rolling green hills of the Snake Pass, the winding road that cut through the valleys of the Peak District National Park.

As they literally snaked through some of the most dramatic and breath-taking scenery on the planet, Phillips marvelled at how different the landscape was just twenty miles from of Manchester city centre. She made a mental note to bring Adam out walking here one day. The fresh country air, and the peace and quiet, would do them both a world of good.

Forty minutes later, they arrived at the headquarters of South Yorkshire Police, located on the edge of Sheffield city centre. The large, purpose-built building was not dissimilar to Ashton House; covered in reflective glass, with well-maintained but uninspiring landscaped gardens surrounding the large car park.

Entwistle pulled into a visitor's bay close to the main reception block and switched off the engine.

Phillips checked her watch. It was 10.11 a.m. 'So we're due to meet Inspector Hayley a 10.15, right?'

'Yes, Guv.'

'And how long did you say we've got?'

'Half an hour, tops. Apparently she's in back-to-back meetings from eleven for the rest of the day.'

'And she doesn't know the specifics about Bradley yet?'

'No. I just said we were following up on a cold case from her time in Manchester.'

'Good,' said Phillips, and reached for the car door handle. 'Let's see what she remembers about November the 5th, 1993, shall we?'

When they reached reception, they explained the purpose of their visit. A couple of minutes later, a petite woman with brown cropped hair, and wearing an inspector's uniform, made her way towards them.

'DCI Phillips?' she asked as she approached.

Phillips held out her hand. 'Inspector Hayley? Thanks for agreeing to see us.'

Hayley offered a firm shake. 'Please, call me Lia.'

'I'm Jane. This is one of my detectives, James Entwistle.'

'Nice to meet you both,' said Hayley. 'Are we ok to talk in one of the conference rooms?'

'Fine with me,' replied Phillips.

Hayley smiled, and led the way to a large room that annexed the reception area. The ceiling lights turned on automatically as they stepped inside the cool, air-conditioned space. After taking seats around the large conference table, Phillips got straight to the point. 'Are we right in thinking you worked as part of the investigating team on the Archie Boothroyd murder?'

Hayley's brow furrowed. 'Archie Boothroyd? Wow, that's going back a bit.'

'November the 5th, 1993,' replied Phillips.

'Yeah, Guy Fawkes night. Boothroyd was shot in the face during a fireworks display. Nobody noticed the gun going off, so his body remained undiscovered for days. It was only when a neighbour reported the smell that he was eventually found.'

'The case was never solved, was it?' said Phillips.

Hayley shook her head. 'No it wasn't, but then the SIO at the time wasn't particularly bothered about finding the killer either.'

'DCI Monaghan?'

'Yes. Somewhat *old school* in his approach, you might say.'

'What do you mean by that?'

'In his eyes, Boothroyd was well known as a gun-toting drug dealer. He was convinced he'd obviously had it coming, and said it was "one less scumbag to worry about". His words, not mine.'

'And was that the feeling of the rest of the team as well?'

'Pretty much,' said Hayley. 'I was the only female detective in the squad at the time, and there was a real macho drinking culture within the team. All the blokes were forever trying to impress Monaghan, so whatever he said was law.'

'What about you?'

'Well, like I said, I was the only woman in the squad and it was my first year as a detective, so I was just happy to have the job. I certainly didn't feel like it was my place to contradict him or go against the team.'

Phillips remembered it being a similar story when she started out. 'So, in your opinion, do you think the case was properly investigated at the time?'

Hayley pursed her lips for a long moment. 'Officially, it was done by the book.'

'And unofficially?' asked Phillips.

'Is this off the record?'

'Of course.'

'Well, in that case, I think it would best be described as a car crash that I'm still embarrassed to be connected to. Monaghan did just enough to appear as though he was taking it seriously, but as more new cases came in, it very quickly slipped down the list of priorities until it was eventually classified as a cold case. Monaghan celebrated that moment by buying everyone a round of drinks at the pub. Said it was a victory for common sense, and justice had been served.'

'Sounds very old school indeed,' said Phillips.

'Believe me, it was. It's one of the reasons I stepped away from detective work. It was a man's world back then, and there was no place for *me* in it.'

'Did you have any dealings with Paul Bradley back then?'

Hayley's eyes narrowed. 'Yeah, I did. Not much really, but he was a bit of a player at the time.'

'Was he in a gang?'

'Yeah. Part of the Moss Side crew, as I recall.'

'Do you remember if he had anything to do with Archie Boothroyd?'

'They were both young lieutenants in the same gang,' said Hayley. 'Both liked the life, the money, cars, and girls, of course. Especially Boothroyd. He was a real ladies' man – always had a different girl on his arm.'

'Anyone you can remember? Someone we could speak to perhaps?'

Hayley appeared deep in thought for a long moment. 'There were so many, but if my memory serves me right, there was one girl who Boothroyd spent more time with.'

'Do you remember her name?'

Hayley shook her head. 'Scarily, it was almost thirty years ago, so I'm afraid not.'

'Well, could you tell us what she looked like?'

Hayley's eyes narrowed. 'Peroxide blonde as I recall, almost white actually. And seriously feisty. One day we turned up to search Boothroyd's flat after a tip off he was storing drugs there. She was staying with him, and it all got a bit heated. She ended up assaulting one of the team, kicking and screaming like a banshee. It took three of us to pull her off him.'

'So, she was arrested? Maybe we could track her that way.'

'No, I'm afraid not. We had our hands full with the actual gang members. Monaghan wasn't interested in arresting the girlfriends. That's what I mean – it was a shit show.'

Phillips flashed a sympathetic smile. 'Sounds that way.'

Hayley sat forward and linked her fingers together on the table. 'Can I ask why you're interested in Boothroyd's murder after all this time?'

'We're not certain at this stage, but we think it could be connected to a murder that happened in Manchester on Sunday night. Like Boothroyd, the victim was shot through the eye, and had a front tooth removed. And we believe the execution took place while the village's 4th of July fireworks display was in full flow, once again masking the sound of the shots.'

'Oh God,' said Hayley.

'Stranger still, the dead man was actually Paul Bradley.'

Hayley's eyes widened. 'I'd heard on the grapevine he'd been killed, but I didn't know the details.'

'Yes. And despite the amount of time that's passed, it feels like too much of a coincidence that two former gang members were executed in exactly the same way.'

Hayley's expression was grave. 'I'd have to agree,'

'We were hoping we might find a clue to Bradley's murder in some of the finer details of the Boothroyd killing. We've checked the historical case files, but so far found nothing that stands out.'

'Well, I'll help you in any way I can, Chief Inspector, but like I said, it wasn't the most comprehensive investigation, and it was a very long time ago.'

'I appreciate that. Thank you,' replied Phillips. She changed tack again. 'Did you ever come across a man called Adders Bahmani during that time? A well-built Pakistani chap. Works in scrap these days.'

Hayley's brow furrowed. 'The name doesn't mean anything to me, I'm afraid.'

'We think he could have been involved in one of the drug gangs back then.'

'Maybe, but there was a lot of gangs and a lot of kids involved in the nineties. If they weren't at the top of the hierarchy, then we rarely got to know their names. He might have been a runner for one of the gangs, moving the drugs around on BMXs.' Hayley checked her watch. 'I don't mean to be rude, Chief Inspector, but is there anything else you need to know? I have a team briefing in ten minutes, so I really need to be going.'

'No. I think that's it for now,' said Phillips.

'I have to say, it's always bugged me that Boothroyd's killer got away with his murder, scumbag or not. So please, do let me know if I can help with anything else. I'd love to see the case finally solved.'

Phillips nodded. 'I will, of course.'

'I'll show you out,' said Hayley, standing.

Phillips and Entwistle followed suit, and a minute later found themselves back in the car park and walking towards the squad car.

'How do you think that went, Guv?' asked Entwistle.

'Well. It filled in a few gaps, I guess, but nothing of real value from her perspective. That said, it is interesting to hear that the Boothroyd case was never properly investigated.'

'I know. I couldn't believe it when she said that.'

'Oh, I can,' Phillips shot back. 'The detective world back then was like the wild west. And the world was very different: very few digital files, no social media, very little CCTV, and ANPR cameras didn't exist. If you wanted to bury a case – or lose evidence that didn't fit with your theory – it was very easy to do. Thankfully, though, we still have all the original case files, or at least what they left in the box. When we get back, I want to go through them with a fine-toothed comb. See if we can find anything lurking inside.'

'I'll get straight on it,' said Entwistle, and unlocked the car.

Thanks to her early start, Phillips's stomach rumbled. 'Are you hungry?'

'I am, actually.'

'Right. I spotted a nice-looking pub on the way over here. Let's stop there on the way back, and I'll treat you to some lunch.'

'A scenic drive and a free lunch? I could get used to this,' said Entwistle as he opened the driver's door.

'See. I told you it pays to get out from behind your desk,' said Phillips, and dropped into the passenger seat.

———

PHILLIPS AND ENTWISTLE took seats at one of the many tables outside the Ladybower Inn as they waited for their food to arrive. The sun shone in a cloudless sky, and they both donned sunglasses as they looked out over the massive expanse of water that was the Ladybower Reservoir, just a few metres away.

'There's a village in there, you know,' said Phillips, and took a sip of her diet coke.

Entwistle looked puzzled. 'In where?'

'There.' She pointed at the water. 'Before the reservoir was built, there was a village in the valley. Houses, a church, shops, even a school. All covered in water now.'

'Surely they demolished them before they flooded it.'

'Why bother?'

Entwistle shrugged. 'I dunno. I guess it seems kind of odd to just leave it there.'

Phillips stared at the water. 'My dad took me for a walk around it once, when we first came back from Hong Kong. He's a bit of a history buff, so he'd been reading up on it. I still remember it all. They started building it in 1935, but construction stopped for a while during the Second World War. Then, because of the strategic importance of the water supply, work started again, and it was completed in 1943. After that, it took until 1945 to fill it with water. Apparently the church tower was still visible three years later, but the rest of the village had disappeared.'

'That sounds kinda creepy.'

'Doesn't it. Since my dad told me that, I've often wondered if anyone took advantage of the flooding.'

'How do you mean?'

'Well, you know. Are there any unaccounted-for bodies lodged down there?'

'In the nicest possible way, boss, you've got one sick imagination.'

Phillips chuckled and took another sip of her drink. 'And that's why I'm a detective, Whistler.'

Just then, a pretty young waitress arrived with their food; a burger for Entwistle and a tuna sandwich for Phillips, each accompanied by mountains of red-hot fries.

'Thank you,' said Entwistle, flashing his trademark poster-boy smile as the waitress placed the plates down on the table.

The girl smiled back and blushed slightly as he held her gaze.

Phillips shook her head. He really did have a gift when it came to women. It was like watching moths around a flame.

With a notable spring in her step, the waitress headed back inside the pub.

Phillips watched her go and turned back to Entwistle 'You still not got a girlfriend?' she asked before taking a bite of her sandwich.

Entwistle swallowed a mouthful of the burger. 'No. Well, nothing serious, anyway.'

Phillips narrowed her eyes. 'So what does "nothing serious" mean, then?'

Entwistle shrugged. 'Just that there's a couple of girls I like to hang out with, but not exclusively.'

'So you've got two girlfriends?'

Entwistle laughed loudly. 'Not quite. More like I'm dating a couple of women but keeping my options open.'

'And do these women know about each other?'

'Yeah, kind of. Like I said, they both know it's not exclusive.'

'I don't know how you find the time,' said Phillips. 'Or the energy, for that matter.'

Entwistle held up his burger in both hands. 'Protein, boss. Protein.'

Phillips smiled. It was good getting to know her DC a little bit better. She'd always been fond of him, and his work was exemplary, but he kept quite a low profile in the team. Not surprising, with two characters like Jones and Bovalino to contend with. But she was glad to see he had started to come out of his shell recently, and she was starting to see there was a lot more to him than just being the 'tech guy'.

By the time they'd finished their meal fifteen minutes later, she knew even more about him; like the fact he'd been a star athlete at university, and a knee injury had stopped him trying out for the British Olympic Team in 2016; he played the drums to help de-stress; and his ideal woman was the movie star, Emma Stone – blaming his Irish roots for his fondness of redheads.

Right on cue, the waitress returned to check on them. As she bent down to clear the plates, Phillips could have sworn she'd recently touched up her make up.

At that moment, Phillips's phone began to ring. It was Bovalino. 'Bov,' she said hitting the green answer button and stepping up from the table.

'I've got something I thought might be of interest, Guv.'

'Ok.'

'I've been looking through all the private CCTV footage we gathered from around the Bradley's house on Sunday night, and I've noticed something odd.'

'Like what?' she asked, pacing around the car park.

'Freddie Bradley's car can be seen driving towards his parents' place at 7.28 p.m., about thirty minutes before his dad was shot. But he didn't appear at the house until after 9.45 p.m.'

'That *is* odd.' Phillips rolled the time frame round in her mind. 'He told me and Jonesy that he was in the city on Sunday night.'

'He was, Guv. In fact, his car was spotted just after 8 in the Northern Quarter, down near his pal Shanks's apartment.'

'So why didn't he go home?'

'I dunno. But I've checked the ANPR feeds and tracked his car from the camera at the traffic junction in Alderley Edge at 7.28, driving towards the Bradley house, then reappearing on the same camera five minutes later, going in the opposite direction and all the way back into the city.'

'What the hell was he doing, and why didn't he share any of this with us when we spoke to him on Sunday night?'

'No idea, Guv, but I can go and talk to him if you like?'

Phillips looked over at Entwistle, still revelling in the attention of the waitress. 'Don't worry about it. I'll take Whistler. We're heading back to Ashton House now, so we can make a detour on the way.'

'No worries.'

'But rather than me trying to track Freddie down, can you call him and find out where he'll be this afternoon? I don't want to waste the rest of the day looking for him.'

'Sure, Guv. I'll do it now and give you a shout back once I know.'

'Thanks.' Phillips ended the call and made her way back to Entwistle. 'Right then, lover-boy,' she said loudly, 'I'll pay the bill and then we've gotta go.'

She noticed Entwistle blush slightly as she headed into the pub, and a devilish grin spread across her face. Well, if she couldn't embarrass her boys every once in a while, what was the point of being the boss?

16

Bovalino had managed to track Freddie to his father's night club in Manchester's gay village. It was late afternoon when Phillips and Entwistle walked through the front door of Vibe. The club wouldn't be open to the public until 10 p.m., and the empty space appeared cavernous with only a few staff members milling about behind the long bar that ran the length of one wall. Phillips made herself known to one of the team, who guided her and Entwistle to the office at the rear of the building. As they approached the open door, Phillips could see Freddie sitting in a large black leather chair behind a mahogany desk, his eyes fixed on an A4-sized journal lying on the desk.

She rapped softly on the door. 'Can we come in?'

Freddie's eyes darted up to meet hers, and he frowned. 'I've been expecting you lot.'

'This won't take long,' Phillips said as she stepped into the office with Entwistle at her rear. There was nowhere to sit, so they remained standing.

Freddie closed the journal, then reclined in his seat. 'What do you want?'

'There seems to be a bit of confusion around your move-ments on the night your dad was killed. I wanted to check them with you.'

'*My* movements?' He folded his arms across his chest. 'Why do you want to know about my movements? Am I a suspect or something?'

'It's just procedure,' replied Phillips coolly.

'Well, if you must know, I was with a girl at my mate Shanks's flat in the Northern Quarter.'

'All night?'

'Most of it, yeah.'

'What about at 7.30? Where were you then?'

Freddie shrugged. 'I don't remember.'

'Because this is where the confusion comes in,' said Phillips. 'See, your car was spotted on one of our cameras, driving towards your parents' house just before 7.30, but never made it there. Instead, we can see it turned around and headed back into the city. Why was that?'

Freddie stared at her in silence for a long moment. 'I *was* heading to Mum and Dad's, but then Letitia called me.'

'Letitia?' asked Phillips.

'A girl I see from time to time. She made me an offer I couldn't refuse.'

'What do you mean by that?'

A wide grin spread across his face. 'It was a booty-call.'

Phillips nodded.

'She wanted sex,' leered Freddie.

'I know what it means,' Phillips shot back.

'She was in the city when she called, so I told her to meet me at Shanks's gaff at 8.15. We got down to it, and about forty minutes later Mum called and told me about Dad. Obviously, I got back home as quick as I could.'

'Why didn't you mention any of this when we spoke on Sunday night?'

Freddie shrugged. 'I didn't think my sex life was any of your business, to be honest.'

Phillips said nothing for a moment. 'You mentioned before that Adders Bahmani had been telling everyone he was planning to take over your dad's businesses. Where did you hear that?'

'Around.'

'Could you be more specific?'

'Just around. You know how it is. Whispers here and there.'

It was obvious Freddie had little love for the police, and was enjoying being deliberately obtuse.

'Has he ever spoken to you directly?' asked Phillips.

'Bahmani?'

'Yes.'

'Just a couple of times. He came in here once to talk to Dad. Walked round like he owned the gaff.'

'The night your dad died, you seemed certain that Bahmani was involved.'

'He was!' spat Freddie.

'What makes you so sure?'

'Because Bahmani had the most to gain from getting rid of my dad. With Dad out of the way, he thought he could steam in here and take over the business. But that ain't happening. Not with me and Shanks around.'

Phillips scanned the office. 'So you're in charge now, are you?'

'Damn right I am, and if Bahmani thinks he can push me around like he did my dad, he's in for a whole world of pain.'

Phillips stared at Freddie in silence for a long moment. 'Look, Freddie, I know you're angry about what happened to your dad – and for good reason – but we can't have things getting out of hand. We don't know for sure Bahmani was involved, and even if we could prove he was, that makes him *our* problem. Not *yours.*'

Freddie sat forward and linked his fingers together on the desk. 'All I'm saying is, if Bahmani comes looking for me, I'll be ready to defend myself and what's mine. And if I *do* find out he tied up my mum and killed my dad, he'd better pray to God that you get to him before I do.'

'Like I said, we're the law, Freddie, *not you*,' said Phillips.

'Depends on your point of view, I guess.'

Phillips glanced towards Entwistle, then back to Freddie. 'Right, well, I think we're finished here for the time being.'

'You can see yourselves out,' said Freddie, and returned his gaze to the ledger.

They walked quickly back to the car. 'He's not winning any awards for charm, is he, Guv?' said Entwistle, once they were outside.

'I've seen it all before, Whistler,' replied Phillips. 'A boy in a man's world, playing at being a gangster. But the problem is, the real villains don't play games. They kill people. And if Freddie Bradley's not careful, he could well end up in the same place as his dad: six feet under.'

As they reached the car, Phillips checked her watch. It was approaching 4 p.m. 'We're not that far from Ancoats here, are we?'

'About five minutes, I reckon.'

'You've never met Adders Bahmani, have you?'

Entwistle shook his head. 'No, I've not had the pleasure.'

'Well, seeing as we're so close—' Phillips flashed a wicked grin. '—I think it's about time you did.'

BAHMANI WAS outside talking to his cousin, Tahir, when they drove into the yard. Phillips could have sworn she saw a snarl form on his lips as he laid eyes on them.

By the time they'd parked up and got out of the car, Tahir had been dispatched and Bahamni stood alone, staring at them. 'What do you want?' he shouted as they walked towards him.

'Just a quiet chat,' said Phillips.

'Well, you can chat to my lawyer. I've got nothing to say to you.'

'Now now, Adders, don't be like that.'

Bahmani looked Entwistle up and down. 'Who's the goon?'

'That's no way to talk about Detective Constable Entwistle. He's one of the smartest young coppers on the force.'

'Wouldn't take much,' Bahmani said with distain.

Phillips ignored the jibe and got straight to the point. 'Where did you go when you were released from custody on Wednesday?'

Bahmani shrugged. 'I came here. The place doesn't run itself, you know.'

'So you didn't take a trip out to east Manchester?'

'No. Not me. I was here all day with Tahir. He can vouch for that.'

'You see, that's funny. Because two men fitting yours and Tahir's descriptions were spotted at the scene of a crime there, about an hour after you left us.'

'There's a lot of Pakistani men in east Manchester.'

'True,' replied Phillips, 'but these two men were driving a van fitted with SORN plates registered to *this* yard.'

Bahmani let out an ironic chuckle. 'Not this number plate shit again. There's no way you can stick that on me.'

'We have a witness.'

'No, you don't, or you'd have a uniform team here to arrest me again. The fact you're on your own means you've got nothing, and this is just a fishing trip.' Bahmani said smugly.

'We've also got the fact the gun used to kill Bradley was a match for the one we found here.'

'And what does that prove, exactly?' Bahmani waved his arm in an arc through the air. 'Look around you, Inspector. This is a big yard with lots and lots of blind spots. Anybody pretending to be a customer could have wandered out of sight, put that gun in the car. You didn't find my fingerprints on it, and unless you've since pulled my DNA from it – which I'm guessing you haven't – then you cannot tie that gun to me, or me to Bradley's murder.'

He was right and Phillips knew it, the smug prick.

Bahmani continued. 'After leaving you lot, I came straight here, where I stayed all day, working with Tahir. I don't know anything about any incidents in east Manchester, and if people are gonna nick number plates from my yard, I can't be held responsible for what they do with them afterwards. And as we both know, *Inspector*, you've got form for trying to pin crimes on me that I had nothing to do with. So, if you've got nothing else, I'd like to get on with my job.'

Phillips clenched her jaw as she stared at him and the smug grin that had spread across his face. 'Actually, it's *Chief* Inspector. Try and get it right.'

'Chief *bitch*, more like,' Bahmani muttered.

'Watch your mouth, mate.' Entwistle stepped towards the big man, who instinctively took a step back.

Phillips shook her head at Entwistle, who continued to stare at Bahmani. The pair resembled a couple of prize fighters at the weigh-in. 'Come on, let's go,' she said, and grabbed his arm.

Entwistle finally acquiesced, and they returned to the

squad car. 'What a prick,' said Entwistle as he slammed the driver's door shut.

'Isn't he just?' replied Phillips, as she stared through the windscreen at Bahmani, who waved at them as Entwistle began to reverse away. 'He's up to his neck in all this, and one way or the other, I'm gonna prove it.'

'Where to now, Guv?' asked Entwistle, as they headed towards the yard gates. 'Back to base?'

Phillips stared out at the main road and the cars passing by for a long moment before speaking. 'No. I've got a better idea. Let's take a drive out to Cheadle.'

'What's out there?'

'Right now, probably the only chink in Adders Bahmani's armour. I think it's time we finally took advantage of it.'

17

With Entwistle just behind her, Phillips led the way up the long, narrow path to the double-width front door of the massive detached house, and rang the doorbell. What sounded like a large dog began barking loudly on the other side.

'I've never liked dogs,' said Entwistle in a low voice.

'Me neither,' replied Phillips.

The dog continued barking ferociously.

'You sure this is a good idea, Guv?'

'No. But that's never stopped me before.'

A moment later, they heard what appeared to be a young man's voice shouting, and then the dog being dragged away on the other side. A few more seconds passed before the front door was opened by a pretty, diminutive woman, no taller than five feet, dressed in traditional Pakistani clothes.

Phillips wasted no time and flashed her police ID. 'Are you Gulsan Bahmani?'

The woman nodded, but appeared unsure of herself.

'I'm DCI Phillips, and this is DC Entwistle from the Major Crimes Unit. May we come in for a minute?'

Gulsan's face fell, and panic filled her eyes. 'My husband is not here.'

'Good, because it's not him we wanted to talk to. It's you. It'll only take a minute.'

Phillips could tell Gulsan wasn't a confident woman, so stepped forward in an attempt to persuade her to let them in. It worked. She took a step backward and opened the door fully, allowing Phillips and Entwistle access to the entrance hall. The dog could still be heard barking, locked in a room close by.

Just then a young man – probably in his late teens – appeared from a door behind Gulsan. 'Who are you and why are you hassling my mum?' he asked, his tone aggressive.

'We're the police, son,' replied Entwistle, flashing his badge.

'I ain't your son, and you can't come in here without a warrant.'

'Calm down,' said Phillips. 'This isn't the movies. We're not performing a search, so we don't need a warrant. We're just here to ask your mother a couple of questions.'

The boy glared at his mother. 'Say nothing, right. I'm calling Dad.' With that, he disappeared back through the door he'd emerged from.

Phillips knew time was against them. As soon as Bahmani heard they were here, he'd be home in a flash, so she pressed on with her questions while they stood in the entrance hall. 'Gulsan. Can I call you Gulsan?'

Mrs Bahmani nodded once more.

'Where were you on Sunday night, around 8 p.m.?'

Gulsan's eyes oozed uncertainty as they darted between Phillips and Entwistle. 'Er, I was here. I'm always here.'

'I see. And was anyone else with you?'

'My mother, my two sons and my daughter.'

Phillips raised an eyebrow. 'So, your husband wasn't here?'

Gulsan scratched her forehead and appeared confused. 'Er...yes, yes of course. He was, Adders was here.'

'You don't sound very sure,' said Phillips.

'He was. We were all here, all night. All of us.'

Phillips said nothing for a long moment as she studied Gulsan's face. The woman was clearly flustered. 'I know you want to protect your husband, but if you're saying he was here, and we find out he wasn't, you could end up in a whole lot of trouble. And I mean *serious* trouble.'

'I'm not lying. I'm telling you the truth.'

'I don't believe you,' said Phillips coldly. 'And I don't think a Crown Court jury would believe you either. Because ultimately, that's where this could end up if you lie to us about where your husband was on Sunday night. Come on, Gulsan. Where was he? Really?'

Gulsan stood straight, a look of defiance on her face. 'Adders was here with me, *all night*. I will vouch for him, my mother will, and so will my children.'

At that moment the door opened again, and the young man reappeared, his chest proud like a peacock as he swaggered across the hallway. 'Dad's on his way, Mum. He was already coming home when I called, so he'll be here any minute.'

Phillips glanced at Entwistle. His expression matched her thoughts. It was clear Mrs Bahmani was not about to give them anything, which meant the best thing to do would be to get out of here before her husband arrived and all hell broke loose. 'Well, thank you for your time, Gulsan. We'll be in touch if we need anything else.'

Entwistle stepped out onto the front step and Phillips followed. They walked briskly down the path and back to the car.

Suddenly, the sound of a powerful engine revving filled the air. A second later, a white Range Rover sped round the corner and screeched to a halt in front of the squad car. 'You've got a fucking nerve!' Bahmani growled as he jumped out of the driver's door.

Phillips's pulse quickened as Bahmani rushed towards her. 'I was just asking your wife a couple of questions,' she said, trying her best to keep her voice even.

Bahmani stopped just inches from her. 'Who do you think you are, forcing your way into my house and upsetting my wife and kids?'

'We're the police, and we didn't force our way in anywhere,' said Phillips.

Bahmani's eyes danced as he pointed a finger directly at her face and leaned closer. 'This is fucking harassment, racial prejudice and racial profiling – and I'm gonna sue you for the bloody lot. You've gone too far this time, Phillips, and you're gonna regret it. Nobody messes with my family and gets away with it. *Nobody!*'

Phillips stood her ground with Entwistle at her side. 'Is that a threat, Adders?'

'You're damn right it is.'

It was Phillips's turn to stepped closer this time. 'I don't take kindly to be threatened, especially by a scumbag like you. Do you hear me?'

Bahmani sucked his teeth with disdain. 'The only thing I hear is your career going down the toilet. By the time Nic Johnson's finished with you, you're gonna wish you'd never heard the name Bahmani.'

Phillips flashed a thin smile as she held his gaze. 'Don't hold your breath, big man.' She turned to Entwistle next. 'Come on. It's time we were going.'

Entwistle nodded, and headed towards with the car.

'I'll be seeing you, Adders,' she said, glancing back at Bahmani before turning and following her detective.

'You can count on it,' Bahmani shouted after her. 'Because this ain't over between you and me, Phillips. Not by a long shot!'

18

Back at the office an hour later, the team debriefed on their progress over the last five days, which had been slow by MCU standards. Phillips had no doubt the guys had been working flat out. They'd just come up against one of those investigations where nothing seemed straightforward, and very little had gone according to plan. As the time approached 6.30 p.m., she ordered them all to go home and make the most of some valuable down time. It would do them good to see their families and friends, let off a little steam.

Phillips followed them out about an hour later, and jumped in the Mini Cooper. Pulling out of the car park, she flicked on the radio and set off for home. Classical music filled the small car, and for the next twenty minutes she drove on autopilot towards Chorlton and an evening in with Adam. Just what she needed.

But ten minutes later, the Bluetooth hands-free kit came alive to the sound of Elvis Presley's 'Are You Lonesome Tonight?' – Adam's ringtone and *their* song. 'Hey, babe,' she said as she pressed the answer button.

'*Hi Janey.*' Adam sounded stressed.

'Everything ok?'

'*Yeah. Well, no. Not really. I'm still at work.*'

Phillips noted the time on the dashboard clock. 'It's almost eight o'clock. You were supposed to be finished an hour ago, weren't you?'

'*Yeah, I was, but there's been a massive RTA on the M62 just outside the city, and they've been bringing them in for the last hour and a half. I thought I might be able to hand over to the next shift, but it looks like they need me.*'

Phillips's heart sank. The way she felt, she really needed one of Adam's hugs.

'*I'm sorry, Janey. I know tonight was the first Friday night we'd both had off in ages.*'

'Don't be daft,' said Phillips, trying her best to hide her disappointment. 'It was just going to be a night on the sofa. You do what you need to do, babe.'

'*Thanks, love. I'll make it up to you.*'

'No you won't. Your job has to come first at times like this. So stop worrying about me and get back and help them. Ok?'

'*Ok,*' said Adam. '*Love you.*'

'Love you too.'

Phillips ended the call and drove for the next few minutes without taking in where she was going as her mind relayed the events of the week, culminating in the standoff with Bahmani. Despite her bravado, she had a growing sense of foreboding that her impromptu visit to speak to his wife was going to bite her on the arse.

Just then, her eyes landed on the exit sign for Wilmslow and Alderley Edge. On a whim, she pulled the car left and headed for the exit ramp. The time was approaching 8.15 p.m. Now she had nothing to do, she might as well use the next few hours to her advantage. Heading for the scene of Sunday night's murder, she hoped it might inspire her thinking. Switching the radio to something livelier and more appropriate for the start of the weekend, she zipped along the A34. It was a beautiful warm night and, without the air-conditioning of modern-day cars, the classic Mini soon began to heat up. Dropping the driver's window allowed fresh air to circulate. The sounds of the salubrious English neighbourhood filled the air around her as birds chirped, and young families laughed and played together in their large walled gardens.

She parked up outside the house of Paul and Melissa Bradley, and switched off the engine. The Bradley house appeared to be empty, with just one car parked on the drive: Paul's large blue Bentley SUV. Staring at the house, Phillips wondered who had broken in and pulled the trigger just five nights ago. She decided to get out and take a walk to see if it might offer some much-needed inspiration.

As she strolled casually up and down the wide, tree-lined street for the next ten minutes, she took in the affluent houses, surrounded by a mixture of high walls, mature bushes and trees. Again, she noted the stillness, and considered the shrewd planning from the killer's point of view. Shooting Bradley at the time of the July 4th fireworks display was a brilliant way of masking the crime, just as it had been on the night Archie Boothroyd had been murdered all those years ago.

As she returned to her car, a car approached slowly from behind. Turning to face it, she spotted Melissa Bradley behind the wheel of a gold convertible BMW M3 coupe. The roof was down and she wore gym gear, her thick dark hair tied back in a ponytail. 'You lost something, Chief Inspector?' asked Melissa.

'My mind, maybe,' said Phillips, stepping next to the car.

'What are you doing all the way out here on a Friday night?'

'Thinking.' Phillips cast her gaze down the street. 'Trying to put a few pieces together on Paul's case.'

'You look like you could do with a drink. Why don't you come in for a few minutes?'

'Are you sure I'm not intruding?'

'Not at all. In fact, you'll be doing me a favour.' Melissa's eyes were filled with sadness. 'The house feels so big without Paul in it, and Freddie's never home. A bit of company would be very welcome right now.'

'Of course,' said Phillips softly. 'I get so focused on the victims, I sometimes forget about the people left behind. In that case, I'll have a cup of tea if there's one going.'

'Follow me.' Melissa smiled before pulling the car noisily onto the long gravelled drive.

Ten minutes later, Phillips found herself in the gargantuan lounge that overlooked the garden and swimming pool, a cup of tea in her hand. Her eyes scanned the vast array of framed photographs that hung around the room – pictures of Paul and Melissa, smiling happily for the camera, in various locations around the world.

Melissa dropped onto the sofa next to her and took a large mouthful of her gin and tonic before exhaling loudly and wiping her mouth. 'God! You cannot beat a gin and tonic after a workout.'

Phillips took a sip of her tea. 'It's been a long time since I stepped foot in a gym, but I know what you mean about an ice-cold G&T.'

'They were Paul's favourite,' said Melissa, before catching herself and staring at the floor for a long moment.

'I'm sure you've been asked this a million times this week, but how are you holding up?'

'Up and down by the hour, to be honest.' Melissa's eyes

were filled with sadness. 'One minute I'm fine and think everything's going to be ok, and then, bam! I'm curled up in a ball on the bed, sobbing.'

'I can imagine.'

'In the blink of an eye, everything has changed. *Everything.*'

'And how do you think Freddie's coping with it?'

Melissa took another drink. 'He told me you'd been to see him today.'

'He seems adamant that Adders Bahmani was involved in Paul's death.'

'That's my fault,' said Melissa. 'I was in shock on Sunday when it all happened, and I mentioned the hassle Paul had been getting off Bahmani. Freddie being Freddie, he's latched onto that and can't let go. He's just like his father in that way.'

'I warned him to stay out of it for his own sake. The last thing we need is any more violence.'

'He told me that – or words to that effect, at least,' Melissa drained her glass before getting up off the sofa and fixing herself another.

When she returned, Phillips decided it wouldn't hurt to do some careful digging. 'I was talking to a colleague of mine this morning who knew Paul back in the nineties.'

'Oh,' said Melissa, eyebrows raised.

'Yeah. She said he was big mates with a guy called Archie Boothroyd.'

Melissa nodded. 'I remember him. A bit of a bad boy. Seriously good looking, but knew it, and a total dog. He shagged anything that moved, that one.'

'Sounds like you knew him well.'

Melissa shrugged. 'Not really. A little flirt here and there, but I knew better than to get involved with him. It never ended well for the girls that dated Archie.'

'So, were he and Paul mates?' asked Phillips.

'Close rivals, more like.'

'Did Paul ever talk to you about Archie's murder?'

'No. Never. Why do you ask?'

'Because Archie and Paul were killed in exactly the same way, but thirty years apart.'

Sadness filled Melissa's face. 'The family liaison officer told me the details of what they did to Paul.'

'I'm sorry. This can't be easy for you.'

'It's fine. Oddly, it helps to talk about it.' Melissa appeared to steel herself. 'So, the same thing happened to Archie all those years ago?'

'Yes. And stranger still, they were both killed while firework displays were happening nearby, in order to mask the gun shots.'

Melissa's expression was incredulous. 'I don't believe it. Surely *that's* not true?'

'I'm afraid it is.'

'So what are you saying? That Paul and Archie were killed by the *same* person?'

'At this stage, we're not sure,' replied Phillips, 'but because no one was ever convicted for Archie's murder, we certainly can't rule it out.'

'Oh God.'

'Can you think of anyone from the past who might have had issue with Archie, who might also want to hurt Paul?'

Melissa's eyes dropped to her knees, and she sat silent for some time. 'To be honest, I didn't really know Archie well enough, and Paul certainly never mentioned anyone. So no, I can't. Sorry.'

'Don't be,' said Phillips warmly. 'I'm sorry I brought it up.'

Melissa's gaze moved to the floor-to-ceiling windows that led out to the garden.

'Look, I should be going.' Phillips stepped up from the sofa. 'I've ruined enough of your Friday night.'

'Will you catch him?' asked Melissa, locking eyes with Phillips now. 'The man who killed my Paulie? Will you catch him?'

'I'm certainly going to do everything I can, yes.'

19

SATURDAY 10TH JULY

The next morning, Phillips crept out of bed and put on a pot of fresh coffee, leaving Adam to sleep off the extended shift. Saturday mornings provided a mix of emotions depending on how her caseload was faring. When she was on top of things, weekends offered a welcome break and a chance to spend time with Adam, relaxing and recharging her batteries. But with a case like Bradley's on her hands, she felt a desperate need to get back into the office and drive the investigation forwards. Not great when it came to maintaining a healthy relationship.

Phillips switched on the radio, poured herself a large mug of coffee, then wandered over to the bi-folding doors at the rear of the house, released the locks and pulled them open. Even though it was only 9 a.m., the air outside was already warm. The sunlight made the array of flowers in her garden seem brighter and more intense. Stepping out onto the lawn, she scrunched her bare toes into the cool grass and looked around the recently landscaped space. It really was a sanctuary on mornings like this. Standing in the garden, with the sun on her face and the smell of fresh coffee and flowers filling the air, she experienced a sudden and unexpected moment of contentedness.

'Is there one of those for me?'

Phillips opened her eyes and spun to find Adam standing in the doorway in just his boxer shorts, a sight she never tired of. 'I thought you'd be having a lie-in.'

Adam moved out into the garden. 'What? And miss spending time with my gorgeous Janey.' He wrapped his arms around her waist and kissed her on the forehead.

She smiled as she looked up into his bright blue eyes. 'Fancy a bacon roll?'

'God, I love you,' he said, with a grin that showed off his chiselled features.

'Come on. I'll get the grill on.'

Phillips led the way inside and began to prepare their breakfast while Adam disappeared upstairs to find a T-shirt to wear. He returned a few minutes later and took a seat on a stool at the breakfast bar in the kitchen.

Phillips placed his freshly made sandwich on a plate in front of him. 'So, what do you want to do today?'

Adam took a bite. 'It looks like it's going to be another lovely day. Do you fancy a run out in car? Maybe get a pub lunch?'

'Sounds great.'

'Maybe we could have a proper chat.' Adam took a bite of his sandwich.

Phillips eyed him suspiciously. 'About what?'

Adam swallowed. 'You know, about us moving in together?'

Phillips felt her shoulders sag as she took a gulp of her coffee.

'Or maybe not, judging by your face.'

Phillips placed the mug down on the countertop. 'Look, it's not that I don't want to move in together—'

'Well, what is it then?' Adam cut her off.

'It's just I've got a lot on my plate with work at the moment, and I don't feel like now is the best time to talk about something as important as this.'

'So when *will* be the right time, Jane? When?'

'Soon. I promise. Once I get this Bradley case into some kind of shape. We can talk about it then.'

'And what if another case comes up in the meantime? Another one you can't solve. Will that get in the way too?'

Phillips opened her mouth to speak but couldn't find the right words. Thankfully, at that very moment her phone began to ring, giving her an excuse to cut the conversation short. It was GMP Control.

She hit the green answer button. 'This is Phillips.'

'Morning, Ma'am. This is Sergeant Sellers from Control. I'm sorry to bother you on a Saturday, but something's come in that I thought you'd want to know about.'

Phillips knew Micky Sellers well. He was an experienced copper who kept his ear to the ground. She respected his opinion.

It seemed Adam had had enough, as he slipped off the breakfast stool and left the room. Phillips watched him go, then turned her attention back to the call.

'What have you got?'

'One of the teams has been called to a body in the park at Pin Mill Brow.'

'Up near Ancoats?'

'Yes, ma'am.'

'And what makes you think I'd be interested as opposed to the on-call SIO?'

'The victim was shot through the eye and had one of his front teeth removed. Like the Bradley murder.'

A shiver ran the length of Phillips's spine. 'Who called it in?'

'A jogger, out for an early morning run. Patrol checked it out and the paramedics just confirmed life extinct. Do you want the case, or should I pass it over to DCI Sullivan? He's the on-call SIO.'

'No. MCU will take it, Micky. You did the right thing bringing this to me first, thanks.'

'My pleasure, ma'am.'

'Can you call in CSI?

'Of course. Straight away.'

Phillips ended the call and immediately dialled Jones.

He answered promptly. *'Morning, Guv,'*

'We've got another body with a gunshot to the eye and a front tooth missing.'

'You're kidding? Where?'

'Pin Mill Brow, over by Ancoats. A jogger found the victim this morning and I just got a call from Micky Sellers in Control. He rang me first to see if I wanted it, which of course I do. It's so similar, it surely has to be connected to the Bradley and Boothroyd murders.'

'What time should I meet you there?' asked Jones.

'To be honest, I wasn't expecting you to come with me. Are you sure you can get away? It is Saturday. I thought you'd have plans.'

'I've got a list of DIY jobs as long as my arm, and absolutely no desire to do them whatsoever. This is the perfect excuse to get out of them. So, what time shall I meet you?'

Phillips could relate. This situation gave her the perfect get-out too.

'See you there in an hour.' She ended the call and headed upstairs to get dressed.

Adam was already in the shower, the door to the en suite locked shut. She raised her hand to knock, but thought better of it. Time was of the essence. Plus, she was in no mood for another argument. So she dressed quickly, pulled her hair into a ponytail and took a slug of the mouthwash she kept in the main bathroom.

Back downstairs, she wrote Adam a note.

Sorry, babe, an urgent case has come in. I've got to go. I'll call you later. J xxx

She pinned it to the fridge with a magnet, then wondered if she was doing the right thing, leaving without saying good-bye? She contemplated waiting for him to finish in the shower, but the water showed no sign of stopping. And the clock was ticking on the new case. Deep down, she knew she was being cowardly, but leaving without speaking to him suited her needs. Plus, a little time apart might well relieve some of the tension. It was time to go.

She arrived at Pin Mill Brow twenty minutes later to find a large grassed area cordoned off with blue and white police tape. A host of patrol cars and vans were parked up at various angles, and quite a few officers had control of the space. In the distance, she spotted the large white CSI tent, erected to preserve the scene around the body. As she got out of the Mini, she spotted Jones's car a few hundred metres away down the road and heading towards her.

He parked up next to her and stepped out of the squad car with a smile on his face. 'I really owe you one, Guv. I bloody *hate* DIY.'

'Glad I could help,' said Phillips, before turning her attention to the crime scene. 'You ready?'

'As I'll ever be.'

After flashing their credentials, they slipped under the police tape and walked briskly towards the tent, where they stopped to put on their protective suits, shoe protectors, masks and gloves. Looking like a couple of nuclear scientists, they stepped inside to find Andy Evans and his team examining the body. It lay face upwards, the damage to the eye socket and mouth evident for all to see.

Evans glanced in their direction as they walked in. 'Morning,' he said – far too cheerfully, Phillips felt. 'Another IC-one male, shot through the eye with a tooth removed. So far, from what we've seen, it's uncannily like the Bradley murder last week.'

'Same shooter?' asked Jones.

'I couldn't tell you for sure at this early stage, but if I was a betting man, I'd say it's a distinct possibility.'

'Was he killed here?' asked Phillips.

'No. There's no fresh blood around the body, so he's been moved and dumped here.'

'Any idea on when he was murdered?'

'Hard to tell exactly. Rigor has passed but the body's yet to start bloating, so I'd say probably somewhere between thirty-six and forty-eight hours.'

'What about ID?'

Evans passed over an evidence bag containing a wallet. 'Credit cards and a driving license identify him as Mitchell Hodge. Lived in Brammall, according to the address on the license.'

'Any other injuries?' asked Jones.

'Nothing that jumps out, but we're only just getting started. I'll be able to tell you more in a few hours.'

Phillips pulled out her phone and took a close-up of the driving licence, then handed it back. She scanned the scene as Evans and his team continued with their work, her eyes finally returning to the body. Dropping to her haunches, she moved closer to get a better look at his face. Where there had once been a right eye, there was now a large fleshy hole. The left eye was filled with the darkness of death. Just below, the mouth was wide open, a large gap where the tooth had been pulled.

'Poor sod,' said Jones.

Phillips pursed her lips. 'What the hell is going on, Jonesy?'

'Like I said the night Bradley was murdered, some weird shit, boss.'

Phillips stood and turned her attention back to Evans. 'Can I get an update as soon you've done the preliminary?'

'Of course,' he replied. 'Oh, and we found a phone in his pocket. Looks like a cheap pay as you go. I'll send you the call log as soon as we can download it.'

'Thanks, Andy,' she said, and led Jones out of the tent.

They removed and bagged their protective clothing, in case they'd unwittingly picked up any trace evidence.

'That's uncanny, boss,' Jones said as they strode back to their cars, 'the similarity between this and Bradley's death.'

'And Boothroyd's.'

'Oh yeah. So that makes three now,' said Jones.

Phillips stopped for a moment and scanned her surroundings. 'Why leave the body here?'

Jones followed her gaze. 'Quiet spot, I'm guessing. Probably no one around at night, so no witnesses.'

Phillips said nothing for a long moment as she rolled a theory round in her mind. 'I wonder if we've been looking at this case the wrong way, Jonesy.'

Jones's brow furrowed. 'How do you mean?'

'Well, so far we've been searching for a link between the historical murder of Boothroyd and the recent Bradley killing.'

'Yeah. So?'

Phillips turned to face Jones now. 'Maybe we're not looking for a gangland hit after all. Maybe it's actually much more primal than that. As you just, rightly, pointed out, we're now looking at *three* identical murders. So, *maybe,* what we're actually looking for is a serial killer. What if we're looking at a killer who's kept his bloodlust at bay for almost thirty years, and now it's finally got the better of him and he's acting on it?'

'I hear what you're saying. But Melissa Bradley said Paul's killer had an accomplice?'

'Maybe he's got an apprentice? Or maybe there were two them in the first place?'

'Maybe, yeah, but serial killers almost always choose vulnerable victims. There's nothing vulnerable about either Bradley or Boothroyd. They were a couple of gangbangers, for God's sake.'

'That's very true, Jonesy, but – as we know better than anyone else – serial killers come in all shapes and sizes, and each one has very different motives.' Phillips glanced back in the direction of the CSI tent, then checked her watch. It was just after 11.30. 'It's time to do some digging.'

'What for, exactly?'

'What links Mitchell Hodge with Paul Bradley and Archie Boothroyd. Because once we have that, I've got a feeling the rest of this mess will finally start to make a bit more sense.'

20

I t didn't take Phillips and Jones long to find the connection. A quick search of Hodge's Facebook page suggested the two men were friends. Close friends, in fact, who had holidayed together in the Spanish resort of Marbella just a month ago. A host of pictures confirmed they'd been part of a lads' trip that had seen them enjoying golf in the sunshine, as well as sea fishing and plenty of lavish dinners and evenings fuelled by heavy drinking. As they scanned the pictures, Phillips began to wonder if it was Hodge who'd made the anonymous call, claiming to be a friend of Bradley's. Was that the reason he was now dead?

Digging into Hodge's profile a little more, they identified a woman he'd labelled 'The Mrs' on a number of pictures dating back as far as 2016 – a Chelsea Winterbottom. With a quick call to Ashton House, they sourced Hodge's police file as well as Winterbottom's address. Jones keyed it into his Sat Nav. The drive to her home would take forty-minutes. She also lived in Brammall, but not in the same house as Hodge.

Leaving Phillips's car in Ancoats, Phillips used the time to scan through Hodge's file while Jones drove. Aside from a few minor run-ins with the law when he was a teenager, his record was clean. Arriving just before I p.m., they parked up on the street just outside Winterbottom's well-presented townhouse. Phillips stared at the front door for a long moment before taking a deep breath and exhaling loudly.

'Everything ok, boss?' asked Jones.

She nodded, but the truth was, she had never got used to telling someone that their worst fears had come true – that the person they loved the most in the world was now dead. It was a task she had first experienced almost twenty years ago as a uniformed beat copper, and it still made her stomach churn with dread.

A minute later, Phillips rapped her knuckles on the front door of the house. Winterbottom answered promptly. Tall and attractive, with long blonde hair, her eyes were filled with fear, puffy and swollen. She clutched a handkerchief in her left hand.

'Chelsea Winterbottom?' said Phillips.

The woman's brow creased. 'Yes?'

Phillips presented her ID. 'I'm Detective Chief Inspector Phillips and this is Detective Sergeant Jones—'

'Have you found him?' Winterbottom cut her off.

'I'm sorry,' said Phillips. 'Have we found who?'

'Mitch, my boyfriend.'

Phillips glanced at Jones, then back at Winterbottom. 'May we come in?' she asked gently.

Winterbottom opened the door farther before stepping back into the house.

Phillips and Jones followed her into her small lounge, where she took a seat on the leather armchair and folded her arms protectively across her chest. They took their positions on the adjacent sofa.

'What did you mean just now when you asked if we'd found Mitch?' said Phillips.

'He's gone missing.'

'Since when?

'Thursday night,' replied Winterbottom, before wiping her nose with the hanky.

'Was that when you last saw him?'

'Yes.'

Mispers were not usually MCU territory, so it wasn't surprising she'd not been briefed on Hodge's disappearance. However, it should have come up on his police file. She made a mental note to ensure the oversight was rectified. Reaching for her phone now, she pulled up the picture of Hodge's driving licence. 'Is this Mitchell?'

Winterbottom stared at the phone. Her voice trembled when she finally spoke. 'Where did you get Mitch's licence?'

Phillips took a long silent breath. 'I'm sorry to have to tell you this, but a body was discovered this morning that we believe to be that of Mitchell Hodge.'

As the words landed, Winterbottom's eyes widened and her mouth fell open. She began to shake her head. 'No...no, it can't be.'

'I'm afraid it is, Chelsea. I'm so sorry.'

Winterbottom's face wrinkled as the tears came, and her whole body began to shake.

Phillips stood and wrapped a protective arm around Chelsea as she began to sob into her hanky.

'I'll make some sweet tea,' said Jones, and disappeared in search of the kitchen.

Ten minutes later, they each sipped from steaming mugs. 'I can't believe he's dead,' whispered Winterbottom staring at the floor.

'Can you think of why anyone would want to hurt Mitchell?'

'Please, call him Mitch. He hated the name Mitchell.'

Phillips nodded. 'Can you think of why anyone would want to hurt Mitch?'

'He had some dodgy friends. Maybe it has something to do with them?'

'Which friends were these?'

'Paul fucking Bradley, for one.' Her voice brimmed with anger. 'I told him hanging out with that guy would get him into trouble one day.'

'You didn't like Paul Bradley?'

Winterbottom shook her head as she took another sip of tea. 'No, I bloody didn't. In fact, I was relieved when I heard he was dead. Finally, Mitch could get away from him.'

'Were Paul and Mitch close?'

'Oh yeah. Went everywhere together. Tweedledum and Tweedledee. But Paul was a bad influence. Had a roving eye for the ladies, if you know what I mean, and a fondness for cocaine.'

'And what about Mitch? Was he the same?'

Winterbottom bit her bottom lip. 'I found a couple of messages on his phone from time to time. You know, from women he'd obviously met when he was out and about. But he always denied there was anything in them. He was very good to me, so to be honest, I looked the other way. What the eye doesn't see and all that.'

'And what about cocaine? Was Mitch into it?'

A look of uncertainty flashed across Winterbottom's face.

'It's ok,' Phillips assured her. 'It won't affect how we view his case.'

Winterbottom blew her nose into the hanky. 'Yeah. Mitch was into it. More so in the last few months, though. In fact, I was starting to worry it was getting out of hand.'

'In what way?' asked Jones.

'It used to be Mitch would do it a couple of times a

month, on nights out with the lads, but recently he seemed to be doing it most days. He must have spent a fortune.'

'So how was he paying for it?'

Winterbottom shrugged. 'I honestly don't know, but you can bet Paul was involved in it somehow. Dodgy as fuck, that one.'

'Dodgy how?' Phillips cut back in.

'You're coppers, surely you know.'

'Well, we heard the rumours about him being involved in drugs, but nothing was ever proven.'

'Pah!' scoffed Winterbottom. 'You can't have looked very hard for proof, cos that club of his, Vibe, is *the* place to score drugs in Manchester. You can't move for bloody dealers in there, and all of them are on the Bradley payroll.'

'We'll be sure to pass that information onto the drugs squad.'

Panic flashed across Winterbottom's face. 'Look, you didn't hear any of that from me. Ok? I don't need anyone thinking I'm a grass.'

Phillips placed her mug down on the coffee table in front of her. 'You said you saw Mitch the night he went missing.'

'Yes.'

'What time exactly?'

Winterbottom took a moment to think. 'He left here just after nine. He said he had a meeting at ten o'clock, but he wouldn't say where or who with – which wasn't like him at all. I *always* knew where he was going. That's why I got so worried when he didn't come home. Something was going on. I could just feel it in my bones. Especially when I found he'd left his phone.'

'Why? Was that unusual?'

'God yeah. He never went anywhere without it, but for some reason that night he'd left it here in the kitchen. I found it when I tried to ring him to see where he was. That's when I panicked and reported him missing.'

Phillips glanced at Jones, who was making notes in his pad. 'We're going to need someone to make a formal identification of Mitch. Is that something you feel up to doing?'

Winterbottom nodded. 'If I don't, no-one else will. Mitch didn't have any family, you see.'

Phillips offered a soft smile. 'We'll organise a family liaison officer to look after you. They'll come and see you later today to make the arrangements.' She pulled a business card from her pocket and handed it across. 'And if you think of anything else that might be of help to us, please call, day or night.'

Winterbottom stared at the card in silence for a long moment. 'How did he die?' she asked without looking up.

'He was shot.'

'Did he suffer?' Winterbottom's voice cracked.

'No. I don't think so.'

'Thank you.' The words were barely audible as the tears returned and Winterbottom fought to hold herself together.

'We'll leave you in peace.' Phillips stood, and Jones followed her lead. 'Is there anyone you can call to come and keep you company?'

'My sister lives in Wilmslow,' said Winterbottom, wiping her nose again. 'She'll come over.'

'We're really very sorry for your loss, Chelsea,' said Phillips, before signalling to Jones to lead them out of the house.

Back in the car, Jones asked, 'You still think we're looking for a serial killer, Guv?'

Phillips blew her lips. 'I don't know what to think right now. The only thing I'm certain of is that all three deaths are connected. But how? And why? That's the question we need to answer.'

'So, where do we go from here?'

'Put the word out around Ashton House. Anyone arrested that's in anyway connected to Bradley or Hodge, I want to know about it.'

'Of course,' said Jones, and fired the engine.

'And the same goes for Bahmani. I want to know everything that's going on as far as that slippery bastard is concerned, no matter how minor it may seem.'

'I'll make sure everyone knows.'

Phillips glanced at the clock on the dash. 'Well, we'd better get back to Ashton House and start writing this up.'

'Excellent,' said Jones.

'And why are you so happy?'

'Because I'd rather be writing reports all day than painting the back fence, that's why.'

Phillips shook her head. 'I don't know how Sarah puts up with you.'

'It's my cockney charm, Guv,' he replied, sounding very much like Michael Caine once more.

'But first things first, we need to get back to Pin Mill Brow and pick up the Mini. If anything happens to that car, you'll be investigating *my* murder before long.'

'Your dad protective of it, is he?'

'Put it this way. If he was asked to choose between saving *me* or the *Mini,* he'd choose the Mini every time.'

'I can understand that,' said Jones playfully as he slipped the squad car in gear and pulled away from the kerb. 'It is a cracking little car.'

21

MONDAY 12TH JULY

The team gathered for their weekly briefing in Phillips's office first thing, taking up their usual positions; Jones and Bovalino sat on the two chairs opposite her, while Entwistle perched on the filing cabinet to her left. After updating Bov and Entwistle on the events of the weekend, she shared her belief that the three murders were all connected. 'I need a full background check on Hodge ASAP,' she said, turning her gaze to Entwistle.

'I'm on it, boss,' he replied.

'And Jonesy, get onto Evans and see if digital forensics have downloaded the call log from the phone they found on him, will you?'

'Sure thing.'

'What about me, Guv?' Bovalino asked.

'Winterbottom claimed Bradley's club was a hotspot for drugs. Find out if that's true, because if it is, it could suggest Bradley was murdered by a rival dealer.'

'No worries,' said Bovalino.

'Right. I should probably head upstairs and brief Carter

on the events of the weekend.' Phillips stood. 'I want updates as soon as you have them. Ok?'

Each of the men nodded and left the room.

Ten minutes later, she entered Chief Superintendent Carter's office. He sat behind his desk, his nose in a pile of paperwork. He looked up as she walked in and smiled. 'Morning, Jane,' he said in his soft Newcastle accent. 'Have a seat.'

Sitting opposite him, it was easy to remember why she liked him so much. He had a kind face under a shock of salt and pepper hair, and she believed he genuinely cared about her and the team. A stark contrast to his predecessor, Fox, who had been promoted to chief constable of the Greater Manchester Police, proving that shit really does float to the top.

'I hear you had a busy weekend,' he said as he dropped his pen on the desk and reclined in his big leather chair.

'Yes sir. Another murder, exactly the same as Paul Bradley: bullet through the eye and a front tooth removed post mortem.'

Carter's brow furrowed. 'Any connection between the victims?'

'Best mates, by the looks of it, and a potential link to drugs.'

'Really? So you think we could be looking at gang murders?'

'Potentially, but I'm not ready to hand them over to Serious Crimes just yet. At this moment, we have three identical homicides over a thirty-year period. Could be gang related, but could also be one killer with an axe to grind. The guys are following up on some leads as we speak, which should hopefully give us a better idea of what we're dealing with.'

'Ok. Keep me posted, won't you?' said Carter. 'You know

what Fox is like for protocols and budget allocation. One sniff of a gangland connection and she'll want these cases out of MCU and over to Serious Crimes sharpish.'

After five years of reporting directly to Fox, Phillips was all too familiar with how the chief constable operated. 'As soon as I know, you'll know, sir.'

'Good stuff. Is there anything else?'

'Not from me. I just wanted to make sure you were across the details.' Phillips stood.

'And I appreciate it.' Carter sat forward and picked up his pen again. 'Well, I'd better be getting back to my favourite thing in the world – *paperwork*.'

'That's why they pay you the big bucks, sir,' Phillips joked.

'Ah, the glamour of life as a chief superintendent in the GMP.'

She chuckled as she left.

Back downstairs, Entwistle beckoned her over as she walked through the doors of the MCU office.

'I've done a preliminary search on Hodge, Guv.'

'And?'

Entwistle angled his laptop so Phillips could see the screen. 'And he's got form for violence and gang involvement. Nothing recent, but plenty back in the mid- to late-nineties. Looks like he was a bit of an enforcer back in the day, running in the same gang as Paul Bradley *and* Archie Boothroyd. The Moss Side Crew.'

'I knew they all had to be connected,' said Phillips triumphantly, slapping him on the shoulder.

At that moment, Jones finished his phone call and replaced the handset. 'That was Evans. We've got a match on one of the numbers from Hodge's phone. Looks like he called the main reception desk here at Ashton House, last Thursday at 11.26 a.m.—'

'Which is when I got the call about the Alderley Edge meet,' Phillips cut in.

'So it looks like Hodge *was* our informant,' said Jones.

Phillips took a moment to process the information. 'So either he was on his way to meet us that night and just happened to be murdered, or his killer knew he was coming to speak to us and that's why he ended up dead.'

'My money's on the latter,' Entwistle chimed in.

'Funnily enough, mine too,' replied Phillips.

'So, who would know he was coming to talk to us?' asked Jones. 'Only you and I were aware of it at this end.'

Phillips frowned. 'God only knows, Jonesy. If this *is* all gang and drugs related, then Mitchell Hodge was living in a world full of snitches. Any one of them could have exposed him.'

'Looks like you were right about that club of Bradley's, boss,' Bovalino interrupted. 'I've just got off the phone to one of the guys in the drug squad and he reckons that dealing is rife in Vibe.'

'So how is it still operating?' asked Jones, shaking his head in frustration.

'Sounds like they've only ever found relatively small amounts on the dealers, and nothing to tie the drugs directly to the club itself,' replied Bov. 'Each time it happens, the owners plead ignorance and promise to be more vigilant. They get a slap on the wrist and the odd fine here and there, and life just carries on as normal.'

Phillips shook her head. 'Sounds just like Paul Bradley, doesn't it? Everyone suspecting he was involved, but no one able to prove it.'

The office fell quiet for a moment as the team digested the latest information.

Phillips broke the silence. 'So, we've got three identical murders, and all three victims connected through their links to organised crime. So, who wanted these men dead? And why?'

'Rival gang members?' said Entwistle.

'Maybe, but why wait thirty years to kill Bradley and Hodge?'

'Maybe the killer has been away for that long?' ventured Jones.

'Prison?' asked Bovalino.

'That would make sense,' said Phillips. 'Bov, check the DOJ records. See if anyone connected to those nineties gangs has recently been released.'

Bovalino nodded and made a note in his pad.

Phillips turned to Jones now. 'There is *one* person still alive who we know was connected to all three men back in the day.'

Jones raised an eyebrow. 'Really? Who?'

'Melissa Bradley.'

'Of course,' said Jones.

'Let's go and see if she can shed any light on who might wanted them all dead.'

Jones picked up his car keys and stepped up from the chair.

'Keep digging, guys,' said Phillips, casting her gaze between Entwistle and Bovalino, 'The answers aren't far away. I'm sure of it.'

22

As Jones pulled the squad car up outside the Bradley house, Phillips once again noted the lack of cars on the drive. At first glance, it appeared that no one was home, but she needed to make sure. So they got out of the car and made their way up the long drive to the front door. Phillips rang the bell over and over, but got no response. They wandered down the side of the house and checked the garden in case Melissa or Freddie were sitting out in the sunshine. There was no trace of either of them, so they returned to the car.

Just as Phillips was about to climb in the passenger seat, someone behind her spoke.

'You looking for Melissa?'

Phillips turned and spotted a man staring at them from over the fence of the house next door. Phillips placed him in his early sixties, and he looked smart in a black suit and tie, suitable for a funeral.

'She's at the memorial in the village,' he said.

Phillips frowned. 'Memorial?'

The man nodded. 'She wanted to do something for Paul.'

He stopped and looked left and right, as if to check no-one was listening in. He continued in a low whisper, 'You know, until they release the body.'

Phillips glanced at Jones, then back to the man. 'Do you know where it's being held?'

'The church in the village. I'm heading there myself, if you'd like to follow me?'

'That would be very helpful, thank you.'

The man turned towards his car, then spun back again, concern etched on his face. 'Can I just check, you're not from the papers, are you?'

Phillips offered him a thin smile and pulled out her ID. 'No, we're the police.'

The man's eyes widened slightly. 'Oh, I see.' An uncomfortable chortle fell from his lips.

'Right, well, we'll follow you then,' said Phillips, and opened the passenger door to the squad car.

The short drive to the village church took just a few minutes. When they arrived, the street was packed with large expensive cars and SUVs. Lots of people dressed in black milled about, with dark sunglasses and lots of gold jewellery. 'Looks like a bloody mafia funeral,' said Phillips under her breath as Jones searched for a parking space.

He found one at the very edge of the village green. After ditching the car, they made their way back to the church. As they arrived at the open doors, people had begun taking their seats. Phillips and Jones followed suit, slipping quietly into the back row just as the church organ sprang to life with the first hymn, signalling for everyone to stand. Glancing down towards the front of the church, Phillips spotted Melissa and Freddie standing in the first pew, hymn books in hand.

The service took no longer than thirty minutes, and to all intents and purposes was almost identical in structure to a funeral, albeit without the coffin. The vicar said nice things about Paul Bradley, as did Freddie – none of which described the man she had come to know since she'd started investigating his death. As their words came over the speakers set around the church, Phillips recalled the saying, 'Never let the truth get in the way of a good story.' She allowed herself a wry smile as she thought about the heroic picture they painted of the man she believed to be a major drug dealer.

The vicar eventually brought the service to an end, and announced that everyone was welcome to join the family back at the Bradley home for refreshments.

'Fancy a drink?' Phillips said to Jones as they walked out of the church amongst the rest of the mourners.

Jones did a slight double take. 'You're kidding, right?'

'Why not?' Phillips hooked her thumb back towards the church behind them. 'We can pay our respects to the ever-so-wonderful-and-caring Paul Bradley we just heard about in there.'

A grave look appeared on Jones's face. 'I really don't think that's a good idea, Guv. Police aren't often welcome at funerals. Especially those connected to gangs and drugs.'

'Nonsense,' replied Phillips. 'And besides, it'll give us chance to check out some of the faces. You never know, we might even drum up a few leads.'

Jones sighed. 'You're the boss, but I've got a bad feeling about this.'

Phillips patted him on the shoulder. 'I'm sure you'll feel much better with a couple of sausage rolls in your belly. Come on, let's get back to the house.'

The parking situation outside the Bradleys resembled the street outside the church when Phillips and Jones pulled up. Phillips lost count of the number of vehicles with blacked-out windows. 'A regular gangsters' paradise,' she said as they walked up the drive towards the front door.

This time it was answered by a petite Asian woman from

a catering firm, dressed in a white blouse and black knee-length skirt, who ushered them inside without question. Her name tag identified her as Stella. They found themselves surrounded by some of Manchester's wealthiest residents, some of whom – based on their potential nefarious business interests – were well known to Phillips and Jones.

A waiter appeared from nowhere and offered them a choice of Champagne or orange juice. Taking an OJ each, they moved slowly through the massive house until they spotted Melissa, standing by the unlit fire in the lounge room and chatting quietly to an elderly couple.

'I hope we're not interrupting,' said Phillips, butting in.

Melissa's face fell ever so slightly as she eyed them both. It was subtle, but Phillips spotted it.

'Would you excuse us?' Melissa said to the older couple before stepping away and drawing Phillips and Jones with her. 'I wasn't expecting to see you here.'

'We wanted to pay our respects,' Phillips lied.

'Great turn out,' added Jones.

'Paul was a great man,' Melissa said sombrely.

At that moment, Freddie entered the room and strode towards them. 'What are *you lot* doing here?' he said, louder than necessary.

Melissa placed her hand on his upper arm. 'Freddie, don't be rude. They've come to pay their respects to your dad.'

'Bollocks they have. They've come for a snoop around.'

Phillips moved closer to Melissa. When she spoke, her voice was low so as not to be overheard. 'Actually, it would be helpful to talk if possible. Is there somewhere private we can go?'

Melissa nodded. 'Paul's office. Follow me.'

Phillips and Jones fell in behind Melissa as she guided them through the throng of guests, with Freddie bringing up the rear. Once they were all inside the office, Freddie closed the door, then turned, arms folded across his chest, his face like thunder.

'I'm sorry to have to ask this today of all days, Melissa, but how well did you know Mitchell Hodge?'

Melissa raised her eyebrows. 'Mitch? I've known him for years. Probably as long as Paul, to be honest. Why?'

'I'm afraid he's dead.'

'Dead?' Melissa was incredulous. 'When? How?'

'Thursday night. He was shot in the face, like Paul.'

'Oh my God. I can't believe it. I was expecting to see him today. Poor Chelsea, she must be devastated.'

Phillips pressed on. 'We have reason to believe Hodge knew the identity of the person who killed Paul, and having that information may have got him killed.'

Melissa shook her head. 'Jesus.'

'What's any of this got to do with Mum?' spat Freddie.

'Your mum is one of the few people who knew all three victims. We're just trying to establish who else might be connected.'

'Three? Who's the three?' replied Freddie.

'Your father, obviously, Mitchell Hodge, and Archie Boothroyd.'

'Who the hell's Archie Boothroyd?'

'He was a friend of your dad's, son,' said Melissa. 'He was murdered in the same way, back in the nineties.'

'How has something that happened thirty years ago got anything to do with Mum now?'

'Your mum knew them all well. Without realising it, she may also know their killer.'

'This is bullshit,' grunted Freddie.

Phillips turned her attention back to Melissa. 'Look, there's no easy way to say this, but we believe Paul's and Mitchell's deaths were potentially drug related. Possibly gang hits.'

Freddie stepped forward now. 'You what?'

Melissa appeared stoic. 'Inspector. My husband was a legitimate businessman. He had nothing to do with drugs or gangs. Nothing whatsoever.'

'What about the club?' asked Phillips.

Melissa recoiled. 'What *about* the club?'

'We have information that suggests a large quantity of drugs is being distributed into the city through dealers operating inside Vibe each week.'

'Are you fucking kidding me?' Freddie snarled, his eyes wild. 'Seriously? You come in here on the day of my dad's memorial and start throwing accusations round about him being a drug dealer? The man's *dead*. You're standing in his office, for God's sake. Have some respect.'

'Look, Freddie. All we're trying to do is find the person that killed your dad,' Phillips shot back. 'If we all carry on pretending Paul was a saint and never did anything off the books, the chances of finding that person are slim to none. *But,* if you're honest with us and start telling the truth about what kind of business he was really involved in, then we've got a much better chance of finding his killers and making sure they spend the rest of their days in prison.'

Freddie took a step closer to Phillips now. 'Who the hell do you think you are, calling my dad a drug dealer?'

'Easy lad,' said Jones, blocking the young man with his hand.

Melissa stared Phillips dead in the eye now. Her voice was measured when she spoke. 'I think you'd better leave, Inspector.'

Phillips matched her gaze, but remained silent for a long moment. 'Very well,' she said finally, then turned towards the door with Jones at her back.

'Please don't come back,' Melissa said after them.

Freddie followed, apparently determined to make a scene

in front of the other guests. 'Get out of our house, you fucking vultures,' he shouted in the double-height entrance hall as they made their way to the front door.

Guests began turning their attention to the noise.

'You haven't heard the last of this, Phillips. I'm gonna make sure you pay for disrespecting my dad's memory. D'you hear me?'

Phillips avoided all eye contact with the other guests as she and Jones strode towards the front door. Pulling it open, she stepped outside and marched quickly away down the gravel drive.

'Well, that went well,' said Jones sarcastically when they'd reached a safe distance.

Phillips turned back to face the house. 'They're playing games with us, Jonesy, pretending Bradley was some kind of saint when everyone knows the man was a gangster hiding in plain sight.'

'With respect, Guv, what did you expect? That they'd suddenly start confessing that all of their wealth has come from crime?'

'I know, I know. It's just so frustrating. There's a killer out there who is showing no signs of stopping, and we're no nearer to catching him. I don't care if Bradley and Mitch *were* dealers. All I wanna know is, who had beef with them, and who stood to benefit the most from their deaths?'

'Half of gangland Manchester could be on that list, Guv.'

'I know. Which is why these idiots playing happily families is so bloody irritating.'

'So, what now?'

Phillips pursed her lips. 'Now we go back to the office and do what we do best. Keep digging.'

'I'll get my shovel,' quipped Jones, and fished the car keys from his trouser pocket before deactivating the central locking.

As Phillips took one final glance towards the house, her eyes landed on Paul Bradley's top-of-the-range blue Bentley, sitting on the drive. At a rough estimate, she reckoned it cost upwards of a hundred-and-fifty-thousand pounds to buy brand new. 'You didn't get that selling cookies, did you, mate?' she muttered under her breath, then turned and climbed into the car.

23

Phillips had been back in her office for a couple of hours when the door was thrust open and Chief Constable Fox strode in with Carter in tow. Fox was clearly in no mood for pleasantries. 'Would you like to tell me just *exactly* what you thought you were doing today?'

Phillips frowned as she stood up from her chair. 'I'm sorry, Ma'am. I'm not following you?'

Fox remained standing, feet planted firmly, as Carter moved adjacent to her. The strained look on his face told Phillips he'd already had a bollocking.

'I just received an official complaint that you were harassing Melissa Bradley at her husband's funeral.'

'Actually, ma'am, it wasn't a funeral. It was memorial service,' Phillips corrected her, and could have sworn she saw Carter wince.

'Don't get smart with me, Chief Inspector.' Fox's eyes bulged. 'Did you, or did you not, accuse Paul Bradley of being a drug dealer at his memorial service today?'

Strictly speaking, the accusation had been made at the

house afterwards, but Phillips decided against correcting Fox twice. 'I can see how this looks when you say it like that, but Paul Bradley was widely rumoured to have been involved in drugs for years, as was the latest victim, Mitchell Hodge. I was merely trying to understand if their deaths could be drug related.'

'At his *memorial service*? You can't go into a situation like that with those kinds of questions. There's a time and a place, Phillips.'

'I was doing my job, ma'am.'

'Stirring up trouble, more like,' Fox shot back. 'Have you ever heard of Travis Tate?'

Phillips thought for a moment. 'It doesn't ring any bells.'

'Well, he's the top man at Tate Law in the city, and Melissa Bradley's attorney; a pitbull of a man who has made all kinds of threats against you, the department and the GMP as a whole if you persist in – as he put it – "slandering his client's late husband".'

'But that's ridiculous. I'm investigating Bradley's murder. It's my job to ask difficult questions.'

'*Not* of Melissa Bradley, it isn't.'

'I'm sorry, ma'am.' Phillips did a double take. 'Are you telling me I'm not allowed to question her anymore?'

'No, you're not.'

'What? So she's off limits?'

'To you, yes. If anyone needs to speak to her, send Jones.'

Phillips was incredulous. 'Since when do we allow lawyers to dictate how we carry out murder enquires?'

'Oh grow up,' said Fox. 'Melissa Bradley has a lot of friends in high places, and could cause all kinds of problems for us if she so wishes. I mean, can you imagine if she takes this to the media? I can see the headlines now: HEAVY-HANDED COPS HARASS GRIEVING FAMILY AT FUNERAL. It's hardly good PR, is it?'

'With respect, ma'am, PR is *not* my concern.'

'No, but it is *mine*, and the last time I looked, I was in charge. So, as of now, Melissa Bradley is off limits to you. Do I make myself clear?'

Phillips did her best to control the rage building in her gut. She clenched her jaw as she stared back at Fox. 'Crystal, ma'am,' she said finally.

'Good,' replied Fox, turned on her heels and marched out of the office.

When Fox was safely out of the way, Phillips locked eyes with Carter. 'Is she for real?'

He raised his hands in defeat. 'I tried to stop her and said I'd talk to you about it, but she insisted. Whatever that lawyer said to her *seriously* pissed her off. She'd already spent ten minutes tearing strips off me before she came down here.'

Phillips dropped into her seat. 'Well, if she thinks I'm going to jeopardise the investigation because Melissa Bradley has got the hump, she's got another think coming.'

Carter frowned. 'Be careful, Jane. Fox isn't messing about on this one.'

'And neither am I,' Phillips shot back. 'Besides, all Fox really cares about is results. As long as I catch the killer, she won't give a shit about my methods.'

'I know you're upset, but do yourself a favour,' Carter said coolly. 'Follow protocol, will you?'

'Is that an order, sir?'

'If it needs to be, yes.'

Phillips stared up at Carter for a long moment. 'Very well. I'll leave Melissa alone, for now.'

'Thank you,' said Carter.

'Is that all?' asked Phillips, trying hard to mask her annoyance.

'Yes. That's it.' He turned and walked to the door before glancing back at Phillips. 'Don't let her get to you, Jane.'

Phillips nodded, but remained silent as Carter followed Fox out.

24

Adders Bahmani pulled his office door closed, then locked it. The recent hot weather had made the air thick and muggy. He glanced at the sky. A heavy downpour was imminent. As he fired the engine of his Range Rover, the first few drops hit the windscreen, activating the automatic wipers. He noted the time on the dash: 7.06 p.m. He should have been home an hour ago, but sorting out his bookkeeping had taken longer than planned. Still, the best way to keep the law out of his business was to appear legitimate, and well-maintained accounts were key.

Tahir had left work an hour ago, so it was down to Bahmani to secure the site for the night. Moving the SUV through the main gates, he jumped out into the now-torrential rain and quickly pulled the gates together before locking the heavy padlock in place. Almost soaked through, he rushed back to the car and climbed inside, pulling the door closed behind him.

It was then that he saw the two men climbing out of a car parked across the street. They both wore dark hooded tops, and scarves hid their faces. With their hands thrust deep into the pockets of their sweaters, Bahmani instinctively knew what came next.

In unison, the two men pulled pistols from their pockets and began firing at his windscreen.

He ducked down left over the passenger seat, slammed the car in drive, and smashed his foot down on the accelerator. The big car shot forwards as the firing continued, then came to a shuddering halt as it crashed headlong into the car the gunmen had exited. The airbags exploded around him.

The firing ceased. He waited for the gunmen, but after some time there was no sign of them. Instead, an eerie silence filled the car.

With caution, he lifted his head high enough to see out through the broken windscreen. One of the gunmen was wedged face down against the bonnet, motionless, his legs and waist trapped between the Range Rover and their car. The gun was still locked in the grip of his gloved right hand, and his body was soaked.

Out of the corner of his eye, Bahmani spotted the second shooter running down the street. Launching himself out from the driver's seat, he grabbed the gun from the man against the bonnet, turned, and began firing. But the second gunman was too far away. A split second later, he ducked left down an alleyway and disappeared out of sight.

'Yeah, you better fucking run!' he shouted after him, 'cos when I find you, I'm gonna kill you.'

He turned back to his car. Taking in the macabre scene, he was sure of two things: his car was totalled, and the shooter was very wet, and very dead.

25

Phillips was working late when Adam called her mobile. 'Hello you,' she said.

'Hi babe.' He was obviously in the car. *'Where are you?'*

'Still at the office.'

'Really? It's gone eight.'

'I know. Jonesy and I are the only ones left. What about you?'

'On my way home. I was just wondering if you wanted me to come over tonight.'

Phillips glanced at the clock in the corner of her laptop screen. 'It's up to you, but I'll probably be here another hour at least. I've got a mountain of paperwork to try and get finished.'

'In that case, I'll have a shower and something to eat, then give you another call to see where you're at.'

'Ok, sounds good. And you've got your key if you need to let yourself in.'

Adam paused for a moment. *'You know, Jane, this would be*

a lot easier if we lived together. At least that way, I wouldn't have to call ahead each time I wanted to see you.'

Phillips opened her mouth to respond, but was distracted by Jones at her door, notepad in hand. 'Can you hang on a minute, Adam?'

'There's been a shooting at Bahmani's yard. One dead,' said Jones.

'Bahmani?'

'No, someone else. I didn't recognise the name.'

'Jesus,' muttered Phillips. She turned her attention back to Adam. 'Sorry, I'm gonna have to go. A new case has just come in.'

Adam sighed heavily. *'Well, I definitely won't be seeing you later, will I?'*

Phillips's mind was already focused on the shooting. 'I'll call you later. Ok?'

'Sure. Talk later. Love you.'

Because Jones stood in the doorway, she felt uncomfortable replying in kind. 'Me too,' she said, and ended the call.

Jones brought her up to speed. 'The uniform team on scene says Bahmani claims two men started shooting at him as he left work, which caused him to crash his car into one of them, killing him. A right mess, by all accounts. CSI are on their way.'

Phillips got up from behind her desk. 'What was the name of the dead man?'

Jones looked down at the notepad. 'Jez Fulton.'

Phillips typed the name into a message in her phone. 'Let's see if DCI Cleverly knows him.' She pressed send, then grabbed the keys to the Mini. 'We'd best take two cars. I have a feeling it could be a long night.'

They arrived at Bahmani's yard twenty minutes later. As Phillips parked up on the street outside, she checked her phone. Cleverly had replied.

Fulton? Gangbanger and one of Bradley's boys.
Works the door at Vibe amongst other odd jobs.
Done a bit of time for GBH and drugs offences.
Why do you ask?

Phillips slipped the phone in her pocket without replying, then stepped out of the car. Jones was waiting for her. In the distance, two ambulances were parked up next to a patrol car and police van. Beyond them, behind blue and white police tape, Phillips could see Bahmani's white Range Rover and the car it had collided with being pored over by the CSIs. 'Where's Bahmani?'

'My guess is, one of the ambulances,' said Jones as they walked side by side.

He was correct. As they reached the rear of the green and yellow ambulance, they could see the big man sitting on a chair in the back. He looked dishevelled and soaked through. A paramedic on the chair next to him typed into her iPad.

'Been in the wars, Adders?' asked Phillips.

'Couple of kids with guns tried to shoot me.'

Phillips frowned. 'And why do you think they wanted to do that?'

Bahmani shrugged. 'Beats me. Maybe they were after my car? It wouldn't be the first time somebody tried to jack a nice motor in this city.'

'You said there were two shooters. What happened to the second?'

Bahmani thumbed over his shoulder. 'Ran off down the road.'

'Did you recognise either of them?'

Bahmani shook his head. 'Nar. They were both wearing scarves over their nose and mouth.'

Phillips scrutinised his face for a long moment to see if he was lying, but the truth was, she couldn't tell. Stepping back, she cast her eyes towards the scrap yard, where she spotted a number of security cameras trained on the street. 'We're going to need copies of your CCTV footage.'

'The cameras are fake,' Bahmani replied.

Jones frowned. 'They look pretty real to me.'

'They're good fakes.'

'I see.' Phillips knew full well that even if they were real, he would never willingly allow them to view the footage. 'So, how badly were you hurt in all this?'

Bahmani rubbed the back of his neck with his thick hand. 'Bit of whiplash, and my ears are still ringing from the airbags going off. Other than that, I'm fine.'

'I've suggested he let us take him into A&E for a proper checkup,' the paramedic cut in, 'but he'd rather go home, wouldn't you, Adders?'

'Damn right. I bloody hate hospitals. Full of sick people.'

The paramedic continued. 'And we can't make him go if he doesn't want to.'

'Well, you watch yourself,' said Phillips, and handed him her card. 'Any sign of the second shooter coming back for a second go, you call me straight away. Ok?'

Bahmani glanced down at the card but didn't reply.

Phillips stepped away and gestured for Jones to follow her. 'Let's take a look at the scene, shall we?'

Evans and his team were busy taking photographs of the Range Rover's bonnet as they approached. 'How's it looking, Andy?' Phillips asked.

'Well, I'm not an expert in traffic accidents, but from what I've seen so far, it happened pretty much as Mr Bahmani described it. Two shooters fired multiple times into the Range Rover before it collided with the dead man and trapped him against his car. Chakrabortty will be able to say for certain, but in my opinion, death would have been pretty much instant.'

Phillips gazed at the two cars mangled together. 'What a way to end your days.'

'At least it was quick,' said Jones.

At that moment, Phillips's phone began to vibrate in her pocket. Fishing it out, she could see it was DCI Cleverly. 'Steve,' she said as she answered.

'I've just heard Jez Fulton is dead.'

'Yeah, I'm at the scene now.'

'Bahmani's yard?'

'Yep. It's a right mess.'

'What happened?'

'Looks like Fulton and another IC-one started shooting at Bahmani, so he drove his car at them, killing Fulton instantly.'

'Did he recognise the other shooter?'

'Apparently not. Claims they wore face coverings.'

'Well, if Jez Fulton is involved, my money's on the second shooter being Shawn Harvey. Where one goes, the other usually follows.'

'Thanks for the heads-up. We'll look into it.'

'Let me know if I can help at all,' added Cleverly.

'I will. Thanks, Steve.' Phillips ended the call and turned to Jones. 'First thing in the morning, get the guys to find out everything they can on a Shawn Harvey. Cleverly reckons he's a likely candidate for the second shooter.

'Will do,' said Jones.

Phillips turned her attention to Evans. 'How long do you think you'll be here?'

Evans shrugged. 'Most of the night, I'm guessing.'

'Right. In that case, seeing as there were no other witnesses, I think we can leave you to it. We'll be in touch first thing in the morning.'

Evans gave her a thumbs up, then got back to work as Phillips and Jones headed for their cars.

26

The sunlight was finally starting to fade when the target parked his car in front of the row of terraced houses, each with a small garden to the front. He'd followed the man here in a stolen car with fake plates. Pulling into a parking space a little farther down the road, he jumped out and quickly made his way to the target's location. Thankfully, no neighbours or passers-by hung about, but he'd covered his mouth and nose with a scarf anyway, to ward off any potential witnesses or private CCTV cameras.

Up ahead, the target opened the garden gate and made his way up the path. He pulled keys from his pocket as he stopped at the front door. In his left hand was a small overnight bag.

Reaching into the pocket of his tracksuit, he rushed through the gate and up the path towards the target. The noise obviously startled the man, because he dropped the bag and spun to face him, the confusion on his face transforming into fear as he spotted the large blade.

'I haven't got any money,' the target shouted, and raised his hands in surrender.

'I'm not after your money,' he spat, and thrust the knife deep into the man's stomach, forcing him backwards and up against the front door. Clamping his hand over the target's mouth to muffle his screams, he yanked the knife out, then thrust it in a couple more times before stepping back and leaving him to fall to his knees.

Blood pooled on the path around his feet as he shoved the broken body sideways. The target slumped in a bloody heap amongst the flowers and shrubs.

'Nothing personal, mate. It's just business,' he said as he bent over and wiped the knife on the man's jeans, then slipped it back into his pocket.

The target let out a low moan as his blood pooled around him.

He scanned the street. It appeared no one had witnessed the attack. It was time to go.

Careful not draw any unwanted attention to himself, he walked slowly down the path and back onto the street before moving as casually as he could towards the car.

As he climbed back behind the wheel and fired the engine, he took one last look around, then pulled away from the kerb at a steady pace. The last thing he needed now was to be stopped for speeding in a stolen car, a bloodied knife in his possession.

Thirty minutes later, he stood on the derelict site of a long-abandoned warehouse in Salford and watched as the stolen car was engulfed in flames. Pulling out his phone, he pressed redial.

'It's done,' was all he said before ending the call.

27

It was dark by the time Phillips arrived home. As she stepped out of the Mini, she suddenly remembered her promise to call Adam and let him know her plans for the rest of the evening. In all honesty, she was exhausted, so hoped he wouldn't mind if they didn't see each other tonight. All she wanted to do was soak in a hot bath, then go to bed. Fishing her phone from her pocket, she pulled up the favourites and hit Adam's number as she walked along the street towards her house. It took a moment to connect but eventually began to ring as she pushed open the front gate. The sound of 'Are You Lonesome Tonight?' by Elvis Presley stopped her in her tracks. Adam's ringtone. Pulling the phone away from her ear, she focused all her senses on locating the source of the music.

What she saw next made her blood run cold. Adam, lying prostrate amongst the shrubs and flowers.

'Adam!' she shouted as she rushed over and dropped to her knees. 'Adam!'

He didn't move.

She placed her fingers to his neck in search of a pulse. It

was there, but only just. 'I'm gonna get help, Adam. Stay with me, babe.' She rolled him into the recovery position. Only then did she notice his blood-saturated T-shirt. 'Oh, Jesus. Please stay with me!'

Even in the darkness, Adam's skin appeared ashen. He had lost a lot of blood. As she dialled 999, Phillips pulled up his bloody T-shirt in search of the source and spotted three large knife wounds on his torso. The call connected.

'This is Detective Chief Inspector Phillips from the Major Crimes Unit. I need an ambulance urgently. My boyfriend has been stabbed at least three times in the abdomen, maybe more. He has a pulse, but he's lost a lot of blood and he's in a very bad way.'

'*What's your location?*' asked the operator, her voice calm and clear.

'Number 11 Beaumont Avenue, Chorlton. *Please hurry.*'

Phillips could hear the operator typing on the other end of the line.

'*They're on their way, ma'am. ETA five minutes.*'

Phillips ended the call, then dialled Jones.

'*Missing me already, Guv?*' he joked as he answered.

'Adam's been stabbed.'

'*What?*' His tone was incredulous. '*Is he badly hurt?*'

'Yes.' Phillips had to fight away the tears. 'I think he could die.'

'*Oh God, Guv. Where did it happen?*'

'Outside my house. I found him lying in the garden when I got home. He wasn't even supposed to be here tonight.'

'*I'll come straight over.*'

'There's no point. The paramedics are only a few minutes out. We'll be gone by the time you get here.'

'*In that case, I'll meet you at A&E.*'

Phillips nodded, but no words would come out.

'And I'll call Bov and Entwistle. We're going to need to secure the scene at your place to preserve the evidence.'

Up until then, Phillips had been oblivious to the fact she was kneeling in the middle of a crime scene. After almost twenty years of forensically poring over bloodied bodies and murder locations, she'd never imagined that CSIs would one day set up their tents in her own front garden. The whole place would need to be searched for any evidence that might help identify Adam's attacker.

Staring down at her left hand, she was suddenly aware it was soaked in blood. 'I can't lose him, Jonesy,' she whispered.

'You won't, Guv. You won't.'

28

TUESDAY 13TH JULY

It was almost 3 a.m. by the time the surgeon, Doctor Li, arrived at the *Relatives' Room*, located close to A&E. Of Chinese descent, he was in his mid-thirties.

Phillips instinctively stood as he entered. 'How is he?' she asked, her voice small with fear.

Li's expression was grave. 'Please, take a seat,' he said, then pulled up a chair opposite Phillips and Jones. 'Adam's very poorly. The next few days will be critical for him.'

Phillips swallowed hard. 'Will he live?'

'At the moment, we simply don't know. We've had to remove a kidney, which was severely damaged in the attack.'

'Oh my God.' She couldn't believe what Li had just said.

Li continued. 'We're now trying to protect him from infection. A lot of toxins were released into his body when the kidney was damaged, and sepsis – blood poisoning – is a real concern right now. We'll know more in the next few days, but for now he's been put into an induced coma to try and help him recover.'

Phillips heard the words, but it was as if he was talking to someone else. Like she was watching a horrifying movie play out with her stuck in it, unable to escape.

'He's in the best possible place, and the ICU team here is second to none.'

Phillips dropped her head into her hands for a long moment before looking up again. 'Can I see him?'

Li nodded. 'Just for a few minutes, though, and only you, I'm afraid.' He glanced at Jones. 'We need to minimise the risk of infection.'

'Of course,' said Jones softly.

Li stood. 'If you'd like to come with me, I'll take you through to ICU.'

As Phillips got up from the chair, her legs felt like jelly. For a moment, she thought they may not carry her.

Jones immediately jumped up from his chair to steady her. 'You ok, boss?'

'Yeah,' she said, barely audible, before taking a deep breath and following Li out of the room.

They passed through a maze of corridors before eventually arriving at the secure entrance to the Intensive Care Unit. Li offered a soft smile as he released the electric lock with his key fob and led the way inside. Adam's room was halfway down the main corridor, on the left. As she followed Li inside, she thought her heart might stop seeing Adam lying in the bed, hooked up to the myriad machines monitoring his vital signs.

'We've ventilated him as a precaution,' said Li, 'to help him breath and his body repair itself.'

He looked so fragile and helpless; tubes were attached to almost every part of his body.

Just then a nurse appeared wearing surgical scrubs. Her name badge stated she was Senior Sister Wilson. She was petite, with fair hair and a warm smile. 'I'm Angela,' she said, and offered a hand.

Phillips shook it. 'Jane.'

Li placed a reassuring hand on Phillips's wrist. 'I need to be getting back to surgery, but Senior Sister Wilson will take care of everything for you.'

Phillips watched him leave before turning back to Wilson.

'I know it all looks pretty scary, but everything in this room is designed to help Adam get better. Including me.' Wilson smiled again.

Phillips had held herself together since discovering Adam lying in the garden over five hours ago, but something in the nurse's tone and manner disarmed her. A moment later, she began to cry, deep, guttural sobs that suddenly engulfed her.

Wilson wrapped a warm arm around her. 'Hey. It's ok. He's in good hands, and he's young and fit. He's got a real fighting chance of coming through this.'

'I can't lose him,' Phillips found herself saying again. 'I just can't.'

'We're doing everything we can to help Adam make a full recovery.' Wilson handed her a tissue. 'I know it's easy to say, but please, try not to worry.'

Phillips moved to the side of the bed and wrapped her hand around the fingers of Adam's right hand before leaning over and kissing him gently on the forehead. 'Please don't die,' she whispered as she rested her head against his.

'Do you have anyone with you?' asked Wilson.

Phillips stood and looked at the nurse. 'Yes, a colleague from work.'

'And what line of work are you in, Jane?'

'I'm a detective.'

'And I understand Adam is a doctor?' said Wilson.

'Yes,' said Phillips as she attempted to fight back more tears.

A flash of pity shot across Wilson's face. 'Well, I'm sure he'd be the first one to tell you how important it is for you to rest. Why don't you head home and get some sleep? Come and see him in the morning.'

Phillips nodded, but in reality, sleep was the last thing on her mind.

Wilson moved to the other side of the bed and opened the small locker, then pulled out a clear plastic bag, which she handed across. 'These are Adam's personal effects. That's quite an expensive watch, so I think it's safer with you as opposed to sitting in his locker.'

'Thank you.' Phillips gazed down at Adam's Tag-Heuer watch, his wallet and mobile phone.

'There's cash in the wallet and everything else seems to be working ok, but I'm afraid his clothes had to be cut off in A&E, so we didn't keep them.'

'I understand.' Phillips looked at Adam.

'I'll give you a minute alone,' said Wilson softly, then left the room.

Phillips once again gripped Adam's fingers with all her might as she moved her face close to his right ear. 'I love you, babe, with all my heart,' she whispered, barely able to get the words out. 'Please live. Please, Adam, you can't go. I need you here with me. By my side, where you belong.' The thought of losing him was too much to bear.

The sound of the machines echoed around the room as tears streaked down her cheeks. For the next couple of minutes, she remained silent as she tried to process the events of the night.

Eventually, Wilson reappeared.

Phillips stood, picking up the plastic bag as she did.

'You can visit any time. There's a special ICU *Relatives' Room* just by the entrance where you came in,' said Wilson. 'You can access that night and day. And rest assured, if anything changes, I'll let you know immediately.'

'Thank you, Sister.'

'Please, call me Angela.'

'Angela.' Phillips offered a faint smile, then walked out the room.

Retracing her steps, she found Jones in the A&E *Relatives' Room*, nursing a hot cuppa.

'How is he?' he asked, getting up from the chair.

Phillips opened her mouth to speak, but all that came were more tears.

Jones placed his cup down on the side, then wrapped his arms around her. 'Oh, Guv. I'm so, so sorry.'

Phillips buried her head in his chest and sobbed, shoulders heaving.

'He's a fighter. He'll get through this,' said Jones softly.

'He's in there because of me.' Phillips pulled her head away now. 'This is my fault. That blade was meant for *me*.'

'You don't know that,' said Jones.

She stepped back now. 'Of course it was. Why else would someone attack Adam? He hasn't got a bad word to say about anyone.'

'Maybe it was a mugging that went wrong?'

'His wallet is full of cash, and his watch was on him when I found him. Anyone looking for money would have grabbed them and made a run for it.' Phillips shook her head. 'No, it was me they came looking for.'

'Well, if that is the case, then we need to speak to Carter first thing in the morning. You're going to need a protective detail at home.'

Phillips suddenly remembered the crime scene. 'What's happening at my house?'

'Bov and Entwistle secured it with uniform around midnight, but Evans was still working on the Bahmani shooting, so Alice Freeman is leading up the CSIs.'

'She's good,' said Phillips. 'Just what we need. But that means my house will be off limits for a while.'

'You're welcome to come to ours. Get your head down for a bit.'

'There's no way I can sleep with Adam like that. No. I may as well go into the office and get started.'

'On what?'

'Finding Adam's attacker, of course.'

Jones's face wrinkled. 'You can't take on the case, boss. It'd be a conflict of interest.'

'Why would it?'

'Because you're too close to it. It'd be almost impossible for you to be objective.'

'Bollocks would it,' Phillips spat back. 'I'm a professional.'

'Come on, Guv. There's no way Carter will go for that.'

'Well, I won't give him a choice. Adam was stabbed at my house, and I'm going to find out who did it.'

Jones shook his head, but clearly knew better than to keep on arguing. 'You're the boss.'

'Yeah, I am.' Phillips could feel the rage building in her gut. 'And I want everyone in the office for an 8 a.m. briefing on the case.'

'Of course,' Jones replied without conviction.

'I'm gonna catch this bastard – *whatever it takes*,' she raged, then stormed out of the room.

29

I t was just after 5 a.m. when Phillips arrived at Ashton House. After freshening up in the women's locker room, she headed up to her office, where she made herself a mug of hot sweet tea before taking a seat at her desk. Spinning the chair to face the window, she stared out at the clear blue morning sky. It was going to be another warm day.

It wasn't long before her mind wandered to the image of Adam, lying in the ICU bed and hooked up to the machines. Her pain was a living thing inside her, growing by the second. Her soul mate was fighting to survive, and there was nothing she could do to help him. She had never felt so powerless.

If she wasn't going to lose her mind thinking constantly about him, she needed to distract herself. The best way to do that was to throw herself into her work. She checked her phone for the first time since finding Adam. There were a number of missed calls from Chief Superintendent Carter, between 10.30 p.m. and 1 a.m. It was 5.37 a.m. according to her watch – way too early to call him back. Plus, the truth was, she didn't want to talk about Adam. If she avoided talking about it, she could almost pretend it wasn't happening. So she muted the handset and placed it on her desk, then headed out into the main office.

Pulling together two large whiteboards on rollers, she began lists of potential suspects, as well as motive and opportunity for each of them. By the time Jones arrived at 7.50 a.m., she had an impressive dossier.

'Someone's been busy,' Jones quipped as he dropped his car keys on the desk and removed his suit jacket. 'Any news on Adam?'

'Nothing since we left, but the surgeon said not to expect much change in the first twenty-four hours.'

Entwistle walked in next, followed by Bovalino, who carried four hot drinks wedged into a moulded cardboard tray, which he handed around.

Phillips was eager to get on. As each of them sat at their desks, she began the briefing. 'As you all know, Adam was stabbed three times, sometime between 8.05 p.m., when I last spoke to him on the phone—' She used a marker pen to point out the times. '—and 10.25 p.m., when I found him. Whoever our suspect is left behind sixty pounds in cash, as well as a Tag-Heuer watch worth around three grand and a brand-new iPhone 13 Pro. So I think it's fair to say we can rule out a mugging.'

Bovalino frowned. 'Sorry, Guv, but I thought this case had been passed over to Serious Crimes? At least, that's what Carter said last night on the phone.'

'I don't know anything about that,' said Phillips. 'So as far as I'm concerned, it's *our* investigation.'

'With respect, boss,' Bovalino continued, 'protocols won't allow for that. You're personally involved here, and that could cause real issues for the CPS. The defence could claim you're not objective and use it against us.'

Phillips struggled to control her emotions. 'I know the

law, Bov, but until I hear otherwise, this is our case and we're doing it *my way*. Understood?'

The big man offered a weak nod, but said nothing as he glanced at Jones and Entwistle. Their expressions suggested they shared Bovalino's concerns.

Phillips continued regardless. Finding Adam's attacker was all she could think about. 'These are the three suspects in the case so far: Adders Bahmani—'

'But he was with *us* when Adam was attacked,' Jones cut in, 'sat two feet away in the back of an ambulance.'

'I know he was, but his goon of a cousin wasn't, was he?'

'So we're looking at Tahir, then? *Not* Adders.'

'Adders made threats against me after we questioned his wife. *He's* in the frame *as well* as his cousin. Tahir doesn't do anything without Adders's say so, so we'll treat him was an accessory.' Phillips pointed to the next name on the board. 'Freddie Bradley also made threats against me at his father's memorial.'

'Fox isn't going to like us going after him, boss,' said Jones.

Phillips glared at her sergeant for a long moment. 'I don't give a shit what Fox does or doesn't like. He made threats against me, so he's a suspect.'

Jones exhaled loudly and folded his arms across his chest.

Phillips ignored him and pressed on. 'And the third on the list is Josh Castillo. He was released from Hawk Green on Friday after serving five years of ten, for the manslaughter of his wife. Until recently, he maintained his innocence. At the time of his sentencing, he made threats against me for putting him away.'

'If it was Castillo, that's a pretty quick turnaround, Guv,' said Entwistle. 'Out Friday morning and attacking Adam on Monday night.'

'So, what's he gonna do?' Phillips shot back. 'Sit and wait for a month before he comes after me? If he'd planned this for the last five years, then I'm pretty sure he'd be chomping at the bit to get back at me.'

At that moment, the main door to MCU opened and Carter walked in. He had a grave look on his face as he stopped next to Phillips's office. 'Have you got a minute, DCI Phillips?'

Phillips nodded. 'Of course, sir.'

As they stepped inside her office, Carter closed the door behind them. 'I've been calling and calling since I heard about Adam.'

'Sorry, sir. I had my phone on silent in the hospital. Must have forgotten to turn it back on,' she lied.

'How is he?'

Phillips really didn't want to talk about it. It was too painful. But he needed to know. 'He's in a bad way. They had to remove one of his kidneys, and they're worried he could end up with sepsis.'

'Blood poisoning?'

'Yeah. It can be fatal if not caught in time.'

Carter blew his lips. 'Jesus, Jane. That's awful. I'm so sorry.'

'Thank you,' said Phillips. She struggled to keep the tears in check.

Carter's face wrinkled. 'So why on earth are you at work? You should be with Adam.'

Phillips shook her head. 'I'm better off here. It breaks my heart to see him like that. Work is a good distraction for me.'

Carter studied her for a moment. 'Ok, I can understand that. But maybe we reduce your caseload? Pass a few over to Serious Crimes.'

'No. That won't be necessary,' Phillips shot back.

'Are you sure, Jane?' asked Carter. 'It's ok to let others help, you know. Especially at a time like this.'

'No. Really, sir. The busier the better for me. It's just how I deal with things.'

'I understand. Well, you'll be pleased to know Fox has assigned DCI Cleverly and SCU to investigate Adam's attack. He's a first-rate detective—'

'But *I've* already opened an investigation into the attack,' Phillips cut him off. 'I was just briefing the team as you walked in.'

'You're not serious?' scoffed Carter.

'Yeah, I am. Deadly serious, sir. We have three potential suspects and—'

It was Carter's turn to cut in now. 'Jane, that's impossible. The victim is *your boyfriend*. Your credibility would be called into question throughout, not to mention your state of mind, impartiality, your judgement, even. You know as well as I do, you cannot investigate Adam's attack.'

Phillips's jaw trembled as the emotions swirled through her body. 'Well, at least let me help Cleverly and the guys at SCU. I can assist, offer another point of view. I was the one who found him.'

'Steve is a great detective, and his team has a conviction rate on par with MCU's. He doesn't need your help, Jane.'

Phillips bit her top lip and nodded silently.

'Look. I know you want to keep busy, but maybe you *should* take some time out. Get some rest. I can see you've not been to bed in the last twenty-four hours.'

Phillips stared him dead in the eye. 'I'm fine, sir. Really I am.'

'Very well. But if it gets too much, you must let me know.'

'I will.'

'Equally, Jane, if I think you're struggling, or this situation is affecting your judgement, you need to know that I *will* take you out of the firing line. Jones is more than capable of leading the team for a couple of weeks.'

Phillips swallowed hard as she glanced out at the team, each of whom had made themselves busy since Carter walked in. 'I understand.'

Carter said nothing for a long moment. 'I really am very sorry about Adam, Jane.'

'Thank you, sir,' said Phillips, her voice cracking slightly as she thought about him lying in that bed, fighting for his life.

'I'll check in later to see how you're doing. Ok?'

'Yes sir.'

Carter offered a warm smile. 'I haven't been to church in over twenty years, but I'll be praying for him,' he said, then opened the office door and headed out.

Phillips watched him leave, then swatted away a tear as it rolled down her cheek. Moving to her desk, she picked up the clear bag that contained Adam's things and pulled out his phone. Keying in the passcode, she searched through his contacts until she found who she was looking for and pressed the call button. A moment later the call connected, and she heard the international dial tone.

It was eventually answered by woman who sounded surprised. '*Adam?*'

'No, Carrie, it's Jane.'

'*Jane? What's up?*'

'I'm sorry, Carrie, but Adam's in hospital…'

arrie, Adam's younger sister, lived in Zurich with
her husband and two young boys. As Phillips had
expected, the news of the attack came as a massive
shock. There were no tears at the other end of the line, just
utter disbelief. By the time they hung up, Carrie planned to
be on the next flight out to Manchester. Phillips warned her
what to expect at the hospital.

Putting the phone down, Phillips sat in her office, staring
down at Adam's watch in her hand. She wondered if he
would ever wear it again. She hoped to God he would.

At that moment, Jones knocked on her door, then stepped
inside.

'What's up?' she asked as she placed the watch in her
pocket.

'We were just wondering what's happening with Adam's
case, Guv.'

'Shit, sorry. I got distracted.'

'Understandable, given the circumstances.'

Phillips laid her hands flat on the desk. 'Fox wants SCU to
lead the investigation. She, like you and Bov, it seems – not to

mention Carter – believes it would be a conflict of interest for us to handle it.'

'It's not just that, boss. No copper should *ever* have to investigate the attempted murder of their partner. It's not right, and it would do more harm than good. We're on your side here, honestly we are.'

'I know,' replied Phillips. 'Anyway, it's out of our hands now, so there's nothing we can do. It's up to Cleverly and his team now.'

Jones breathed an audible sigh of relief.

Just then, Bovalino appeared at her door. 'Guv, I've got an update on the Bahmani shooting.'

'That was quick,' said Phillips. 'What do you have?'

'I've managed to get hold of some council CCTV footage and identified the guy who legged it.'

'Shawn Harvey, by any chance?'

'How did you know that?' He handed over a mugshot of Harvey, taken after a recent arrest.

'Cleverly mentioned him last night. Apparently Harvey and Jez Fulton were thick as thieves, so it makes sense. And they both worked for Paul Bradley, apparently.' Phillips stared down at the photograph for a moment. The man looking back at her emanated an air of violence and intimidation, with facial scars to match. 'Why do all wannabe gangsters look the same?'

'They practice from a young age,' joked Jones.

Phillips handed the photo back to Bovalino. 'I want a copy of this, please, and get his name circulated to every copper in Manchester. I want him in here ASAP.'

'On it,' said the big Italian before heading back to his desk.

Phillips turned her attention to Jones. 'Bring the team up to speed on Adam's case, will you? And then get your car keys. We're heading out?'

'Anywhere nice?'

'Bahmani's yard. I want to talk to him about Harvey.'

Jones left the room, and returned a few moments later.

Phillips let out a huge yawn.

'You look knackered, boss,' said Jones.

'I'm fine, and besides, *you* were up half the night too.'

'Yeah, but *I* got a couple of hours on the couch this morning, *and* a shower. You've been here since five.'

'I'm fine.' She waved him away as she stood. 'Come on. Let's go see what Adders has to say.'

THEY ARRIVED at the Ancoats yard forty minutes later, in part due to heavy traffic on the M60. An accident had caused a long tailback anti-clockwise, and it was only thanks to Jones's knowledge of the back roads that the journey wasn't a great deal longer.

Bahmani was outside in the yard as they parked up.

Phillips said nothing as she climbed out of the car and stared at one of the men she suspected in Adam's attack.

'Back so soon?' he said, his tone contemptuous.

Phillips and Jones walked over and stood opposite him.

She pulled out Shawn Harvey's mugshot and held it in front of his face. 'Do you recognise this guy?'

Bahmani glanced at it for a moment. 'Should I?'

'We think he was the second shooter last night.'

'Like I said, the two guys wore masks, so I never got a look at their faces.'

Phillips scanned the yard. She spotted Tahir as he walked out from behind one of the compactors. She gestured in his direction. 'Where was your cousin last night?'

Bahmani turned to follow her gaze. 'Why do you wanna know?'

'Because a man was stabbed multiple times in Chorlton, sometime between eight and ten p.m.'

Jones shot Phillips a look that made his thoughts clear: these questions were off limits to MCU.

Phillips deliberately ignored him.

'Your boyfriend, you mean?' asked Bahmani.

Phillips recoiled. 'Who told you that?'

Bahmani shrugged. 'Big city, small town. Word gets around.'

Phillips's rage burned through every fibre of her being. 'Never mind word gets around, how do you know about my boyfriend? That information hasn't been released to the public.'

A lopsided grin spread across Bahmani's face and he shrugged nonchalantly. 'I can't remember now.'

'If you know anything about the attack, you need to tell us now,' said Phillips, squaring up to Bahmani.

'Guv, can I have a word?' asked Jones.

Phillips blanked him and nodded in Tahir's direction once again. 'So where *was* your cousin between eight and ten p.m. last night?'

Bahmani's eyes narrowed, and he paused before answering. 'He was at my house doing some odd jobs.'

'And I'm guessing your wife will vouch for him, will she?'

'Correct.'

'Can we talk to him?'

'He doesn't speak English.'

'Of course he doesn't,' said Phillips flatly.

'Have you got a minute, Guv?' Jones cut in again. His expression had not changed, and it was clear he was pissed off she was pushing this line of enquiry.

Phillips knew exactly why he wanted to talk, and decided it would be best to back down – for now. 'You sure you've never seen this guy?' she asked, returning the conversation to the shooting.

'Never,' said Bahmani flatly.

'Well, if you do come across him, let us know, won't you? We don't want you taking things into your own hands now, do we?'

'You'll be the first to know, but like I said last night, I'm pretty sure they were just after my car. I can't think of any other reason they'd want to come after me.'

'That's right, I keep forgetting.' Phillips's tone was facetious now. 'You're just a humble scrap merchant, aren't you?'

Bahmani's grin reappeared. 'Got it in one.'

'Pah,' scoffed Phillips as she turned and walked away.

Jones followed hard on her heels, but waited until they were back in the car before delivering the inevitable reprimand. 'What the hell was all that about?'

'What?'

'You know damn well what, Guv. Adam's case has *nothing* to do with us.'

'Really? Last time I looked, he was *my* boyfriend,' Phillips spat back.

'Exactly. And that's exactly what I'm saying. Fox and Carter were clear that MCU getting involved could jeopardise the chances of getting a conviction, so we *have* to leave it to Cleverly and the rest of SCU. I know that's tough for you, and I totally understand why, but you've got to get a grip on this otherwise *you* could be the reason his attacker gets off.'

Phillips knew he was right, but it didn't make it any easier to hear. Some scumbag had tried to murder Adam, and all she wanted to do was catch him and make him pay. Doing nothing was destroying her. 'Ok, ok. I hear you, and I'm sorry. I wasn't thinking straight.'

Jones's tone was instantly softer. 'Are you sure you should be at work, boss? This can't be easy for you.'

Phillips choked back the tears that threatened to over-whelm her. 'Work's all I've got, Jonesy. I can't sit in the hospital and watch Adam die.'

'He's not gonna die. He's a fighter and he will come through this. I can feel it in my gut.'

Phillips locked eyes with him and offered a weak smile. 'I hope you're right.'

'I am.' He smiled back. 'I'm always right.'

Phillips let out a low growl as she rubbed her face before exhaling loudly. 'Right. Let's get over to see Freddie Bradley.'

Jones shot her a sideways glance. 'You *do remember* Fox said he's off limits?'

'To *me,* yes, but not to you. I'll stay well out of the way.'

'Well, I'm not asking him about last night, if that's what you're after.'

'It's not. I just want to know a little bit more about Fulton and Harvey. If they worked for his dad, chances are he knows them well enough.'

Jones fired the engine. 'As long as that's all I'm going to be talking to him about.'

She raised her hands in mock surrender. 'It is, I promise.'

31

When they arrived at the Bradley home, Freddie was out on the drive waxing his father's Bentley, which sparkled in the sunshine.

Jones parked up on the pavement adjacent to the house, then turned to face Phillips. 'Why don't you stay in the car, boss? I can handle this on my own.'

Without warning, her anger got the better of her. 'I'm not a bloody child, Jonesy. I said I wouldn't get involved and I won't. Equally, I'm not going to sit here peeping out like a spare part. What kind of message does that send to pricks like Freddie Bradley?'

'Ok, ok. It was just a suggestion,' he replied as he switched off the engine and opened the car door.

As they approached, Freddie stopped what he was doing. 'To what do I owe the pleasure?' He sounded unusually cheery as he stood staring at them, a soft polishing cloth held in his right hand.

'We were hoping to talk to you about a couple of your employees, if that's ok?' said Jones.

Phillips folded her arms but remained silent as she looked on.

'Oh? Which ones?' asked Freddie.

'Jez Fulton and Shawn Harvey.'

'They don't work for us anymore,' Freddie replied without missing a beat. 'Right pair of headbangers, so we got rid of them. What they done now?'

'Well, I'm sorry to tell you, Jez was killed last night, and Shawn is wanted in connection with the same incident.'

'Oh God, really? That's a shame, but I can't say I'm surprised.' Freddie appeared unmoved by the news.

'When did you last see either of them?' asked Jones.

Freddie didn't answer. Instead, he turned his attention to Phillips. 'Cat got your tongue, Chief Inspector?'

'Just answer his questions,' she shot back.

A wide grin spread across Freddie's face. 'So does this mean the rumours are true, then?'

'And what rumours would those be?' said Phillips.

'Well, that after your little performance at my dad's memorial, you've been muzzled.' He opened his arms wide. 'That the Bradleys are off limits to *you*.'

Phillips opened her mouth to respond, but Jones beat her to it. 'As I was saying, when was the last time you saw either Jez or Shawn?'

Freddie shrugged as he opened the driver's door of the Bentley and began rubbing the metal with the cloth. 'I dunno. Can't really remember.'

'Could you maybe hazard a guess?' Phillips could hear Jones's irritation in his tone.

'A few months ago, I'd say. They worked the doors for us a few times at Vibe, but they were both too fond of a fight. Plus, neither of them was what you'd call tolerant of the LGBTQ community. So not a good mix for a club in the Gay Village. We got a lot of complaints about them being too rough with the punters, so we let them go.'

'So they've not worked for you in any other capacity since?' asked Jones.

Freddie frowned. 'And what exactly is that supposed to mean?'

'Well, you have other business interests besides the club, don't you?' replied Jones.

'Nothing I'd let either of those two near.'

'What about your mate, Shanks? The one who's apartment you were at when your dad was killed?' Jones asked, changing the subject.

'What about him?'

'Did he have anything to do with Fulton and Harvey?'

'He works at the club, so he'll have come across them from time to time, but no more than me.'

'If we wanted to talk to Shanks, where can we find him?' asked Jones.

'I haven't seen him for a few days, but try his flat in the Northern Quarter. He spends most of his time there.' Freddie turned his attention back to Phillips now. When he spoke, his tone was mischievous. 'I heard another rumour, actually.'

Phillips remained silent as she glared back at him.

Freddie continued. 'Yeah, I heard that *somehow* you've got a boyfriend, Chief Inspector...'

Phillips swallowed hard as her adrenaline spiked.

'...and that last night somebody had a go at him, right outside your house. Apparently they really did a number on him. Almost killed him.'

'Where did that information come from?' asked Jones.

There was a glint in Freddie's eye as he turned back to face him. 'It's all over town. Big news in some circles.'

Phillips took a couple of steps forward as rage threatened her sanity.

'We're not here to discuss that incident,' said Jones.

'So it's true, then?' Freddie smiled as he rested his left elbow on the roof of the Bentley and moved behind the open door. His tone was one of mock concern as he stared at Phillips. 'Oh dear. How awful for you, Jane. I hope he doesn't die.'

Without thinking, Phillips took a step forward, grabbed the handle of car door and pushed it shut against Freddie's arm, which dangled down from the roof.

There was a sickening thud as the door connected, and he cried out in agony.

In a flash, Jones pulled Phillips back and released the door.

'You fucking bitch!' Freddie growled as he protectively bent double around his wrist.

'Oh dear, I hope it's not broken,' Phillips said, mimicking Freddie's mock concern.

Jones locked eyes with Phillips, his expression grave.

'I'll have you for this,' Freddie raged.

'It was an accident,' replied Phillips flatly. 'I tripped.'

'Like hell you did!'

Jones stood between the pair. 'Would you like us to call an ambulance, Freddie?'

'No!' He was evidently in immense pain. 'I'd like you both to get the fuck away from me.'

'Well, if that's what you want,' said Phillips nonchalantly, and headed for the car.

Jones joined her a few moments later, and slammed the door once he was inside the car. 'Are you deliberately trying to get yourself fired?'

'What was I supposed to do?' Phillips shouted back. 'He was bloody laughing about Adam being stabbed, for Christ's sake!'

Jones started the engine and drove away at speed. 'Look, I

get the fact you're upset, but you can't go around assaulting arseholes just cos they got under your skin.'

'It was an accident.'

'Oh, pull the other one, Guv. You pushed the door into his arm. I saw you do it.'

Phillips locked eyes with Jones. 'I tripped and fell into the door.'

'So that's your story, is it?'

'Yes, and if that's different to yours, then so be it.'

Jones shook his head. 'We need to get out in front of this before it gets out of hand.'

'And we will. As soon as we get back to base, I'll go and see Carter.'

'Good!' replied Jones. 'At least that's something.'

Phillips gazed at the offside wing mirror as the Bradley house grew smaller in the reflection. 'He knows who attacked Adam. He absolutely does.'

'Well, that's down to Cleverly and his team to find out, not us.'

'So you keep reminding me,' said Phillips as they reached the main road and merged with the traffic.

32

B y the time Phillips walked into Carter's office suite, she'd calmed down somewhat and was beginning to regret her actions. She knew better than to lose her cool, but the images of Adam lying in hospital were never far from her mind's eye. Her emotions were starting to get the better of her.

Carter's executive assistant, Diana Cook, greeted her with a soft smile. 'Hello, Jane. I was so sorry to hear about Adam. How's he doing?'

'I've just got off the phone to ICU. He's stable. That's all they would say.'

'Well, I'm keeping everything crossed for him.'

'Thank you.'

Cook glanced in the direction of Carter's office door. 'He's been expecting you.'

Phillips raised an eyebrow. 'That can't be good.'

'Go straight in.'

Carter stood by the window with his back to the room. He was well-built, and in great shape for a man in his mid-fifties.

He turned to face her as she walked in, his expression dour. 'I thought we had a deal, Jane?'

'What do you mean, sir?'

He gestured for her to sit, then dropped into his large leather chair. 'That you were to stay away from Freddie Bradley?'

'I did, sir.'

'Really? Then how come I've just had a call from Travis Tate, Melissa Bradley's attorney?'

'Look, it was an accident—'

'You smashed Freddie's arm with a car door!' Carter cut in before she could finish.

'I tripped sir.'

'Oh come on, Jane. If I'm going to help you sort out this mess, you need to at least be honest with me.'

Phillips let out a loud breath. 'Ok. The truth is, he knew about Adam's attack and started goading me, saying he hoped he wouldn't die. I lost it for a split second and pushed the door against him.'

'And Jones saw all this?'

'Yes, sir, but he had nothing to do with it. In fact, he gave me quite the rollocking when we got back into the car.'

'Were there any other witnesses?'

'No. I'm pretty sure it was just the three of us.'

'Well, that's something, at least.' Carter pursed his lips and said nothing for a moment, evidently deep in thought. 'Look, Jane. The reality is, Tate has been instructed by Freddie's mother to make an official complaint for the assault, which naturally will have to be investigated by the IPCC.'

'Jesus. They didn't mess about, did they?'

'No. Tate called me as a courtesy ten minutes ago – at least, that was his excuse. I have to say it felt more like a fishing trip to see if I knew about the incident, which of course I didn't.'

'That's why I'm here, sir, to debrief you on it.'

'You should have called me as soon as it happened, Jane.'

'I know, but I was still so angry,' said Phillips. 'I needed some time to clear my head. And I never expected them to react so quickly.'

Carter's expression softened. 'Are you sure you want to be at work, Jane? Like I said this morning, there's no shame in taking some personal time to be with Adam.'

'I appreciate your concern, but like *I* said, I'm better off at work.'

'Well, judging by today's incident, one could argue that's maybe not the case.' The room fell silent for a long moment. 'Look, if you're telling me it was an accident, then that's the line we'll stick with.'

'You don't have to do that, sir.'

'I know I don't, but I'm going to. Will Jones back you up?'

'I honestly couldn't say, sir. He was pretty angry.'

'Well, I'll have a quiet word. As I understand it, Freddie Bradley is as crooked as his dad was purported to be. Anyway, from what you said, sounds like the little shit had it coming to him.'

Phillips offered a weak smile. 'I take it Fox doesn't know, yet?'

Carter shook his head. 'No, but that'll be my next job.'

'She's certainly not going to be happy.'

'No, she's not, but then again, she never is. One thing in your favour is that she knows as well as I do that our best chance of catching Bradley's and Hodges's killer lies with you.'

Phillips felt her neck flush. She wasn't great at accepting compliments. 'Thank you, sir.'

'So, I'm guessing she'll do her best to avoid a suspension at this stage – for the time being, at least. Providing you are actually fit for duty, Jane.'

'I am, sir. Honestly, I am. Today was a stupid mistake. It won't happen again.'

Carter said nothing for a moment. 'Look, Jane, I know you want to work and that you'd rather be busy, but if there's a chance the attack on Adam is somehow linked to the Bradley and Hodge murders, maybe it's best you step away from those cases. Jones can carry on as SIO.'

Phillips dropped her chin to her chest momentarily before she looked up and locked eyes with Carter. 'Please don't do that, sir. You said so yourself, I'm the best chance of catching the killers.'

'I know, Jane, but you're also emotionally involved now. My worry is, can you really remain objective? Could anyone in your position? I know I couldn't.'

'You don't have to worry about me, sir. I can do this.'

Carter offered her a sympathetic smile. 'I'm not going to talk you out of it, am I?'

'No. You're not.'

'Very well.' Carter sighed. 'But if it all gets too much, you must tell me immediately. Ok?'

'I will, sir.'

'And no more *accidents*. MCU's creditability is at stake here, and that doesn't just affect you. Your actions reflect on me as well as the rest of your team.'

'I understand. And I promise, I'll bring my A-game from now. You can count on me.'

Carter checked his watch. 'Ok. Look, it's been a long twenty-four hours for you. Why don't you go home and get some rest?'

'What about the CSI team at my place?'

'I spoke to Alice Freeman earlier. They finished at the house a couple of hours ago. You're free to go back home.'

Images of Adam, lying in her front garden covered in blood, flashed into her mind's eye. 'Actually, I'm not sure I'm quite ready to face that just yet. I think I'll head to the hospital first, check how he's doing.'

Carter nodded. 'Let us know if there's any improvement, won't you?'

'Of course,' Phillips said, then stood. 'And thank you, sir. For going in to bat for me on this.'

'I'll always have your back, Jane, you know that. Just keep it by the book from now on. Ok?'

'I will,' said Phillips, then left the room.

33

Phillips waited to be buzzed through the secure door to ICU, then made her way down the long corridor to Adam's private room. The familiar smell of industrial-grade disinfectant was pervasive. As she walked through the door, she stopped in her tracks when she saw a strikingly attractive woman – likely in her thirties – sitting next to Adam's bed, holding his hand.

The woman looked up. Her eyes were red and swollen from crying. 'Jane,' she said softly, then burst into tears.

Carrie looked very different from the last photo Phillips had seen of her, but her voice was unmistakable – a female version of her brother's. The two women embraced, and their bodies shook as they both allowed the tears to flow unabated.

After a few minutes, Phillips pulled back and stared into Carrie's big blue eyes that were so like Adam's.

'The doctor said he's very poorly,' Carrie managed to whisper before the tears returned once more.

Phillips hugged her again, squeezing her as tightly as she could. 'I'm so sorry, Carrie.'

After a few more minutes, Carrie was able to continue

with her update from the doctor. 'His blood pressure is very, very low, and he's got a urine infection, which is quite common when they use catheters. He's fighting it, but he's so weak.'

Phillips stared down at Adam as the rhythmic sound of the ventilator managing his breathing filled in the air. 'This is all my fault.'

Carrie's brow furrowed. 'What is?'

'Adam was attacked because of me. Because of what I do.'

'You can't blame yourself, Jane.'

'We split up once, you know.' Phillips turned her gaze back to Carrie. 'If I hadn't asked him for a second chance, this wouldn't have happened. He'd be living a normal life, safe, away from me and the scum I share my days with.'

Carrie squeezed Phillips's hand. 'He's been in love with you since the moment he met you at the dinner party. And he told me all about the time you split. He was so happy when you turned up at the hospital that morning. He wouldn't have had it any other way.'

Phillips was surprised to hear how much detail Adam had shared with his younger sister. She knew they spoke every few weeks, but he rarely shared what they had talked about. She offered a faint smile. 'I want him to live so badly.'

Carrie returned her smile, and used a tissue to wipe her nose as she retook her seat. 'Me too.'

Phillips took the seat on the other side of his bed and held his left hand. 'You look very different from the last photo Adam showed me.'

'A lot of people have said that.' Carrie smiled. 'I've gone back to my natural brown hair. I was blonde for so long, I didn't recognise *myself* for the first few days.'

'It really suits you.'

'Thanks.'

Phillips glanced at Adam, then back at Carrie. 'Have you thought about telling your mum what's going on?'

'No. The dementia's getting worse and she doesn't know who we are anymore. There's no sense in upsetting her at the moment. Let's see how things pan out over the next few days.'

'Fair enough. So, have you thought about where you're going to stay? I would offer you a bed at mine, but I've not been back since the attack. The crime scene investigators have been all over it, and I really don't know what I'm going to find when I get home tonight.'

'Actually, I was thinking I could use Adam's flat if you have a spare key.'

Phillips fished her keys from her pocket. 'I have one on here.' She picked through the bunch until she found the key, released it and passed it over.

'Thank you,' said Carrie.

'The alarm code is 445678,' added Phillips.

For the next ten minutes, they sat in silence, watching Adam.

Phillips wondered where he was right now, if he could hear their conversations at all. 'I do love him, you know,' she said, locking eyes with Carrie.

'I know you do. A blind man could see that.'

'I wish I'd said it to him more often.'

Carrie swatted away a tear from her cheek. 'He knows you love him, Jane. From everything he's told me about you and how you are together, I'm pretty sure of that.'

Phillips suddenly felt an overwhelming sense of fatigue. The total lack of sleep and the events of the last twenty-four hours had finally caught up with her. 'Look, I've not slept for a couple of days and I'm pretty much running on empty right now. I think I should go home.'

'Yeah, you look worn out.'

'Can I give you a lift to Adam's place?'

'If it's ok with you, I'll stay a little longer.'

'Of course,' said Phillips. 'Can I get you anything before I go? A cup of tea or a sandwich?'

'The nurse said they'd get me something if I wanted it, but to be honest, I'm really not hungry.'

Phillips handed across her business card. 'My mobile's on there if you need anything. Call me any time.'

'I will. Thank you, Jane.'

The two women embraced one last time before Phillips made her way back to the car.

THIRTY MINUTES LATER, Phillips pushed open her garden gate. She couldn't shake a sense of foreboding. The CSI team had done their best to return the space to normal once they had finished, but the plants and shrubs where Adam had fallen were still flattened. Steeling herself, she made her way over to the spot where she had found him, and looked at the ground. There were still traces of blood soaked into the grass. She prayed for some of Manchester's ubiquitous rainfall to wash it away. Standing there, she was filled with a sense of powerlessness she had never experienced before. An empty hollowness and overwhelming dread. Moving to the house, she unlocked the front door and stepped inside the hallway.

In an instant, her Ragdoll cat, Floss, was snaking round her legs and meowing, desperate for attention. Phillips bent down and picked her up. 'Sorry, baby. You must have wondered what the hell was going on today with all these strangers in the garden.' She went through to the kitchen. The framed picture of herself and Adam smiling, taken outside the Horse and Jockey pub on their very first date, greeted her. Sadness washed over her like a tidal wave, and the tears streaked down her cheeks.

Opening the fridge, she pulled out a tin of food for Floss, and spooned some into her bowl on the floor. Then she returned for an ice-cold bottle of Pinot Grigio. Grabbing a glass from the shelf, she made her way into the lounge, passing more framed pictures of herself and Adam, taken in various locations over the last twelve months.

Dropping down onto the large sofa, she filled her glass almost to the brim before taking three large mouthfuls. 'Please don't die,' she whispered to the empty room before gulping down another mouthful. 'You can't die, Adam. You can't fucking die.'

34

WEDNESDAY 14TH JULY

P hillips arrived at Ashton House feeling the after-effects of a night of drinking. She'd even fallen asleep on the sofa, an old habit she'd thought long behind her.

Mercifully, it was Jones who appeared a few minutes after she'd unlocked her office, hot coffee in hand. 'You look knackered, Guv.'

'Gee, thanks,' she said sarcastically as she took the steaming cup.

'Any news on Adam?'

Phillips dropped into her chair. 'Nothing good. He's got a urine infection and his blood pressure is very low. I was at the hospital last night, and called them again this morning. All they keep saying is he's stable, and the next few days are critical.'

'Shit. I'm sorry, boss.'

'I did finally get to meet his sister, Carrie, yesterday. She flew in from Zurich as soon as she heard about the attack.'

'And how was that?'

'It was really sweet, actually. She's lovely, and just like

Adam.' Tears welled in her eyes again. She placed her cup on the desk. 'God, I wish I could do something to help him. All this sitting around and waiting for news is driving me mad.'

Jones took a sip of his peppermint tea. 'Carter came to see me yesterday, after you'd gone for the day.'

'Oh,' said Phillips, trying hard not to appear sheepish.

'Talked to me about the incident with Freddie and how we, as a department, are going to deal with it.'

'Look. I was totally out of order, Jonesy. I let him get to me, and I should know better.'

Jones took another sip of his drink. 'Like you said, boss, it was an accident.'

Phillips eyed him for a long moment. 'You don't need to lie on my account.'

'I'm not. I've had some time to reflect on what happened, and I'm simply saying it as I saw it. Freddie's a spoilt little brat playing at being a gangster. He got what he deserved for being a prick about Adam and besides, it's his word against ours.'

'As long as there's no CCTV footage from the cameras at the house. I keep thinking about that.'

'I'm pretty sure there won't be.' A wry smile formed on Jones's lips. 'I checked the angle of the cameras before we left.'

'Really? I never saw you do that.'

'No. You were storming off towards the car at that point.'

Phillips let out a loud sigh of relief. 'Oh thank God. I thought I was in real trouble for a minute there. Thanks, Jonesy. I owe you one.'

'Well, you can repay me by staying out of trouble from now on, hey?'

'It's a deal,' said Phillips.

'Anyway, in other news, after Carter's visit I went down to SCU to see Cleverly.'

Phillips tilted her head slightly and her eyes narrowed. 'Oh yeah?'

'Briefed him on our friend Josh Castillo as a potential suspect in Adam's case.'

'And what did he say?'

'Not much. They were dealing with a potential kidnapping, so I didn't get long with him.'

'A kidnapping?'

'Some gangbanger had been beaten up in the street and bundled into the back of a van yesterday afternoon, apparently.'

'Just another day in Manchester, hey?' Phillips sat forward and clasped her hands together under her nose. 'Do we really think Castillo could be behind the attack on Adam?'

'Murdered his wife, didn't he?'

'Well, strictly speaking it was manslaughter, but that was a crime of passion. This was clearly planned.'

'True, but like you said, boss, he'd had a lot of time in prison to think about revenge if it was him.'

Phillips remained silent for a long moment. 'Is there any way we could talk to Castillo without prejudicing the case?'

Jones's face was incredulous. 'You're not serious, are you? After everything we've talked about, Guv.'

Phillips shook her head. 'Just thinking out loud.'

'Not thinking *straight,* more like.'

She knew he was right, but it didn't make it any easier to swallow. During the investigation into his wife's death, Phillips had come to know Josh Castillo well. She was sure that if she could speak to him directly, she would be able to tell if he was the man behind Adam's attack or not. But like Jones said, as a possible suspect, he was off limits to MCU. She checked her watch; it was approaching 8.15 a.m. 'Cleverly's usually at his desk by 8. Let's go and see if he's in.'

Five minutes later, they found him huddled around a

laptop in his office with his 2IC, DI Kerry Benner. She was diminutive but athletically built, with short dark hair, and was widely regarded across the GMP as a DCI in waiting.

Cleverly looked up as they approached his open door. 'Jane, we were just talking about you.'

'All good, I hope?'

'We think we've identified our kidnapping victim.'

Phillips raised her eyebrows. 'Oh really? What's that got to do with me?'

'We're pretty sure it's Shawn Harvey.' Cleverly turned his laptop round so they could see the screen. 'CCTV from a convenience store across the street where he was snatched.' He pressed play.

They all watched as a man fitting Harvey's description, and wearing identical clothing to the person seen running away from Bahmani's scrap yard, was set upon by two men – wearing hooded tops, and scarves to hide their faces. After knocking him to the ground, they began beating him with baseball bats until he stopped moving. Then they bundled him into the back of a white Mercedes van parked up outside the store, before jumping in the front and speeding off.

'We're checking ANPR cameras to see where they went, but we've already identified that the van was stolen about thirty minutes before the attack,' said DI Benner.

'Can you play it again?' asked Phillips.

Benner obliged.

'Pause it there.' She leaned in to get a closer look. Tapping the screen, she turned to Jones. 'These two look familiar to you?'

Jones stepped forward and examined the footage.

'They're a perfect match for the two suspects who attacked Dillon Wilton.'

'God, yeah. You're right,' said Jones.

Phillips turned her attention to Cleverly. 'When we

mentioned Bahmani's name to Wilton in the hospital, he nearly shit his pants. Whacked a load of morphine into his veins to knock himself out so we couldn't ask any more questions.'

'You think Bahmani tortured Wilton?'

'Don't you?' Phillips shot back.

'Well, he's one on a very long list of suspects. Wilton was widely known as a police informant, so any number of the faces could have had beef with him.'

'If Shawn Harvey *was* the second shooter at the yard, then this could be Bahmani taking his revenge, along with his cousin, Tahir.'

'Makes sense,' said Cleverly.

Phillips folded her arms across her chest. 'So, the question now is; whose case is this?'

'Ours, of course,' Cleverly shot back. 'It's a kidnapping, and last time I looked, that fell under our jurisdiction.'

'Yes, but the kidnapping victim is already a suspect in a murder case, which means it belongs to MCU all day long,' countered Phillips.

Cleverly opened his mouth to speak, but stopped himself. He thought for a long moment. 'Why can't we work together?'

Phillips recoiled slightly. 'And why would you want to do that? SCU aren't known for sharing the glory.'

'I'm hurt,' said Cleverly, placing his fist against his chest playfully. 'But I think the same could be said for Major Crimes.'

Phillips produced a wry grin. 'I'll give you that.'

'Look, we both want to find Harvey, and both have a fair claim to the case. Unless we collaborate, we're going to be stepping on each other's toes and it'll all become a bit of a clusterfuck. We've both got enough open cases to deal with, so we don't need to make our lives any harder than they already are.'

Phillips guessed Cleverly was being strategic. As Harvey was already under investigation by MCU, the case was rightly theirs, but he didn't want to lose face by handing over an investigation. At the same time, from her point of view, Major Crimes had enough on their plate trying to find the killer of Bradley and Hodge. The added support could only be of help. 'Ok,' she said. 'So how do we split it?'

'We'll follow the van and see if we can track where Harvey was taken. You guys chase down Bahmani and see what he's been up to.'

'I can live with that,' said Phillips.

A wide smile appeared on Cleverly's face. 'Excellent.'

'Right, no time to waste,' said Phillips, signalling to Jones it was time to leave. As they reached the door, she turned back. 'Could you send us a copy of that CCTV footage?'

'Of course,' said Cleverly.

Phillips continued, 'Oh, and I meant to say, Jonesy said he'd briefed you on Josh Castillo as a potential for the attack on Adam.'

'Yeah. I've got a team going to interview him as we speak.' A sympathetic looked flashed across Cleverly's face. 'And please believe me, Jane, when I say finding his attacker is a major priority for us. We'll catch the bastard. Kerry and I will make sure of that.'

Phillips offered a thin smile. 'Thanks, Steve,' she said in a low voice, before turning and heading back to MCU.

35

Back in Major Crimes, Phillips and Jones brought Bovalino and Entwistle up to speed on the joint operation to find Shawn Harvey.

'So, we're thinking he was snatched in retaliation for the Bahmani shooting?' asked Bovalino.

'It would make sense, wouldn't it?' replied Jones. 'I mean, it's a bit of a coincidence if not.'

Phillips shot him a look.

'I know, I know. We don't believe in them in this department.'

Phillips stifled a grin. 'When we spoke to Freddie about Fulton and Harvey, he claimed they no longer worked for him. Hadn't for some time. But I don't believe him. We know they were his associates, and Jonesy and I heard Freddie make threats against Bahmani. He had to have been the one to sanction the hit.'

'They worked the doors at Vibe, didn't they?' asked Entwistle.

Phillips nodded.

'In that case, it shouldn't be too difficult to find out when they last worked there.'

'How?' asked Jones. 'Freddie's certainly not going to tell us.'

'Council CCTV. The cameras are all over the village, and Vibe sits on the corner of the busiest junction down there. I'll get the footage from the nearest cameras sent over from the last month, see if we can find them.'

'Great idea,' said Phillips.

'So, does this mean another visit to Bahmani's yard, then? We'll be paying rent next,' said Bovalino with a chuckle.

'No. That would be a waste of time,' replied Phillips. 'He'll just pull out the same old bullshit about being either at work or at home all day, with his family as alibis. If we're going to implicate him, we need proper proof. I think the best way to do that would be digitally. Bov, see if you can track where his mobile was when Harvey was snatched.'

'Will do,' said the big Italian.

'Right. I'd better brief Carter on the plans to work with SCU,' said Phillips, then made her way upstairs.

She returned half an hour later.

'How did he take it?' asked Jones.

'He actually seemed quite impressed. Said if we can get a result, it would give Fox something to crow about down at the town hall when she launches her gang task force – "cross departmental co-operation", he called it.'

'You gotta love the political bullshit at times,' Jones quipped.

'Quite,' said Phillips. She headed to her office to update the lengthy decision logs for the Bradley, Hodge and Fulton cases.

Towards the end of the day, her paperwork was just about up to date when Bovalino's massive frame filled her doorway.

'I've tracked Bahmani's mobile, Guv. As far as the records show, it remained in Ancoats the whole day yesterday.'

Phillips dropped her pen on the open log in front of her. 'Damn it!'

'Obviously that doesn't mean he was actually with the phone,' Bov added as he stepped inside.

'No, you're right. But how do we prove it?"

Just then, Entwistle joined them, carrying his laptop. 'I've got something for you, boss.'

Jones followed him in and moved to a position behind Phillips's right shoulder.

Entwistle placed the laptop on the desk in front of her and pressed play. 'Footage from just last week, showing Fulton and Harvey working the door at Vibe.'

Phillips watched as the surprisingly high-quality black and white images played on the screen. The timestamp in the corner clearly stated the date and time of the footage as a few days before the Paul Bradley murder. 'So my guts were right. Freddie *was* lying about them not working for him.'

'Wait for the next bit, Guv,' Entwistle added eagerly.

Phillips focused on the screen as she watched Freddie Bradley step out of the front door of the club and strike up a conversation with the two men. Whatever he said made them laugh. 'They look pretty tight to me,' said Phillips as she watched Freddie embrace Fulton and Harvey in turn, before walking away down the street and out of shot. 'It *had* to be Freddie who ordered the hit.'

Entwistle nodded.

'Gotta be,' said Jones.

Phillips pursed her lips and remained silent for a long moment as she figured out their next move. 'If it *was* Bahmani who kidnapped Harvey – and everything would suggest it was – I would guess that his motives for snatching him were twofold: firstly, to find out who ordered the hit, and secondly to punish Harvey for trying to kill him.'

'Jesus. I wouldn't want to be in Harvey's shoes right now.'

'Jonesy's right,' said Phillips. 'Having seen the injuries we suspect Bahmani inflicted on Dillon Wilton, we can assume Harvey's in for a rough ride of it. Nobody could sustain that level of torture for long, so I think it's safe to assume that Harvey will eventually reveal who put him up to it. Which means Bahmani will likely move his attention to Freddie next.'

'So, what do you wanna do, Guv?' asked Jones.

Phillips rolled the options around in her mind. 'I'm not sure it's going to advance our investigations into the deaths of Bradley and Hodge, and even though he's a little toe-rag, our priority has to be preservation of life. That means we need a team outside the Bradley home for at least the next twenty-four to forty-eight hours. If Bahmani's gonna exact his revenge, then I doubt he'll waste much time.'

'There is another possibility, boss,' said Jones.

'And what's that?'

'Well, if Freddie believes Bahmani did kill his father – as well as Fulton, and now potentially Harvey – he may want to strike first.'

'Which is even more reason to watch his every move,' said Phillips.

'Well, I'm happy to take the first shift,' said Jones.

'And me,' added Bovalino.

'Good stuff.' Phillips checked her watch; 5.13 p.m. 'Look, there's no time to waste. Get over to Alderley Edge as quick as you can.'

Jones and Bovalino nodded, then hurried out of the room.

'First rate work again, Whistler,' said Phillips. 'How did you get the footage so quickly from the council?'

Entwistle produced a lopsided grin.

'Wait. Let me guess. You know a girl in the office over there?'

'Something like that. Let's just say, I'm cooking dinner for *two* tonight.'

'You really are something else,' said Phillips with a chortle.

Entwistle shrugged as he picked up his laptop. 'Whatever it takes, Guv. Whatever it takes,' he said, then turned and walked out of the room.

36

W hile Jonesy and Bovalino headed to the Bradley home, Phillips made her way back to the MRI to see Adam. Her guts churned with nervous anticipation as she wandered along the ICU corridor, past rooms occupied by unconscious patients and desperately worried relatives. Despite the amazing work they did in this unit, she hated having anything to do with it, and prayed she would soon be free of its vice-like grip. When she walked into Adam's room, her hopes were dashed at the sight of Carrie's tear-stained face sitting in a chair next to his bed.

'Any updates?' she asked, fearing the worst.

Before Carrie could answer, Sister Wilson appeared.

Phillips turned to face her. 'I was just asking if there were any updates?'

Wilson's eyes betrayed her genuine concern. 'Why don't you sit down, Jane.'

Phillips's adrenaline spiked, and an icy shiver ran down her spine as she dropped into the large chair next to the bed.

Wilson continued. 'Adam is very, very poorly right now.

We've managed to get the urine infection under control, but, as we feared, he's now developed sepsis—'

'That can be fatal, right?' asked Phillips, fearing the answer.

Wilson nodded softly. 'Yes, but we've spotted it very early, and already started him on antibiotics. He's got every chance of beating it, but the next forty-eight hours are critical.'

Phillips bit her bottom lip as her jaw trembled. She tried her best to hold back the tears that threatened to overwhelm her.

'We're doing everything we can to keep him comfortable and rest assured, he's not in any pain.'

Carrie began to cry on the other side of the bed. Phillips got up from her chair and made her way round the bed to comfort her. The two women embraced.

'Can I get either of you a cup of tea?' asked Wilson.

The British cure-all: tea, thought Phillips, as she turned and shook her head.

'Not for me,' said Carrie.

'I'll leave you to it. I'm just down the corridor if you need anything,' Wilson added, before disappearing out of sight.

For the next hour, Phillips and Carrie sat through a mixture of silence – punctuated by the machines keeping Adam alive – and 'getting to know you' topics of conversation, which Phillips found quite comforting. A much-needed distraction from their grim reality.

Finally, when she could watch Adam's broken body no longer, Phillips made her excuses and left, promising to call Sister Wilson later to check on him.

Stepping outside the hospital into the warm evening air, the sounds of the city around her assailed her heightened senses. She felt nervous and edgy, as if on high alert. Symptoms she recognised as the onset of anxiety and panic, something she had struggled with since being shot at point-blank range during the Marty Michaels investigation. Like Adam, she had also spent time in ICU and for at least a week had been in a critical condition. She hoped and prayed that he too would make it through. God, she missed him.

Pulling out her phone, she rang Jones for an update on Freddie. 'Any news?' she asked when he answered.

'*All quiet on the western front. How's Adam?*'

'I'd rather not talk about it,' she replied, her voice flat.

Jones seemed to take the hint and changed the subject to something a little lighter. '*Bovalino was just regaling me with his recipe for seafood linguine. Sounds nice, but not a patch on Sarah's steak and ale pie, which, incidentally, I'm missing tonight to keep this arsehole safe.*'

'You should go home,' said Phillips.

'*Chance would be a fine thing,*' laughed Jones.

'I'm serious,' Phillips shot back. 'I'll come and relieve you.'

'*I was only joking, boss.*' Jones sounded confused now. '*You've got enough on your plate.*'

'That's just it, *I haven't.* All this sitting around waiting for Adam to improve is driving me insane. I need to be doing something, otherwise I'll just end up diving into a bottle of wine at home. Which never ends well.'

'*I can understand that, boss. But after the incident the other day, it's probably not the best idea for you to be anywhere near Freddie Bradley right now. You know, with the impending IPCC investigation and all that.*'

'I'd be there to protect him, Jonesy. The IPCC could hardly have an issue with that now, could they?'

'*Honestly, Guv. It feels like a bad idea to me.*'

'Well, luckily I'm the DCI here, not you. I'm coming over whether you like it or not. So, if you've got any sense, take advantage of my offer and get yourself home to that steak and ale pie.' With that, she ended the call and headed for the car park.

A couple of hours later, the time approached 10 p.m. Phillips and Bov sat chatting idly in the squad car, parked in the shadows on the corner of an adjacent street, when a dark Ford Mondeo parked up not far from the Bradley home. They watched on as two tall, well-built men wearing dark clothing and hooded tops climbed out of the car and began walking towards the Bradley residence. As they moved closer, it became obvious their faces were covered. One of the men carried a backpack, and both wore gloves.

'Shit,' said Phillips. 'This pair look just like the guys who snatched Shawn Harvey. I think it's on. We need backup.'

Bovalino grabbed the police radio and requested that uniform support to be despatched to their location. The team at Control quickly confirmed there was a car in the area that would arrive within eight minutes.

Phillips watched as the two men turned left onto the Bradleys' drive before disappearing out of view. 'We should go after them,' she said as adrenaline coursed through her veins.

'No, boss. We've done that too many times in the past and look where it got us. You, me and Jonesy, all with life-threatening injuries. Let's play it safe for once and wait for backup.'

'Well, I think we should at least call in TFU. If that *is* Bahmani and Tahir, I'm not sure what help a couple of beat coppers are going to be.'

'You make a good point, boss.' Bovalino picked up the radio once more to request the immediate support of a Tactical Firearms Unit.

37

Adders Bahmani led the way quietly up the long gravel drive to the front door of the house, Tahir in tow. As usual, he'd taken the precaution of wearing a hooded top, as well as a scarf over his nose and mouth. Still, he wanted to make sure all bases were covered, so, pulling a small can of black spray paint from his backpack, he reached up with his gloved right hand and sprayed the lenses of the two CCTV cameras positioned just above the front door. Returning the bag to his shoulder, he turned to face Tahir, then headed towards the side of the house. Mercifully, the path to the back garden was lined with mature fir trees which cast thick shadows and offered complete cover from the neighbouring house.

Taking great care not to make any noise, he soon heard a TV playing what sounded like some kind of sports programme. As expected, someone was home. As he reached the end of the path, he peered around the corner of the house and took in the scene. The patio directly in front of him was illuminated by the lights pouring out through the French doors of the lounge room. A large outdoor dining area and stone-built pizza oven were located on the other side of the patio, just in front of a lit swimming pool, which glowed in the darkness. Steam rose from the water.

Standing in the shadows for a moment, he listened to the sounds filtering through the night air: the TV from inside the house, traffic from the nearby road, and the ever-present drone of planes flying to and from Manchester Airport, located just six miles away.

He turned to face Tahir and, whispering in Urdu, reiterated his instructions. Tahir nodded his agreement.

Stepping softly along the rear of the house, Bahmani stopped at the edge of the French doors. He craned his neck to peer through the glass. Freddie Bradley sat, the back of his head partially visible above the back of the sofa, watching the flatscreen TV on the opposite side of the room. As far as Bahmani could tell, he was alone.

Bahmani tiptoed across the patio and, very gently, tried the handle of the French doors. They were locked, which irritated him. Still, that wouldn't stop him. With one last nod to Tahir, Bahmani pulled the Glock G17 from the small of his back and took aim at the back of Freddie's head. A second later, he squeezed the trigger. With an ear-shattering bang, the French doors exploded. A split second later, he charged over the broken glass and continued firing into the room.

———

PHILLIPS PHYSICALLY JUMPED in her seat when she heard the first shot being fired. 'Shit! That sounded like gunfire!' A moment later, as multiple shots rang through the night air, it was clear they originated from the Bradley House. 'We've really gotta go in now!'

Bov grabbed the radio. 'Control, this is Mike Charlie One.

We need an urgent ETA on our firearms support. Shots fired at our location.'

There was a moment's pause before the response came. *'Mike Charlie One, this is Control. The patrol team are four minutes out. TFU approximately eight minutes. They're on their way from the airport now.'*

'That's too long,' said Phillips. 'We have to go in *now*.'

Bov's face betrayed his fears. 'We should wait for the TFU, Guv.'

'It'll be too late by then. I'm not gonna sit here and let anyone else get killed.'

Phillips pushed open the door and jumped out. A moment later, Bov followed suit.

Phillips ran as fast as she could across the street and onto the drive of the Bradley home, Bovalino just behind her. With no sign of life at the front door, she could hear what sounded like American accents coming from the rear of the property. Ducking down the side of the house, she spotted movement on the path up ahead. Someone was running towards them.

'Stop!' she shouted. 'Police!'

The man stopped in his tracks, then spun on his heels and ran in the opposite direction.

As Phillips reached the back garden, she stopped for a second to take in the scene of devastation to her left; broken glass, and a man lying on his back on the patio.

Bovalino rushed past her and after the man they'd been chasing.

Phillips's gaze followed the big Italian for a moment. Despite his size, he was quick on his feet. He would catch the suspect. She focused her attention on the man on the ground. Blood pooled around his torso. Kneeling, she pulled the scarf away from his face. To her surprise, she recognised him. Tahir Bahmani. Checking his pulse at the neck, she confirmed the obvious: he was dead. Getting back to her feet, she moved across the broken glass to the edge of the lounge and scanned the room. It appeared empty. A large TV blared out commentary to a baseball match.

'Look who I've found,' said Bovalino from behind her.

Phillips turned to see Adders Bahmani standing in front of Bov, hands cuffed behind his back. His customary cockiness and swagger seemed to have deserted him.

Bovalino held the backpack up. 'Packed full of tools, Guv, including a crowbar.'

'Freddie just went fucking mad!' spluttered Bahmani. 'I came to talk, and he just started shooting!'

'You came to talk, wearing a mask and carrying a crowbar?'

'It's true, I'm telling you. It's Freddie. He's a bloody lunatic, man.'

Phillips glanced into the empty room, then back at Bahmani. 'Who else was in the house?'

'I dunno. I just saw Freddie.'

At that moment, the sound of police sirens filled the air. 'That'll be uniform. Hand over our friend here and make sure they bag all his clothes for forensics when they book him in. I'll wait for the TFU so we can check inside.'

'You got it,' said Bovalino. He shoved Bahmani in the back and pushed him towards the side of the house and the street.

38

The TFU was comprised of four officers, with Sergeant Aiden Knight leading. They arrived a few minutes after the uniform team and joined Phillips at the rear of the house. Bovalino, having handed Bahmani over to the uniform team, was hot on their heels.

Phillips wasted no time briefing Knight. 'So far we have one fatality that we know of. I need you to sweep the house and radio through as soon as you find anything. We suspect Freddie Bailey, who lives here, is still inside and likely armed. It's a big property with lots of blind spots, so be careful. Ok?'

'Yes, ma'am,' said Knight. He led his team into the house through the French doors.

Phillips and Bovalino remained outside, but could hear the shouts of 'Armed Police' echoing through the house as the TFU boys moved steadily through it.

Three minutes later, Phillips's radio buzzed into life. *'Ma'am, we've found a woman claiming to be Melissa Bradley. She's very distressed.'*

'Any sign of Freddie?'

'No, ma'am. The house is clear.'

'Where are you now?'

'Master bedroom.'

'We're on our way,' said Phillips.

A minute later, Phillips strode into Melissa Bradley's bedroom to find her sitting on the bed, sobbing. 'Melissa, are you ok? Are you hurt at all?'

Melissa fixed her red, bloodshot eyes on Phillips. 'You're not allowed to be here!' she growled, and turned to Sergeant Knight. 'Get that bitch out of here!'

'Look, we haven't got time for all that now,' said Phillips. 'There's a man lying dead in your garden, and we need to know what happened to him. Where's Freddie?'

'I don't know!'

'He's not in the house,' said Knight.

'Any idea what happened here tonight?' asked Phillips.

Melissa shook her head. 'I have no idea. I was up here reading when I heard the shots. Then all hell broke loose. After what happened to Paul, I dived into the bathroom, locked the door and dialled 999.'

'Ok,' said Phillips. 'Well, from what we can ascertain so far, a man's been fatally shot downstairs, and we suspect Freddie fired the gun that killed him.'

'Freddie wouldn't do that,' Melissa protested.

Phillips ignored her. 'Does he own a gun?'

'No. Not that I know of. Paul used to keep one, but I doubt very much that Freddie would know how to handle it.'

'Was Paul's gun registered?'

'Yes,' said Melissa. 'All legal and above board. There's a gun cabinet in his office.'

Just then, one of the uniformed team came over the radio. *'DCI Phillips, we've found a firearm in the front garden.'*

'Ok, I'm on my way.' Phillips turned to Bovalino. 'Finish taking her statement, then call CSI, will you?'

'Sure,' said Bovalino. He pulled his notepad from his pocket.

Outside, Phillips made her way to the corner of the front garden to the right of the house, where she was met by PC Kate Lynch, a surprisingly tall woman at well over six feet, who held a heavy-duty torch.

'It's over here, ma'am.'

Phillips followed her to a large flower bed nestled next to the high wall that surrounded the property.

'There's large footprints in the soil.' Lynch shone the torch onto the flowers and the gun. 'Looks as if the pistol could have fallen out as he was climbing over the wall.'

Phillips pulled on a pair of latex gloves, then grabbed the torch. Careful not to disturb the footprints, she stepped forward and picked up the pistol. Shining the torch over it, she could see the serial number had been filed off. 'Illegal firearm,' she muttered before carefully laying the pistol down on the grass. 'Get that bagged into evidence, will you?'

'Right away, ma'am.'

Phillips made her way back to the rear of the property and surveyed the scene. Paramedics had arrived and were attending to Tahir's body, still on the patio amid the broken glass. 'What an almighty fucking mess, Jane,' she whispered.

It was at that moment nausea assailed her. Her blood ran cold and her mouth filled with saliva. Overwhelmed by anxiety, time slowed. She had to get away.

Rushing back towards the street, she avoided all eye contact with the various uniformed and TFU officers positioned around the front door, and headed for her car. She opened the door to the Mini and dropped into the driver's seat, exhaling loudly as she did. Closing her eyes, she rested her head against the headrest, placed her hands on the steering wheel and began taking deep breaths. *Breathe, Jane, breathe,* she thought to herself.

From experience, Phillips knew that no single thing triggered her panic attacks. They always arrived when she was overwhelmed, overworked and under stress. It was her nervous system's way of telling her she had moved into the danger zone. Hardly surprising, given current events.

A few minutes later, with her breathing under control and her pulse slowing, she opened her eyes. Then her phone began to ring. Panic engulfed her again. Was it the hospital? Had something happened to Adam?

Fishing it out, she saw Carter's ID. She breathed a sigh of relief, then pressed the answer button. 'Sir?'

'What the hell are you doing at the Bradley house?'

'How do you know about that?'

'It doesn't matter how I know. What on earth is going on, Jane?'

'It's a long story, sir.'

'I'm all ears.'

'Ok. Well, this afternoon we received information that led us to believe Adders Bahmani may have kidnapped Shawn Harvey. It was possible his next target could be Freddie Bradley. With imminent threat to life in play, I asked Jones and Bovalino to watch the Bradley House.'

'Why didn't I know about this?'

'With everything going on, it slipped my mind, sir.'

'So how did you end up there?'

'I relieved DS Jones.'

'And why would you do that?'

Phillips swallowed hard as she struggled to hold off another wave of panic. 'I needed the distraction, sir.'

Carter exhaled loudly on the end of the phone. 'I understand there was a fatality?'

'Yes, sir. Tahir, Bahmani's cousin, was shot dead. When we saw the two men enter the Bradley property, Bov called for

TFU backup, but the shooting started before they could get here.'

'Jesus Christ, Jane. This is a disaster. Not only did you ignore strict instructions not to go anywhere near the Bradleys' home, but you sat outside as a gunfight broke out! Do you know how bad this looks?'

'I know, and I'm sorry.'

'Fox is going to go fucking mental when she finds out about this.'

'I know.' Phillips closed her eyes and dropped her chin to her chest. She had royally screwed up. It was time to take responsibility. 'Sir, I'd like to offer my resignation.'

'What? No, you bloody won't!'

Phillips opened her eyes.

Carter continued. *'I'm sorry, Jane, but you've made this mess. Now you're going to have to clean it up. If you walk away, then we're all left picking up the pieces. I warned you that you carried the reputation of MCU on your shoulders. It's down to you to protect that reputation. Luckily Fox is at a policing conference in Birmingham tomorrow, so she won't want to be disturbed. But I'll be debriefing her first thing Friday morning. I expect you to somehow have sorted this mess out by then. Do I make myself clear?'*

'Yes, sir. You do.'

Carter ended the call.

Phillips threw her phone onto the passenger seat and growled in frustration as she placed her head against the steering wheel. It was then that the tears came. And wouldn't stop.

39

'How was the steak and ale pie?' Phillips asked as Jones joined her and Bovalino in the interview observation suite at Ashton House ninety minutes later.

'Delicious as ever, but I'm really starting to wish I hadn't let you talk me into leaving.' Jones gazed at Adders Bahmani on the big screen attached the wall, alone behind the table in Interview Room Two. 'Jesus, what a mess.'

'That's exactly what Carter said.'

'He's not happy then?' asked Jones.

'You could say that.'

'I'm sorry, Guv. I should have been there.'

'No, you shouldn't. *I* told you to go home. This is on me. And besides, the reality is, we did this by the book. Right, Bov?'

'Yeah, we did.'

'And that's the ironic thing. If we hadn't, Tahir might still be alive.' Phillips shook her head in dismay. 'Anyway, you really didn't need to come back in, you know. Bov and I have got this.'

'You're kidding, aren't you? After your call, there's no way I could sit at home and do nothing. And besides, Bahmani on the hook? There was no chance I was missing this.'

Phillips gathered her files. 'Bov and I will go in as soon as Johnson arrives. I'm told she's on her way. You can stay here and keep an eye on things. As ever, make an excuse and pull us out if you spot anything that might be useful.'

'Sure,' said Jones.

Phillips checked her watch. 'Well, it's almost midnight and I'm really flagging. Don't know about you two, but I need a coffee.'

Jones and Bovalino nodded their agreement, and all three headed for the vending machine in the canteen.

As soon as Nicolette Johnson arrived half an hour later, she whisked Bahmani into a private consultation room as was her legal right. They emerged an hour later and were sitting side by side behind the table in Interview Room Two when Phillips and Bovalino joined them.

Phillips remained silent as she took her seat and slowly, and deliberately, laid out her files and notepad on the table. When she was ready, she went through the usual formalities and explained the protocols of the interview, including the DIR and video recordings. With everyone fully briefed, she started. 'Mr Bahmani, can you tell us what you were doing at the home of Melissa and Freddie Bradley this evening?'

Johnson sat forward in her chair. 'My client has prepared a statement which he'd like me to read.'

'Of course he has.' A snarl threatened to break out onto Phillips's top lip as she sat back and folded her arms across her chest.

Johnson remained stoic as she opened her leather-bound notepad and began reading from the page. '"This evening at approximately 10 p.m., Mr Bahmani visited the home of Freddie Bradley for the purpose of a business meeting;

specifically, to resurrect a deal he had initially proposed to Paul Bradley a number of months ago. The meeting, time and venue had been Freddie's idea. Taking into account Freddie's reputation for unpredictability, Mr Bahmani took along his business associate and cousin, Tahir Bahmani, to act as his security. Upon arriving at the house, Mr Bahmani and his cousin Tahir received no answer when they rang the bell at the front of the house, so, hearing what sounded like a television playing to the rear of the property, they made their way down towards the garden, where they spotted Freddie watching television in the lounge. Mr Bahmani knocked on the French doors to alert Freddie to their presence, at which point Freddie turned and opened fire with a handgun. Unbeknownst to Mr Bahmani, Tahir was also carrying a gun and fired back in response. Sadly, Tahir was shot in the stand-off, at which point Mr Bahmani, fearing for his life, fled the scene. As he made his way down the side of the property back to the car, he spotted two people running towards him. Concerned the two individuals were part of Freddie's plan to kill him, he turned and ran back into the garden in an attempt to find another route to safety. It would become clear sometime later that the two individuals he ran from were actually DCI Phillips and DC Bovalino of the Major Crimes Unit. Had he known this, he would have had no reason to run. DC Bovalino recovered a bag containing a number of tools. The reason Mr Bahmani was carrying this bag was because he had come straight from work and did not want to leave tools in his car as they are very expensive, and he feared they could be stolen. Finally, Mr Bahmani did not know his cousin owned or carried a weapon, and would never condone their use in any situation. He is devastated that Tahir's decision to carry a gun has resulted in the tragic loss of his life and the effects this will have on his family." That is all Mr Bahmani has to say at this time, and he is invoking his right to answer no comment to any further questions.' Johnson closed the leather notepad and placed it flat on the table as she locked eyes with Phillips.

'Wow. That's some story,' said Phillips.

'The truth is often stranger than fiction, Inspector,' Johnson spat back.

Phillips turned her attention to Bahmani, who appeared to have rediscovered his smugness – the lopsided grin was back. 'So, if you were there for a business meeting, why did you rock up wearing gloves and a mask.'

'No comment.'

'Forensics are going through the Bradley home as we speak. You do know they'll be able to tell us who fired first, don't you?'

'No comment.'

'I'm intrigued. Freddie told me and DS Jones that he believed you were responsible for the death of his father. In fact, he'd made it known across the city that he wasn't going to be bullied by you. So why would you believe he wanted to do business with you?'

'No comment.'

'Isn't it true you went to the Bradley home to cause Freddie harm?'

Bahmani yawned loudly as he slouched in his chair. 'No comment.'

Phillips's frustration and irritation grew by the second. She'd been here before many times, with suspects playing the 'no comment' card in their first interview. It was a standard legal tactic that allowed the defence to understand exactly what their client was up against. It offered them time before the second interview to create an alternative explanation to counter the evidence in court, and ultimately create doubt in the minds of the jury; the difference between a guilty and not guilty verdict.

Phillips passed across a still CCTV picture. 'These two men were pictured yesterday during the kidnap of Shawn Harvey. They look pretty much identical to you and Tahir, don't you think?'

Bahmani avoided looking at the picture, keeping his eyes fixed on Phillips instead. 'No comment.'

And so it continued for the next forty-five minutes, with Bahmani replying 'No comment' to every question put to him. When she'd work through the required list stipulated by the Crown Prosecution Service, she ended the interview and left the room with Bovalino in tow.

Back in the observation suite, they debriefed with Jones.

'We knew he'd do it, Guv,' said Jones. 'He was always going down the no comment route.'

Phillips dropped heavily into the leather chair next him. 'I know, but I haven't got time to mess about with this bullshit. I need to charge him as soon as I can.'

'Surely you've got enough?' asked Jones.

'Yeah, but for what? You heard Johnson. He's dumped everything on Tahir and Freddie. The way she puts it, Mother Theresa got caught up in the crossfire between Al Capone and Billy the Kid. You know how the CPS can be. If there's no hard evidence, they'll release him on bail. And a man like Bahmani could be out of the country in less than twenty-four hours, off to his family estate back in Pakistan.'

The room fell silent for a moment as they processed the situation.

Phillips glanced up at the large digital clock on the wall. It was after 2.30 a.m. and she was exhausted. If she'd learnt one thing over the years, it was that knackered coppers didn't make great detectives. She was in danger of burning out the whole team. 'Look, no matter how good Johnson *thinks* she is, Bahmani's not going anywhere for another eighteen hours or so. Let's get some kip and start with fresh eyes in the morn-

ing. CSI will have assessed the scene by then, and we'll hopefully have something specific we can pin on Bahmani.'

'Sounds like a plan,' said Bovalino, stretching his arms
and back.

'Let's debrief at eight. Ok?'

'Yep,' said Jones.

Phillips stood and led them out of the room. As they
wandered down the ground floor corridor towards the rear
exit and staff car park, her guts churned. The clock was literally ticking, and she prayed CSI could dig her out of the shit
by morning. If not, Bahmani would likely walk, leaving MCU
looking like downright amateurs, and the careers of the
people she cared about most in tatters. The mounting pressure was like nothing she had ever known.

40

THURSDAY 15TH JULY

Phillips felt an overwhelming urge to be with Adam, so instead of going home, she returned to his bedside. Thanks to the late hour, and much to her relief, Carrie was nowhere in sight. It was hard enough to see him like this without having to feel her grief too.

Angela, Adam's specialist nurse, appeared with a cup of coffee. 'I thought you might want a hot drink,' she said as she placed the mug down on the cabinet next to the bed.

'Thank you,' said Phillips softly.

'Carrie left a few hours ago. Said she needed to get some rest, which I agreed with. She's not left his side for the last couple of days.'

Phillips gazed at Adam. His body was still wrapped up in tubes and intravenous lines, and the ventilator continued to deliver its rhythmic beat at the side of the bed. 'How is he, Angela? I mean how is he *really*? What are his chances?'

Angela's sad eyes betrayed the truth of Adam's condition without her having to say a word. 'He's extremely poorly, Jane.' She squatted in front of Phillips, so their eyes were at the same level. 'We would have expected him to be showing some signs of improvement by now, but he seems to be struggling.'

Tears welled in her eyes as she stared into Angela's.

'I'm not here to take away your hope, but equally, I have to be honest with you about his condition. The doctors are starting him on an experimental treatment tonight to help fight the sepsis, but you need to be aware that it might not work. And if it doesn't, then the prognosis doesn't look good.'

'You're saying he could die?'

Angela nodded softly. 'I'm afraid so, yes.'

Phillips could no longer hold back the tears that streaked down her cheeks.

Angela leaned forward and wrapped her arms around Phillips. 'I'm sorry, Jane.'

A minute passed before she let go.

Phillips wiped her eyes with a tissue. 'God. I wish there was something I could do.'

Angela stood now. 'I know. And please believe me, we're not giving up either. We won't stop until we've explored *every* avenue.'

Phillips flashed a faint smile, then blew her nose into the tissue.

'Look, I'll give you some space,' said Angela. 'But I'm just outside if you need me.'

'Thank you,' Phillips turned to face Adam. Grabbing his left hand, she held it against her cheek. It felt surprisingly warm, and had the unmistakable scent of the man she loved more than she had ever believed possible. 'Hey, babe,' she whispered. 'Time to come back to me now. Enough of all this lying around, hey?'

The room remained silent but for the hiss of the ventilator and a couple of machines feeding drips into his arms.

'Please come back to me. I really can't cope without you.'

As had been the case since he arrived in the ICU, Adam remained unresponsive, his eyes fixed shut, his mouth half open thanks to the breathing tube in his throat.

For the next hour, Phillips sat and watched him in silence, interrupted every fifteen minutes or so by Angela as she checked each of the machines for any signs of change. Finally, when the doctor arrived just before 4 a.m. to start the new treatment, Phillips decided it was time for her to go home. After kissing him on the forehead, she walked out of the room as the medical team got to work behind her. She prayed that whatever they were putting into him would work. The alternative was unthinkable.

When she reached the Mini on the fourth floor of the hospital car park, she realised she had no recollection of how she'd got from the ICU to where she now stood. Her mind was numb with pain and disbelief.

Opening the car door, she got into the driver's seat and sat in silence for a long moment as she tried to process her life. She felt like she was stuck in a bad movie that needed to stop so she could escape it. If only that were true. God, she had never felt so powerless or as terrified. She wished with all her heart that it had been her they'd attacked, that she was the one lying in that bed, not Adam. He didn't deserve this, a man who saved lives every day. Now he fought for his own.

As she fired the ignition, the radio sprang to life, filling the car with Elvis's 'Are You Lonesome Tonight?' – Adam's ringtone. Her heart ached for their old life together. Images of him flitted through her mind, upset and angry at her, walking away when she refused to talk about moving in together. How could she have been so selfish? Why had she let work dictate her happiness? Without realising it, she'd finally got everything she'd ever wanted, but had pushed it away. And now she might never get it back, or ever get the chance to tell him how much she loved him.

Switching off the engine she dropped her head into her hands and began to cry, softly at first, but a moment later her body began to shake as she sobbed her heart out.

41

The team reconvened at 8 a.m. sharp. Entwistle, who'd got the heads-up from Jones in an early morning call, was at his desk and raring to go. Bovalino handed round hot drinks and bacon rolls.

'Any news from forensics?' asked Phillips, standing in front of the two large rolling whiteboards she'd commandeered the previous day.

'Evans and his team attended this one, Guv,' said Jones. 'I spoke to him in the car on the way in. He's still there, and says it's pretty clear from the position of the glass that it was broken from the outside. Which means either Bahmani or Tahir fired first.'

'Just as we suspected, which contradicts Johnson's little fairy tale last night.'

'She didn't really think anyone was going to fall for that shite, did she?' said Bovalino through a mouthful of sandwich.

'It only takes one juror, Bov,' said Phillips.

'True,' he replied before taking another large bite.

'Anything on the gun found near Tahir?'

'No prints, but then they were both wearing gloves,' said Jones.

'And the gun in the front garden?'

'They've found prints on it, but as yet unidentified.'

Phillips took a gulp from her coffee. 'Has Freddie got a record?'

'Nothing came up in the searches this week,' Entwistle cut in.

'Which would explain why they haven't shown up on the system if they're his,' said Phillips. 'Anything else of significance we can pin on Bahmani?'

'Well, the car they turned up in was stolen,' Jones replied.

'Which will help, but it's hardly going to warrant remanding him to Hawk Green. We need something else.' Phillips blew her lips and dropped into the spare chair.

The room fell silent for a long moment, aside from the sound of eating.

As ever, Bovalino made light work of his food. 'Thanks, boss. That was just what I needed.' He tossed the wrapper into the bin.

Phillips turned her attention to Jones. 'There are CCTV cameras at the Bradley house, aren't there?'

'Yeah, they're positioned above the front door.'

'Can you call Evans and see if he's checked them yet? If not, we need to see the footage of Bahmani and Tahir as they approached the house.'

'They were wearing masks, Guv. I'm not sure what else it's going to offer us.'

'I know, but check all the same, will you?'

'Sure.' Jones picked up the phone.

The team watched on as Jones passed on Phillips's instructions, then replaced the receiver. 'They've not been checked as of yet, but he's getting one of the team straight onto it.'

'Great,' said Phillips, standing. 'Shout me as soon as he comes back to you.'

Phillips headed to her office and closed the door. Moving over to the window, she pulled out her mobile and pressed redial to call the ICU team at the MRI.

It was a different nurse who answered. She explained that the treatment was still ongoing but as yet there had been no improvement in Adam's condition.

With a heavy heart, Phillips took a seat at her desk and opened up her laptop. Next, she called Cleverly for an update.

As ever, he answered promptly. *'Jane. How you doing?'*

'I'm ok, thanks.'

'And how's Adam?'

'No change, I'm afraid.' She was in no mood to get any deeper into that conversation, so got straight to the point of the call. 'How did you get on with Castillo?'

Cleverly blew his lips on the end of the line. *'Well, he's an angry man and he really doesn't like you, but we doubt he's the person who attacked Adam.'*

'Does he have an alibi?'

'No, but he does have motive for staying out of trouble. He's not seen his kids for six years, and he claims he's doing whatever it takes to get access to them now he's out.'

'Ex-cons make great liars, Steve. You know that as well as I do.'

'True, but DI Benner called the shrinks at Hawk Green, who confirmed he's been making all the right noises for the last couple of years. Mentally stable, no incidents of violence or issues with other prisoners. He was a trusted inmate and given access to different areas of the jail for work; a real privilege given only to the most responsible prisoners. They state he was totally focused on getting out and getting his life back on track, and access to his kids. Stab-

bing Adam in a frenzied attack two days after walking out of
Hawk Green doesn't fit with any of that.'

Phillips could feel her jaw clench as she tried to control
her growing agitation. 'So what? He's off the hook?'

'Not at all. We'll be keeping an eye on him. But at this moment
in time, he's not looking likely,' replied Cleverly. 'Look, Jane. I
can't imagine what you're going through, I really can't. But I
meant what I said the other day; catching Adam's attacker is a
priority for the team. That said, I've been doing this a long time –
just like you – and if there's not enough evidence, then there's no
case to answer. My focus is on catching the right man, not the first
man. Ok?'

Phillips knew he was right. 'I'm sorry. I just want the head
of whoever did this on a spike!'

'As do I – well, maybe not a spike – but you know what I
mean.'

'So, what about the Shawn Harvey case? Any joy in
tracking the van?'

'We followed it on the ANPR cameras for about two miles east
from where he was snatched in Woodhouses, but it disappeared off
the grid somewhere near Daisy Nook Country Park.'

'Do you think that's where they took him?'

'It's a possibility, but we found the van burnt out and empty on
the banks of the River Medlock, out near Waggon Road. So that's
been our starting point.'

'You thinking they dumped him in the river?'

'We have to consider it as a strong possibility. There's a dive
team on site just now.'

'Jesus,' Phillips whispered into the phone.

'I know. It's a lovely world we live in.'

'Isn't it just.'

'So what happened last night with Bahmani?' asked Cleverly.
'I heard Tahir was killed.'

'You're remarkably well informed.' Phillips tried her best

to hide the irritation in her voice. Nothing remained secret in the GMP for very long.

Cleverly scoffed. *'This is Ashton House, Jane. If it wasn't for gossip, no one would have anything to say to each other.'*

The last thing Phillips wanted was to share the full details of the events the previous night, so she offered up just enough to suggest she was a willing team player. 'We arrested Bahmani at the Bradley home around ten p.m. There was an exchange of gunfire and Tahir was shot dead. Adders is sitting in the custody suite as we speak.'

'Got anything that'll finally stick?'

'So far, only on minor misdemeanours. I still need to tie him directly to the shooting, but you know what his lawyer's like.'

'Nic Johnson? Oh yeah. Our paths have crossed many times. Sharp as a tack and tough as a cat's head.'

'Exactly. Well, she's already painting him out to be an innocent victim, caught up a gun battle between Freddie and Tahir.'

'Jesus. You've gotta laugh, haven't you? No wonder he's called The Teflon Man.'

'Yeah. But this time he's not getting away with it.'

'Well, good luck with that,' said Cleverly, his tone facetious.

Phillips was keen to wrap things up. 'Look, I'd better go, Steve. If I'm gonna have any chance of keeping this bastard locked up, I've got a lot of work to do today.'

'Keep me posted, won't you?'

'Sure,' replied Phillips. 'And same here with the search for Harvey.'

'Of course. I'll update you as soon as I hear anything.'

With that, she ended the call.

Phillips spent the next hour updating the decision logs for the events of the previous night, which made grim reading despite the fact she had followed the proper protocols. Just as she was filing the paperwork away, Entwistle appeared at the door carrying his laptop.

'Evans has sent over some footage from last night.'

'Have you looked at it?'

'Not yet.' He walked round her desk, placed the laptop in front of her and pressed play.

They watched on as silent images of the masked Bahmani and Tahir appeared on screen, walking slowly towards the front door. It appeared as if Bahmani was looking for the CCTV cameras. Once he spotted them, he took off the ruck-sack and pulled out an aerosol can. After checking the surrounding area, he pulled off the cap and reached up towards the camera. A second later, the screen went black. 'What the hell was that?' asked Phillips.

'Looks like spray paint.'

'We've got him,' said Phillips, clasping her hands together. 'This goes towards intent. There's no way he can claim he was there for a business meeting now, or that he was an innocent party. He deliberately vandalised the CCTV cameras to stop anyone seeing what happened next. That act, along with the tools we found and the fact he rocked up in a stolen car, mean we've got enough for remand. I'm sure of it.'

'That's brilliant, boss.'

Phillips picked up the landline receiver and dialled the number from memory. 'I'm calling CPS now. Thanks, Whistler. You may have just dug me out of a hole.'

Entwistle flashed that perfect smile of his as he picked up his laptop. 'Thanks, Guv, but I think Evans deserves the credit on this one.'

At that moment, the call connected. 'Sandra? It's Jane Phillips. I need you to review some charges for a suspect we have in custody.'

42

It was after 7 p.m. and Phillips was just about ready to leave for the night when Carter paid her a visit. 'Working late, sir?'

His grave expression suggested this wasn't a social trip. 'I've just got off a call with Chief Constable Fox. She was in the car on the way back from Birmingham.'

'I'm guessing you told her about the incident with Bahmani at the Bradleys'?'

'Yes. I was going to wait till the morning, but somehow she already knew something had happened. I just filled in the gaps.'

Phillips let out a frustrated sigh. 'She's got eyes everywhere, that woman.'

'Certainly seems that way.'

'So, what did she say?'

Carter folded his arms across his chest. 'Oh, you know, the usual: that MCU has gone to pieces since she left. That *I've* taken it backwards, *you're* a loose cannon, and how the whole thing is an almighty clusterfuck and a PR nightmare. She also thinks it makes her look bad personally.'

'And how did she work that one out?'

'Because she made so much noise when she was first appointed chief constable about ending the gang violence in the city. This makes it look like it's only getting worse, and that's down to her.'

'So, as usual, it's all about Fox, then?'

'Pretty much. But to be fair, Jane, a suspect being shot whilst a senior officer sits in a car outside the crime scene doesn't look good in anyone's eyes.'

Phillips twisted her face. 'That's bloody typical, that is. I followed protocol. *I* wanted to go in but Bov talked me down. Said we should wait for backup. Which we did – and look where that got us. If I'd followed my instincts, Tahir might still be alive.'

Carter's eyes closed as he dropped his chin into his chest for a long moment before looking up again. 'Well, at least the CPS have agreed to the charges against Bahmani.'

Phillips nodded. 'Accessory to attempted murder, carrying tools, possession of a dangerous weapon – plus he was travelling in a stolen car. So, plenty to keep him in Hawk Green for now. And if we can prove the firearm found next to Tahir was his, he'll get five years minimum.'

'*If,*' said Carter with feeling.

'Well, it's all we've got right now. But with a bit of luck, Cleverly can tie him to the kidnap of Shawn Harvey too.'

'Any news on that front?'

'The divers have been in the river all day, but so far they've not found anything,' said Phillips.

'If anything changes, you'll let me know, won't you?'

'Of course, sir.'

'And any news on Freddie Bradley's whereabouts?'

'Not yet, but his picture has been sent to every copper on the force. If he's still in the city, we'll find him eventually. I've also issued an all-ports warning, so if he tries to leave the country, he won't get very far.'

'Ok. Well, as ever, keep me posted.'

Phillips got up from her chair as she made ready to leave.

'There is one more thing, Jane. Fox wants to see us both in the morning. She has a breakfast meeting at the Town Hall at eight, but then wants us in her office at 9.30.'

'Ooohh goody.' Phillips's tone was sarcastic. 'Another bollocking.'

'That would be my best guess, so best to be prepared for a rough ride.'

'I always am when it comes to Fox.'

'If you can provide a status report on the Bradley and Hodge murders, preferably with some solid progress since we last debriefed her, she might go a little bit easier on you.'

Phillips picked up her keys and slung her bag over her shoulder. 'There goes my evening, then.'

'Sorry, Jane, but you know how she operates better than most.'

'Yeah. Yeah, I do.'

Carter produced a sympathetic smile. 'Come on. I'll walk you out.'

43

FRIDAY 16TH JULY

Phillips had worked until almost midnight the previous evening, going through the case files on the Bradley and Hodge murders. But all her effort was to no avail. She was thoroughly depressed, accompanied by an overwhelming sense that both investigations had stalled. With her confidence at an all-time low, the last thing she needed was a dressing down from Fox.

As she unlocked her office door just after 8 a.m. she wished she was anywhere but Ashton House. With a heavy heart, she took a seat in her chair and fired up her laptop.

Jones appeared about twenty minutes later and, as ever, presented her with a steaming cup of coffee. 'You look like you lost a tenner and found a penny, Guv.'

Phillips sighed. 'I have a meeting with Fox and Carter at nine-thirty. She wants to bollock me for the Bahmani shooting.'

'Ah.' Jones took a seat opposite her. 'Not the ideal start to your day.'

'No, not at all.' Phillips took a sip of her drink.

'How's Adam?'

'The same. Still no signs of improvement.'

'Shit. I'm sorry, Guv.'

If truth be told, Phillips struggled when it came to talking about Adam. It was the first question everybody asked her, and repeating the same bad news over and over was taking its toll on her mental health. 'Look, I'd rather not talk about it, if you don't mind. It's just too painful.'

'Sure,' said Jones with a sympathetic nod.

'Anyway, I'd better get on with finishing these status reports.'

'I'll leave you to it.' Jones got up from the chair. 'Shout if you need anything.'

'I will.' Phillips turned her attention to the latest forensic reports from the shooting at the Bradley home.

An hour later, Phillips sent the final reports to the printer in the main office. As it chattered to life, she wandered out to collect the printouts. Standing by the large, noisy machine, she considered the meeting that lay ahead. Her stomach turned like she was a naughty schoolkid waiting to see the headmaster.

Jones, Bovalino and Entwistle were busy at their desks, each doing their bit to try and crack the Bradley and Hodge cases. Just then, Jones's phone rang. He picked it up and listened for a short while.

'Freddie Bradley? And you're sure it's him?'

Phillips turned and locked eyes with Jones as her pulse quickened.

He stuck a thumb up.

'Call me as soon as you get here, ok?' he said, then replaced the receiver.

'What is it?' asked Phillips.

'A uniformed team have just picked up Freddie for running a red light in Ashton. When his name flagged up on the system as a priority suspect, they arrested him. They're bringing him in now. Should be here in the next five minutes.'

'Fucking get in!' said Phillips, her relief palpable.

'Nice one,' Bovalino added as Entwistle clapped his hands together.

'Some good news to take to your meeting with Fox,' Jones said with a wide grin.

'Sod that. The meeting can wait. My priority is interviewing Freddie.'

Jones's brow furrowed. 'Is that a good idea, boss? I mean, it sounds like Fox is pretty pissed off about the shooting at the Bradleys'. I don't think she's gonna take kindly to you being a no-show.'

Phillips fixed Jones with a steely glare. 'Right now, my priority is to find out what happened to Tahir and figure out how he was killed. I'd much rather take a bollocking for missing a meeting than head in there now with my arse in a sling.'

Jones shook his head. 'It's your call, Guv, but she's not gonna like it.'

'Tough,' said Phillips. 'As long as I'm in the custody suite, I'll be fine. She never goes down there.'

'True,' Bovalino cut in. 'She's never been one for mixing with criminals, has she?'

Phillips burst out laughing. 'We can always rely on you to tell it like it is, Bov.'

The big man grinned. 'It's the Italian in me.'

44

Phillips called Fox's assistant, Ms Blair, to make her excuses for missing the meeting, then headed down to the custody suite. Freddie had just been processed and was on his own in a police cell.

Jones stood ready as she walked into the observation suite. 'He's asked for his lawyer, so we'll have to wait to interview him.'

'To be expected.'

'How did Ms Blair take you pulling out of the meeting?'

'Did her usual job of talking to me like I was shit on her shoe in that oh-so-condescending way that she has.'

'A real charmer, isn't she?' chuckled Jones.

Phillips checked her watch; it was 9.43 a.m. 'Have Freddie's fingerprints been taken?'

'Ahead of you, boss. I've sent them through to forensics to check against the other gun we found at the house. I expressed the urgency, so they said they'd get straight onto it. Shouldn't be long.'

'Good work.' Phillips took a seat. 'Now all we have to do is wait for the lawyer.'

Jones dropped into the chair next to her. 'The desk sergeant said it was one of the partners at Tate Law.'

'That's the same firm that Melissa uses, isn't it?'

'Yup. Very expensive, so I'm guessing they should be here pretty quickly.'

'Good,' replied Phillips. 'The sooner the better, as far as I'm concerned.'

TWO HOURS LATER, Phillips entered Interview Room Four carrying a large Manila folder and took her seat at the desk opposite Freddie and his lawyer, Julie Simpson, whose face was fixed with an austere expression that matched her dark suit and straight black hair, which was pulled back in a ponytail.

Phillips quickly explained the recording protocols, then got straight down to business. 'Adders Bahmani has given us his side of the story, so why don't you give us your version of what happened on Wednesday night?'

Freddie glared back at Phillips, a snarl on his top lip, arms folded across his chest. 'They shot at me and I ran away.'

'So you didn't shoot back?'

'No. I don't own a gun.'

Phillips picked up her phone and pulled up an email that had landed a couple of minutes before she had left the observation suite. 'This is a report from our forensics team. It confirms that the fingerprints we found on a gun in your garden are a perfect match for yours. So why don't we start again, hey? What really happened that night?'

Freddie glanced at Simpson, who nodded her approval.

'They fired first. I fired back in self-defence.'

'I see.' Phillips made a note in her pad. 'But can we just back it up a little? You see, it would really help to know what happened leading up to the shots being fired. Where you were sitting. What – if anything – was said in the lead-up to the incident. That sort of thing.'

Freddie shrugged. 'I was watching baseball on TV – the Dodgers vs The White Socks – when I heard the gunshot and the room exploded around me. Glass flying everywhere. I dived for cover, grabbed the gun, and shot back a couple of times before making a run for it out of the lounge.'

'So, there was no warning? No communication from either Adders or Tahir before the shooting started?'

'No. It was a fucking cunt's trick. I had my back to them when they started firing, the sneaky bastards.'

'How come the gun you used was so close by?' asked Phillips.

'I've been carrying it since Dad was killed. I'm not taking any chances, unlike him.'

'And where did you get the gun?'

'It was one of Dad's.'

Phillips frowned. 'Really? Because your mum reckons your dad had a gun that was fully registered and locked away in the safe. Whereas the one *you* used that night was unregistered.'

Freddie shrugged again. 'He had a few guns. That was the first one I found.'

'And where did you find it?'

'In the glove box of the Bentley. I thought it was legit.'

Phillips opened the file and pulled out a picture of the gun recovered from the shrubbery at the Bradley home, spinning it round so Freddie could see it. She tapped on the picture just above the grip. 'That's where the serial number should be, but as you can see, it's been filed off. That makes it illegal.'

Freddie curled his bottom lip. 'So, I've been carrying an unregistered firearm. So what? It's not mine.'

Phillips smiled. 'Clearly you're not one for the finer points of the law, Freddie. You see, the gun doesn't have to *belong* to you; just being in possession of an unregistered firearm comes with a mandatory five-year jail term.'

Freddie's expression suddenly changed, his usual cockiness momentarily deserting him.

Phillips continued. 'In fact, I think it's fair to say you're in quite a lot of trouble. So, if I were you, I'd be doing everything I could to get on my good side, because as a detective chief inspector, I can have quite a lot of sway with judges when it comes to sentencing.'

Freddie swallowed hard.

'I'm intrigued, Freddie,' said Phillips. 'Every time we've spoken, you've gone to great lengths to tell me how important family is to you.'

'It's *everything*.'

'So, why flee the house and leave your mother to the mercy of Bahmani?'

'They didn't come for her.'

'You sound very sure of that.'

'Why would they?' spat Freddie. 'I'm looking after the business now. It's me Bahmani wanted dead. And besides, Mum can look after herself.'

'Somehow I don't doubt that.' Phillips decided to change tack. 'Tell me about your dad's relationship with Adders Bahmani.'

'What do you want to know?'

'When we first met, you claimed Bahmani was the person behind your dad's murder. Why would you think that?'

'Because he wanted to buy the business, but Dad wouldn't sell. So, he started making threats, throwing his weight around, And then, finally, he killed him. He probably thought that after that, Mum would want rid of it all and hand the business over.'

'But Bahmani hadn't counted on *you*, had he?'

Freddie sat forward now. 'No, he hadn't. With me and Shanks looking after things, there was no way he was going to get his hands on the business. And *that's* why he came for me that night.'

Phillips recoiled theatrically for effect. 'Really? Because I heard it was a revenge attack after you sent Jez Fulton and Shawn Harvey to kill *him*.'

Freddie sat back again. 'I don't know what you're talking about.'

'Oh come on, Freddie. We know they were still working for you the night they started shooting at him. We've even got CCTV footage that proves it. So why not cut the crap and tell the truth for once.'

Simpson chimed in now. 'My client is not responsible for the actions of his employees. Whatever those men did or didn't do has nothing to do with him.' She flicked through her pad for a moment. 'DCI Phillips. It is a known fact that Mr Bradley has made a complaint about you regarding an assault on his person—'

'Alleged assault,' Phillips corrected her.

Simpson continued. 'Is this arrest merely a crude attempt to deflect attention away from that incident?'

'The two events are totally independent of each other.'

'And you're sure of that?'

'Oh yes. Quite sure.' Phillips glared at Simpson for a long moment, then turned her attention back to Freddie. 'When you spoke to Detective Sergeant Jones last week outside your house, you mentioned you'd heard about an attack on a man outside my home–'

'Your boyfriend, you mean?' Freddie leered.

Despite an overwhelming urge to smash his face into the table, Phillips remained stoic. 'How did you know about that attack?'

Freddie's arrogance had returned full force. 'Like I said, it was all over town. Big news in the criminal fraternity, so I'm told. Seems you've made a lot of enemies over the years, Chief Inspector.'

Phillips nodded silently, her eyes fixed on Freddie. 'That's what happens when you put scum behind bars for a living.'

'And how is poor Adam?' asked Freddie, feigning concern.

'That's none of your business,' Jones cut in.

Freddie fixed him with a smug grin, then turned his attention back to Phillips. 'When can I see my mother?'

Phillips took a moment as she picked up her phone once more and clicked on the email from forensics again. She deliberately took a long look at her watch. 'It's now approaching 11.15 a.m. You were arrested at 9.05 this morning, which means we have just under twenty-two hours to hold you without charge.' She held the phone up in front of him. 'But thanks to this little email here, when you go back to your cell, I'm going to get straight on the phone to the CPS. You know, the Crown Prosecution Service? I'm going to ask them if they'll agree to *me* charging *you* with the possession of an unregistered firearm. And do you know what they're going to say?'

Freddie didn't respond as the snarl returned to his lips.

'They're going to say "yes please, DCI Phillips. Thanks to those lovely clean fingerprints you found that match the suspect's, please proceed and charge Freddie Bradley with possession of an unregistered firearm – and please be sure to let him know that he'll probably be spending at least the next five years in Hawk Green prison."'

Freddie remained silent, but his clenched jaw and wide eyes betrayed his anger.

Phillips closed the Manila folder. 'DCI Phillips is terminating this interview at 11.16 a.m.'

She stood, a thin smile on her face. 'So, if you really do

want to see your mother, I'd suggest you put her on the prison visitors' list. Perhaps she can bring you cigarettes, and maybe some sugar. I hear those things are very popular amongst your fellow inmates.'

With that, she left the room with Jones following behind.

45

Carter was sitting silently in the observation suite alongside Bovalino when Phillips and Jones entered. The dark shadows that framed his eyes, along with the thick creases in his brow, betrayed the stress he was under working for Fox. He glanced towards the video feed of the now-empty Interview Room Four. 'One more gangster off the street.'

'For now, at least,' replied Phillips.

Carter stood. 'Fox is expecting us.' His voice had lost all its charm now.

Phillips nodded and followed him out.

As the lift door closed, Carter spoke. 'Jane, I am trying to support you here, but there's only so much I can do. Fox is livid you missed the meeting.'

'I can imagine. And I'm sorry if she's taken it out on you. But I needed to interview Freddie immediately. There was no point losing precious time in custody when we're so up against it.'

'I get that. But you know as well as I do, Jones, Bovalino or Entwistle could have done that interview. Like it or not, Fox is the chief constable, and we need her on-side. She's determined to cut costs, and I'm told she's considering merging MCU with Serious Crimes, which means one thing – redundancies or reassignments. And I for one don't want to go back to the North East with my tail between my legs, having failed down here.'

'She wouldn't do that, sir. Surely?'

'She would and she could. So, if you want to keep your team together, you need to start playing the game a little better. I know you're an ace detective, but you're not bulletproof. And as I've said before, you're the face of MCU. When you fuck up, we all fuck up.'

Phillips took a moment to digest his words. 'You're right. I'm sorry, sir. I'll toe the line, I promise.'

Carter laughed sardonically. 'No you won't, and I'm not asking for that. I know your methods are sometimes unorthodox, but they get results. The results matter, so keep doing what you're doing. But when it comes to Fox, please just play the game. Ok?'

'Ok,' said Phillips with a soft smile as the lift stopped and the doors opened.

A minute later, Carter led them into Fox's office, where the chief constable sat behind her desk in full uniform.

She appeared to be perusing some paperwork, glasses perched on the end of her nose. As ever, her dyed-blonde hair looked overcooked, as did her sunbed tan. She glanced up as they came to a stop in front of her desk. 'Ah, the elusive DCI Phillips. Glad you could join us at last.'

'Yes. Sorry about missing the meeting earlier, ma'am.'

Fox gestured for them to take seats.

Phillips continued. 'I needed to attend an urgent interview with a murder suspect.'

Fox raised her eyebrows. 'In the Bradley and Hodge cases?'

'No, ma'am. The shooting of Tahir Bahmani.'

'Oh? You mean the disastrous surveillance operation you led a couple of nights ago, despite my orders to stay away from the Bradley home?'

'Yes, ma'am,' said Phillips.

'And who have you arrested?'

'Freddie Bradley.'

Fox's face fell. 'Melissa Bradley's boy? The one who made the official complaint against you?'

'That's him.'

'Well, that's all we need, isn't it? You do realise his mother's lawyers will likely have a field day on this one? Say you're singling him out to deflect from your own behaviour.'

'They may have mentioned something to that effect in his interview.'

'Damn it, Jane.' Fox threw her pen down on the desk.

'It's just noise, ma'am. His fingerprints were found all over an unregistered firearm we found at the scene of the shooting – which, as you know, carries a mandatory five-year sentence. And ballistics are currently running tests to see if it's the gun that was used to kill Tahir Bahmani. If it is, we could add murder, or at the very least manslaughter, to the charges.'

Fox sat forward and rested her elbows on the desk as she clasped her hands together under her nose. 'That's as maybe, but we can't afford to muddy the waters on this. The fact is, he made a serious allegation against you, and his lawyers could use that to sway the jury. You need to step down from the investigation.'

Phillips stuttered slightly. 'I'm sorry, ma'am, but I don't think that's necessary.'

'Oh yes it is,' Fox spat back. 'I'm not saying you can't have an influence on the case, but you cannot be seen to be directly involved. So, as of now, Jones is the SIO on the Tahir Bahmani shooting. Ok?'

Phillips opened her mouth to protest, but as she glanced at Carter, the look on his face said it all. *Stand down, Jane.* 'As you wish, ma'am.'

'And what about Adders Bahmani? Where are we at with him?'

'The CPS have agreed to the charges we put to them,' said Phillips. 'Accessory to attempted murder, carrying tools, possession of a dangerous weapon, as well as travelling in a stolen car.'

'What about possession of a firearm?' asked Fox.

'We're working on it, ma'am. The gun used to shoot at Freddie was found next to Tahir, but both men wore gloves, so we don't know who actually fired it. Knowing Adders, my money's on him. And I certainly wouldn't put it past him to ditch the gun next to his dead cousin and make a run for it.'

'I'm inclined to agree,' said Fox. 'He's always been a slippery bugger.'

'The good news is, he's been remanded to Hawk Green for the foreseeable, so he's finally off the streets.'

'Well, at least something good has come out of this mess.' Fox stared at Phillips for a long moment. 'As you may well know, Jane, I made certain promises to the public when I got this job, notably around my stance on gang crime. I need to be seen to be delivering on those promises, so having gangland murders splashed across the front pages of the newspapers is not a good look. We need to make all of this go away quietly. I'm relying on you and your team to make that happen. Do you understand?'

'Yes, ma'am.'

'Good. Because if the opposite were to happen, I'd have to think very hard about what kind of future Major Crimes has within the GMP. I'm under a lot of pressure to rationalise the organisation, and merging departments is not out of the question.' Fox glanced at Phillips and Carter in turn. 'Am I making myself clear?'

Phillips nodded. 'Completely.'

'Yes, ma'am,' said Carter.

Fox's trademark Cheshire Cat grin appeared under her dark, shark-like eyes. 'Good. In that case, that'll be all.'

Phillips needed no encouragement. She was out of her chair in an instant, with Carter not far behind. As they stepped out into the fifth-floor corridor, they stopped.

'Thank you,' said Carter.

'What for?'

'For playing the game in there.' Carter lowered his voice. 'She may be a bitch, but she is the boss.'

'Yeah, you're right...' Phillips cracked a childish grin. '... she is a bitch.'

Carter chuckled as Phillips turned away and headed for the stairs back to MCU.

46

Back in MCU, Phillips dropped into the chair at the spare desk next to Jones.

'How was your meeting with Fox?' asked Jones.

'To be honest, it actually went ok. On Carter's advice, I played the apologetic underling. She seemed to buy it, and the bollocking was fairly light by her standards. I think the fact Bahmani is sitting in Hawk Green for the first time ever helped. Mind you, she was very uncomfortable with us charging Freddie.'

'Why?' asked Entwistle.

'Thinks it could be seen as me covering my tracks around my alleged assault on him and the subsequent IPCC investigation.'

'But that's nonsense. He killed a man and ran away from the scene.'

'Whistler, you know that, and I know that, but juries can be persuaded otherwise. After all, it's rarely the truth that matters. It's usually down to which lawyer tells the best story in court.'

'So, how did you leave it with her?' asked Jones.

Phillips smiled. 'Looks like you've been promoted.'

Jones recoiled. 'You what?'

'You, my friend, are the new SIO on the Tahir Bahmani shooting.'

A look of confusion flashed across Jones's face.

Phillips continued. 'I can support you in an advisory capacity – off the record, of course – but everything goes through you. All decision logs, briefing notes, etc. All yours.'

'I don't know whether to be flattered or feel like I've been tucked up,' said Jones.

'Well, it's less paperwork for me, which isn't such a bad thing right now,' replied Phillips, folding her arms across her chest.

'Will he be getting a pay rise to match his new lofty position, Guv?' quipped Bovalino.

'From Fox? What do you think?'

'Ah well,' said Jones. 'I'll cancel that order for the fishing boat.'

Phillips shifted in her seat and leant forward on the desk. 'Look, on the subject of budgets, there is something else you should know that could potentially affect all of us.'

She had their full attention.

'Fox was making noises about restructuring and rationalisation just now.'

'Sounds like bullshit bingo to me,' joked Bov.

Phillips continued. 'She claims she's getting pressure from above to save money, and she's looking at different options.'

'Did she say what those options were?' asked Jones.

'No, but Carter reckons she's considering merging MCU with Serious Crimes.'

'What?' Jones was aghast. 'That's bullshit!'

Phillips raised her hands in defence. 'I know, I know.'

'So, what would that actually mean for us?' asked Entwistle.

'Depends, really. I'm guessing here, of course, but I'd say best case scenario, *we* continue in our current roles under a new department banner with the cream of the SCU guys joining as part of the team. Worse case, SCU take the lead, some of us stay on, and those that don't get reassigned to another unit – or maybe even another force.'

'Jesus. That's all we need,' said Jones.

'Look. I'm not telling you this to unsettle you. I'm giving you the heads-up so we can keep our fate in our own hands. MCU has one of the best – if not *the* best – conviction records in the GMP. That *has* to count for something. The lack of leads on the Bradley and Hodge investigations is unusual for us, and all the mess around Tahir's death isn't helping right now either, but things can change quickly in this game, as we know.'

'So what can we do?' said Entwistle.

'Simple. We do everything we can to find the killer, *and fast*. If Fox is looking to merge floundering departments, let's make sure it's not ours.'

Each of the men nodded.

Phillips stood and walked over to the incident board allocated to the Bradley and Hodge murders, and tapped Bahmani's mugshot. 'I hate to say it, but I'm starting to think Freddie might be right about his dad's murder. After what Bahmani pulled the other night, he's elevated himself to prime suspect. According to Freddie, he'd been strong-arming Paul Bradley into selling him the business at a cut price for a while. So, when Paul refused for the umpteenth time, maybe that's when Bahmani decided to take matters into his own hands.'

'It makes sense, Guv,' said Jones. 'And, based on the

description Melissa gave of Paul's killers, they're dead ringers for Bahmani and Tahir when they turned up the other night looking for Freddie.'

'Yeah. And they're also a match for the two men pictured kidnapping Shawn Harvey, as well as the two fellas who tortured Dillon Wilton,' said Phillips. 'Right now, Bahmani's looking at a couple of years maximum for his current charges – five more if we can tie him to the gun used to shoot at Freddie. But that's not nearly enough. I want Bahmani to be an old man by the time he's released from prison. He's been running around taking the piss out of the police for years. Everyone's tried to catch him, and everyone's failed. That stops with MCU. Our focus right now needs to be on finding the evidence that proves he killed Bradley and Hodge. And if we can tie him to the kidnap and torture, more's the better. So, let's start by going back through the case files for both murders from the beginning. We're looking for anything we might have missed. No matter how small. I want you to check one another's reports. It's much easier to spot things in other people's work.'

A chorus of 'Yes, Guv' filled the room, following Phillips back to her office.

LATER THAT EVENING, Phillips paid another visit to ICU. Carrie was once again seated at Adam's bedside. She looked as exhausted as Phillips felt. Sadly, as Sister Wilson had explained, there was little improvement in his condition. That said, she'd also pointed out that the new treatment was not something they'd expecting would work miracles. It was simply another tool in the fight to save Adam's life.

Phillips and Carrie chatted as best they could for an hour

or so before Phillips began to feel an overwhelming sense of fatigue. She was dead on her feet.

After making her excuses, she kissed Adam on the forehead and told him how much she loved him, then headed home for the night.

47

MONDAY 19TH JULY

Phillips's weekend had been relatively uneventful. In between visits to the hospital – which offered nothing new and no fresh hope – she'd spent Saturday and Sunday going over the case files desperate to find a breakthrough, but to no avail.

Despite her physical and mental exhaustion, sleep remained hard to come by, and it was no surprise that she found herself wide awake in the early hours. Getting out of bed at 5 a.m., she headed for the kitchen and made her now-ritual early-morning call to ICU. Unsurprisingly, Adam's condition remained the same.

Itching to get back into the office and reconnect with the team, she arrived just after 6 a.m. and buried her head in the Archie Boothroyd case files. She couldn't put her finger on why, but her gut was telling her they'd missed something, something that could help shed some light on the Bradley and Hodge murders. They were, after all, almost identical crimes, even if they had been committed almost thirty years apart.

For the next couple of hours, she pored over the witness statements as well as the decision logs from the investigating team, but came up with nothing of note, much to her mounting frustration. After making herself a coffee in the small MCU kitchen, she headed back to her office and slipped back into her chair. Spread out on the desk were a bunch of photographs taken around the time of the Boothroyd murder. The collection consisted of shots of Boothroyd and his fellow gang mates, as well as a number of people who had been identified as known associates. Frustratingly, the original investigators had not bothered to log who had been photographed – something that would never happen in the modern world of policing. As she sipped her coffee, she took in each of the individuals pictured. All together, it was a host of nefarious-looking characters in various locations around the city: huddled in doorways or standing next to expensive cars, including BMWs, Mercedes and Range Rovers, to name a few. The purposes of the meetings had not been recorded either.

Scouring the main subjects of the images, Phillips's eyes landed on a woman with peroxide blonde hair standing in the background of one of the photographs. Could this be the woman Inspector Hayley had mentioned, Boothroyd's feisty flatmate who had attacked the police? Whoever she was, she looked familiar.

There was obviously no zoom feature on printed pictures. To get around the issue, Phillips took a photo of the photo on her phone, then zoomed in for a closer look. 'How do I know you?' she whispered as she stared at the woman's face.

Jones arrived a few minutes later. As he hung up his coat, she wandered out to get his take on it.

'Any idea who this might be?' She handed him the phone. 'She looks really familiar.'

Jones eyes narrowed. 'Yeah, I know what you mean. Where'd you get it?'

Phillips thumbed over her shoulder towards her office. 'She was in the background of one of the photos I was looking at from the Boothroyd file.'

'I feel like I've seen her before, but I can't think where.'

'Me too.'

Her eyes wandered to the Paul Bradley incident board next to Jones's desk. Slowly scrutinising the images there for a couple of minutes, one photo suddenly stood out to her. Moving closer, she tapped on a recent picture of Melissa Bradley. 'Is it me or does the woman in the photo have a bit of a look of Melissa?'

Jones craned his neck to follow her line of sight, then studied the image of Melissa for a long moment himself. 'Give me your phone,' he said.

She handed it to him.

Jones studied the image on the phone, then Melissa's picture, then back and forth a couple more times before nodding. 'There's definitely a close resemblance, but even if it is her, we already knew she ran with that crowd.'

'Yeah, but we didn't know she was blonde, did we? Like Boothroyd's *girlfriend*.' Phillips felt her adrenaline spike as she grabbed the phone back and began searching through her contact list. She found what she was looking for a moment later, and pressed dial.

'Who you calling?' asked Jones.

'Inspector Hayley in Sheffield.'

'From the original investigation?'

'That's the one.'

Hayley answered promptly. *'DI Hayley.'* It sounded noisy wherever she was.

'Lia, it's Jane Phillips from Major Crimes in Manchester.'

'Hello, Jane. Sorry about the noise. I'm trying to get the kids sorted for school. What can I do for you?'

'I was wondering. I know you said you couldn't remember the name of Archie Boothroyd's girlfriend – the peroxide blonde who attacked your officers. Does the name Melissa ring any bells with you?'

'Melissa? Sorry, Jane.' Hayley sounded harassed. 'Can you hang on a second?'

Hayley covered her phone as she spoke to someone nearby. Phillips could just about make out that one of her kids was looking for something.

A minute or so later, Hayley came back. 'Sorry about that. My eldest can't find her P.E. kit, which is somehow my fault.'

'The joys of parenting,' quipped Phillips.

'Honestly, it's a bloody battle just to get them out the door each morning. Anyway, we're all sorted now. So, what were you saying?'

'I was wondering if Boothroyd's blonde girlfriend was called Melissa.

'Melissa?' Hayley repeated, and went quiet for a moment. 'I can't say I ever knew her as Melissa, but now you mention it, she may have gone by the name Mel. I do recall it was a short name, so that would fit.'

Phillip's pulse quickened. 'I'm going to send you a picture of a woman we think could be Mel. Can you check it and let me know if you recognise her?'

'Of course, I'd be happy to.'

'Great, I'll send it through now.' Phillips ended the call and immediately fired across the photo of the girl.

A couple of minutes later, her phone pinged. She stared down at Hayley's response.

That's her. Very hot-headed and a real handful.

'Bingo!' shouted Phillips, just as Bovalino and Entwistle walked through the office doors.

'Everything all right, Guv?' asked Bovalino.

Phillips flashed him a satisfied grin. 'I think we might have just got a break on the Bradley and Hodge murders.' She presented the image of Mel to them both. 'We suspect this woman is actually Melissa Bradley. She was captured in the background of a photo taken of Archie Boothroyd. We now have reason to believe Melissa was actually his girlfriend, though she's always maintained she hardly knew him.'

Both men scrutinised the picture.

'Whistler, get online and see if you can find any historical images of Melissa from this period to back it up: early-to-mid-nineties.'

Entwistle fired up his laptop.

'Shout me when you find anything,' said Phillips, returning to her office to study the remaining photographs for any further clues. Jones joined her in her search.

Fifteen minutes later, Entwistle beckoned them out into the main office.

'What have you got?' asked Phillips.

'Well, I tried Google but couldn't find anything on there. And her Facebook page only goes back a couple of years.'

'Right,' Phillips could feel her impatience building. 'So, what *did* you find?'

'Freddie's social media, and an old picture posted by him on Melissa's fiftieth. "Happy birthday mum, a true nineties Raver! Love, your boy, Freddie."'

Phillips gazed at the laptop. The same women from the Boothroyd photo looked back at her.

Entwistle mistakenly clicked to the next picture in the album, a shot of Freddie at his eighteenth birthday. 'Sorry, Guv,' he said as he clicked back to the image of Melissa.

'Go back,' said Phillips. 'To the picture of Freddie.'

Entwistle did as requested. Phillips gazed at the image of the young man, beer in hand, leering at the camera in the centre of a crowd of lads of the same age. 'Well, I'll be damned.'

'What is it, Guv?' asked Jones.

'Take a look at Freddie.'

Jones stared at the screen for a long moment. 'What am I looking at?'

'Remind you of anyone?' asked Phillips.

'Should it?'

Phillips moved across to the whiteboards and stopped next to a police mugshot of Archie Boothroyd, taken a few months before he was murdered. 'Archie was about twenty when this was taken, and Freddie was eighteen in that photo. They look like they could be twins!'

Jones's eyes darted back and forth between the two images. 'Bloody hell. I hadn't seen it before, but you're right.'

'So what are you saying, boss?' asked Entwistle. 'That Archie Boothroyd is actually Freddie's dad?'

'That's exactly what I'm saying. What's Freddie's date of birth?'

Entwistle pulled up his file on the laptop. '23 July 1994.'

Phillips took a moment to do the maths in her head. 'Which means Melissa could have been a month or so pregnant with Archie's child when he was killed.'

'If that is the case, then she's been lying to us all along,' said Jones.

'Exactly,' Phillips shot back. 'Melissa Bradley is the first substantial link we have between the Boothroyd and Bradley murders. And for all we know, she could be connected to Hodge's death as well. He was a good mate of her husband, after all. We need to speak to her as a matter urgency.'

Jones's face wrinkled. 'Let's think this through, Guv. Fox was very clear on how we're supposed to handle Melissa. We need to be very careful we don't do anything to prejudice the IPCC investigation.'

'Oh, bollocks to Fox! This has nothing to do with that. This is about the murders.'

Jones raised his arms in defence. 'I know that, boss, but we need to box clever on this one. Before we go charging in, maybe we need solid evidence that actually ties her to the murders.'

'Like what?' Phillips was exasperated.

'I don't know, but there must be something.'

Phillips took a long moment to think. 'Freddie said he wanted to see his mum, right?'

'Right,' said Jones.

'I'm betting if Melissa is somehow involved in all this, then her shit-bag of a son is too.' She turned to Entwistle. 'Are you still connected to that girl who works at Hawk Green?'

'Sophie? Yeah. We still chat from time to time.'

Bovalino grinned and made air quotes with his fingers. '"Chatting". Is that what they call it these days?'

'Piss off, you blockhead!' Entwistle fired back. 'It is possible to be friends with women and not try and shag them, you know.'

'Aye, right,' drawled the big Italian.

'When you two have quite finished,' Phillips interjected. 'Whistler, get onto Sophie and ask her if Melissa has been added to the visitors' list, and if so, when is she due to see him.'

'No problem, boss. I'll call her now.'

'Great. Let me know what she says.' Phillips checked her watch; it was coming up for 9 a.m., and for the first time in days, she felt hungry. 'I'm going to get some breakfast from the canteen. Anyone need anything?'

'Not for me, thanks,' said Entwistle as he searched his phone for Sophie's number.

'I could do with a drink,' said Jones. 'I'll come with you.'

Phillips turned to Bovalino. 'Bacon roll?'

A wide smile spread across the big man's face. 'You read my mind, Guv.'

Phillips returned his smile, then headed for the door with Jones close behind.

48

W hile Jones took his place in the long queue for the food and drinks, Phillips found a quiet corner just outside the canteen and called Carrie to check on Adam. Whilst his condition hadn't improved, neither had it deteriorated. That at least gave them a tiny slither of hope. After promising to keep in touch, Phillips finished the call, then took a moment to gather herself. A few minutes later, she joined Jones in the queue. By the time they returned from the canteen, Entwistle had made the call.

'Sophie says Melissa is booked in to see Freddie at midday.'

Phillips handed Bovalino his sandwich. 'Right. Call her back and tell her that as soon as the visit is done, we need her to send across any CCTV footage they have of the meeting room.'

Entwistle frowned. 'Are we allowed to ask for that, Guv? I mean, is it legal?'

'Probably not, but then neither is murder, and that still happens.'

Jones's grave expression matched Entwistle's. 'Whistler's right, boss. We can't use anything like that in court.'

'I'm not planning to. I just need to see what they talk about.' Phillips folded her arms. 'Look. Since Bahmani tried to shoot Freddie, Melissa's not seen her son, right?'

'Right,' Jones replied.

'And Freddie's a little gobshite; a mummy's boy. Whatever happened that night at the Bradleys is more than likely going to be high on the list of things they need to discuss. If we can check the footage, it might just tell us something we don't know.'

'Are you going to run this past Carter?' asked Jones.

'Not yet, no.'

'It's a big risk, boss.'

'I know it is, Jonesy, but we did things by the book the night Tahir died and look what happened. It's a risk I'm willing to take. If it comes back on us, I'll make sure it's all on me, ok?' She turned back to Entwistle. 'So call Sophie and set it up.'

Entwistle nodded reluctantly and picked up his phone as Phillips returned to her office.

Ten minutes later, he appeared in the doorway. 'Sophie's agreed to send it over, boss.'

'Excellent,' said Phillips. 'Was she ok about doing it?'

Entwistle screwed his face up as he stepped inside. 'Not at first, but she came round eventually.'

'Fell for the famous Whistler charm, did she?'

'Yeah, maybe. The thing is, she says she's ok to send it over, but she's going to need an email from you to confirm the request. Just in case it comes back on her.'

'Fine,' replied Phillips. 'What's her address?'

Entwistle handed across a yellow Post-It Note with the details scribbled on it.

Phillips took the note. 'I'll send it now.'

'There is one more thing.'

'Oh?'

'Sophie says the footage doesn't have sound. For legal reasons, apparently, so we won't be able to hear what they're saying.'

'Ah,' said Phillips, blowing her lips. 'Well, that's not ideal, is it?'

'No. But I was thinking, the digital forensics team have a lip-reading specialist for this very thing. Should I see if we can borrow them later today?'

Phillips banged her hand down on the desk. 'Bloody great idea! What would we do without you, Whistler?'

Entwistle appeared to blush slightly. 'I'll get it sorted now,' he said, then headed back to his desk.

JUST AFTER 2 P.M., Entwistle announced that the footage had landed via an encrypted transfer link. Phillips wanted to see the images on the big screen, so told him to set up his laptop in the conference room.

Half an hour later, they all sat round the table, joined by the digital team's lip-reading specialist, Sergeant Debbie Coulson.

Phillips briefed her on the subjects' names. Then, with everyone ready and staring at the screen, Entwistle pressed play.

They watched in silence as footage of Melissa and Freddie appeared on the massive 70-inch TV fixed to the wall. As luck would have it, the images had come from a camera positioned to the side, which allowed both their mouths to be seen.

'It's general chit-chat just now,' Coulson said as she watched the screen intently.

The video continued for another couple of minutes.

'Can you pause it there?' asked Coulson.

Phillips turned to face her. 'What is it?'

'Just rewind back thirty seconds, will you?'

Entwistle obliged, and pressed play.

Coulson narrated the footage. 'Freddie's saying, "What are you doing to get me out?" but Melissa's saying he needs do his time like a man and keep his mouth shut.'

'What else?' asked Phillips.

'He's saying he could get five years for the gun, which is down to her because she gave it to him.'

'Did she now?' said Jones.

The video continued for another ten seconds or so until Coulson once again began narrating. 'Now she's telling him to stick with the story that the gun belonged to his father, that way the police can't pin it on either of them.'

'And the Mother of the Year Award goes to...' Bovalino quipped.

Coulson continued. 'She's angry now, saying he was stupid for attacking the copper's boyfriend.'

Phillips's blood ran cold and her stomach flipped as she watched Freddie laughing at his mother. It took all her strength to remain in control of her emotions.

'He's saying it's all good because it wasn't him, it was Shanks – whatever that means.'

'Are you ok, Guv?' asked Jones, his voice filled with concern.

'Keep going,' she replied, her voice flat.

'She says it was reckless, but he says the bitch got what was coming to her.'

The rage burning in Phillips was like a living thing, coupled with the guilt of knowing that her actions had led to Adam's attack.

'Do you need to take a break, boss?' asked Entwistle.

'No,' said Phillips, without taking her eyes off the screen. 'Keep going.'

'She wants to know where the knife is. He's saying not to worry, Shanks took care of it. She's not happy. Shanks is an idiot and can't be trusted, he could talk. He says Shanks is not a grass.'

As the footage continued, Coulson narrated the remainder of conversation as Freddie brought Melissa up to speed on what happened the night Bahmani and Tahir turned up at the house. The details appeared to match his statement during interview and it was evident – as Phillips had suspected – that there had been no invitation from Freddie to Bahmani regarding any business discussions.

When the video was finally complete, Phillips took a deep breath before turning to face the team. 'Thanks, Debbie. That was very helpful. Right, I want Melissa and Shanks in for questioning immediately. Jones, you and I will take Melissa. Bov, organise a firearms team to go with you to pick up Shanks. He's likely armed and, as we suspect, extremely dangerous.'

'Do you want me to pass this footage over to Serious Crimes regarding the attack on Adam?' asked Entwistle.

'Not just yet. I need time to think about how I explain it to Carter.'

'Whatever you say, boss.'

Phillips stood. 'Right. Let's go round 'em up.'

49

Phillips and Jones arrived at the Bradley home forty-five minutes later. Alarmingly, the place appeared deserted. After ringing the doorbell repeatedly with no answer, they headed to the back of the house. Large wood panels had been fitted as temporary cover for the missing French doors. And no sign of Melissa.

Returning to the car, Jones spotted the neighbour they had spoken to previously, mowing his front lawn. As they approached, he offered a friendly smile and switched off the mower.

'Have you seen Melissa recently?' asked Phillips.

'Just this morning,' he replied cheerily. 'I wished her well and helped her put her cases in the car.'

'Cases?' Jones cut in. 'Was she going somewhere?'

'Dubai. Moving out there full-time, apparently. We'll miss her. She's been a great neighbour.'

Phillips's pulse quickened. 'I don't suppose you know what time her flight is, do you?'

'About six, I think. Etihad Airways, judging by the tags on her luggage.'

Phillips looked at her watch; 4.43 p.m. She glanced at Jones. His grave expression matched her concern. If Melissa made it out of the country, getting her back would be almost impossible. 'Thanks for your help,' she said, then hurried back to the car.

Jones jumped in behind the wheel a split second after she landed in the passenger seat, and fired up the engine as Phillips called Entwistle.

'*Have you got her, Guv?*'

'No. Looks as if she's trying to get out of the country. Her neighbour says she's booked on the 6 p.m. flight to Dubai.'

Jones screeched away from the kerb as he floored the accelerator and switched on the siren and lights, hidden in the unmarked squad car.

'Jones and I are heading to the airport now.'

'*What can I do?*'

'Call the border team. Ideally, we need them to stop her getting through security, but looking at the time, it's probably too late for that. If that's the case, we need security to try and track her down.'

'*No problem.*'

'And I want backup from one of the armed units already stationed there, as well as access to the entire building. We haven't got time for security checks, so we're going to need waving straight through. We're about fifteen minutes out.'

'*I'll make sure they're ready for you, boss.*'

'Finally, what terminal do Etihad fly out of?'

There was a moment's silence on the other end as Entwistle searched for the information on his laptop. '*Terminal 2.*'

'Thanks,' said Phillips, and ended the call.

DRIVING under blues and twos always seemed to heighten the senses. As Jones sped up the ramp to International Departures at Terminal 2, Phillips's body seemed to be on high alert, her heart racing in her chest.

At that moment, Phillips's phone rang through the car speakers. 'Whistler?'

'She's already through Customs but she's flying business class with Etihad. Her ticket shows she checked into the lounge just after four, so hopefully she's still there.'

'Great. And what about the TFU and security?'

'All set. Sergeant Matthews and his team are waiting for you by the entrance to Terminal 2. They'll escort you through to Departures.'

'Perfect. In fact, I can see them just up ahead. We'd better go.'

'Good luck, Guv.'

Jones screeched to a halt just behind the BMW X5 belonging to the TFU. As they jumped out, Sergeant Matthews and three of his officers approached, holding their Heckler and Koch G36 submachine guns against their chests.

'Roy,' said Phillips as she got out of the car.

Matthews got straight to it. 'Ma'am, we believe the target is currently in the Etihad lounge on the third floor of the building. However, her flight is due to board in the next fifteen minutes, so she may already be on the move.'

'Best get in there, then.'

'Yes, ma'am,' replied Matthews. He turned on his heels and marched towards the automatic entrance doors to Departures.

Thanks to the TFU team, they navigated security quickly, and soon found themselves in the belly of the airport, racing up the stairs towards the business lounges. As they reached the top, Matthews pointed to the large gold Etihad logo positioned above a pair of frosted glass doors to their right and led them towards it, stopping just outside.'

'I don't want to spook her unnecessarily, so you guys wait here,' Phillips said. 'Jones and I will go in alone.'

'Yes, ma'am,' replied Matthews.

Phillips pulled open the door and stepped inside the windowless space, with Jones just behind her. To their left was another set of smoked glass double doors, each pane marked with the word *Lounge* in gold lettering. Ahead was a large counter with flat screens positioned above it, communicating the status of all flights out of the airport. As she approached, she was greeted by the hostess, smartly dressed in a uniform that combined the Western and Middle Eastern styles.

'Can I help you?' she asked through a sparkling white smile. Her name badge indicated she was Cathy.

Phillips flashed her ID. 'I'm looking for one of your passengers. Melissa Bradley. I believe she checked in about an hour ago.'

Cathy began typing into her desktop computer. 'Ah yes, Mrs Bradley. She's booked on the 18.05 to Dubai.'

'Can you tell me where she is at the moment?'

Cathy checked her computer once again. 'It looks as if she checked into the lounge with my colleague just after 4. I've not been on the desk long myself, so I'm afraid I don't what she looks like. She may still be in the lounge, but she could have already left. We start boarding in ten minutes through Gate 17.'

Phillips glanced towards the doors to the lounge. 'Would you mind if we have a look inside?'

Cathy smiled. 'Please, go on through.'

Phillips and Jones moved through the doors and found themselves in a calm, quiet space that oozed opulence. Thick carpets covered the floors, and there was more smoked glass coupled with soft leather chairs facing large flatscreen TVs on the walls around them. Beyond was a restaurant and bar, and a handful of well-dressed men and women enjoying the free food and drinks on offer. There were signs on the walls giving directions to showers and a spa, and yet more screens flashing flight statuses.

'How the other half live, hey boss,' said Jones.

'Quite,' said Phillips, scanning the room for any sign of Melissa. She pointed to the room filled with TVs. 'You check that room. I'll take the bar and restaurant.'

Jones nodded and stepped away.

Careful not to draw too much attention to herself, Phillips moved slowly amongst the passengers. If Melissa was there, she wanted to take her as quietly as possible. But after checking the entire space – including several annexed rooms set aside for families – she could find no sign of her.

Retracing her steps, she met Jones back at the entrance to the lounge. 'No luck?'

Jones shook his head. 'I even checked the shower and the spa. Nothing.'

'She must have already left.' Phillips checked the screens on the wall. 'Come on. It says the 18.05 to Dubai has started boarding. We need to catch her before she gets on that flight.'

Back outside, Phillips quickly updated Matthews. As the whole team set off towards Gate 17, he radioed through to all armed officers in the vicinity of the boarding gates, asking them to be on the lookout for Melissa.

By the time they reached the main gates area, they were almost running, drawing inquisitive looks from passengers as they rushed by.

It was then that Phillips spotted Melissa, walking casually ahead of them. She slowed, signalling for the rest of the team to follow suit.

Without warning, and for no apparent reason, Melissa

suddenly stopped in her tracks. A second later, she turned slowly and looked directly at Phillips. For a moment she stood motionless, just staring back, then spun and set off running.

Phillips and Jones gave chase. Matthews barked into his radio as he followed behind. 'Suspect is on the run, heading away from Gate 17 towards the main shopping area. IC-one female, with dark hair, wearing a white shirt, blue blazer and jeans, carrying what looks to be a brown Louis Vuitton handbag.'

Melissa was surprisingly quick as she darted and side-stepped through the myriad passengers milling around the space.

'Where the hell does she think she's going?' asked Phillips.

'God knows. She's as good as locked in here with us!'

Jones was right. Once a passenger was inside a British airport, it was virtually impossible to get out without the approval of security. Realistically, there was no way Melissa could escape, but if they lost her, the whole airport would need to be shut down until she was located. That scenario could cause untold delays – not just in Manchester, but around the globe. Not a situation Phillips wanted to be responsible for. 'Melissa! Stop!' Phillips shouted again as they chased her.

If Melissa heard, she didn't react.

'This is ridiculous. She's quicker than a bloody grey-hound!' puffed Jones as he struggled to keep up.

It was then that Phillips spotted two armed officers about thirty metres ahead, running straight for Melissa, their G36s ready, the extended stocks pulled hard into their shoulders. 'Armed Police! Stop!' they shouted in unison.

Melissa finally stopped.

The armed police officers edged closer, and the officer at

the front began barking orders. 'Drop the bag and put your hands behind your head! Do it now!'

Melissa reluctantly complied just as Phillips arrived. 'Melissa Bradley, I'm arresting you on suspicion of perverting the course of justice and possession of an unlicensed firearm.'

'This is outrageous!' Melissa protested. 'My lawyer is going to have your pension for this.'

Phillips was still breathless as she pulled the handcuffs from her pocket and clamped them onto Melissa's wrists. 'You do not have to say anything, but it may harm your defence if you do not mention, when questioned, something which you later rely on in court. Anything you do say may be given in evidence.'

Melissa glanced down at the cuffs, then back up at Phillips, her eyes dark and cold. 'If I miss my flight, you'll be paying for it! Now, get me my phone so I can call my lawyer.'

Phillips flashed a thin smile. 'Sorry. We'll be keeping it as evidence. But don't worry. You can call Mr Tate when we get back to Ashton House. There's a shared phone you can use in the custody suite.'

50

As Jones escorted Melissa to the car, Bovalino's number flashed up on Phillips's phone. She dropped back out of earshot to answer it. 'Have you got Shanks?'

'Yes, Guv. I've just loaded him into the car.'

'Can he hear you?'

'No. I'm outside on the street.'

'Good. We've just picked up Melissa at the airport, although she didn't make it easy.'

'And why doesn't that surprise me?'

'How long will it take you to get to Ashton House from where you are?' asked Phillips.

'About thirty minutes, I reckon.'

'We'll be there in about forty. Look, I need you take the long way back to make sure we all land at Ashton House at the same time. I've had an idea, and it relies on Melissa and Shanks crossing paths in the custody suite.'

'No worries, Guv. I'll drive through the city. That should slow us down a bit.'

'Perfect. We'll see you back at base,' said Phillips before ending the call.

———

Just before 7 p.m., Jones guided the squad car through the security gates to the rear of Ashton House and into the car park that served the custody suite. As they came to a stop, Phillips jumped out and opened the back door before leaning in and pulling Melissa out of the seat. A couple of minutes later, they marched her up to the desk and briefed the custody sergeant, Mike Allinson.

Allinson was into his thirtieth year on the force and planned to retire at the end of the year. A cheerful man, he knew instinctively how to handle prisoners at a time when stress was often heightened and emotions threatened to get the better of them. 'Now then,' he said with a soft smile from his elevated position behind the desk, 'who have we got here?'

'Melissa Bradley,' replied Phillips.

'And why have you brought her to see me today?'

'Mrs Bradley has been arrested on suspicion of perverting the course of justice, as well as possession of an unlicensed firearm.'

'I see,' said Allinson, tapping away into the computer.

Over the next ten minutes, Allinson elicited personal details from Melissa, including the name and number of her lawyer, before photographing her from various angles in order to create her mugshot.

Just as the process was drawing to a close, the door behind them opened and Bovalino walked in, his thick hand attached to the handcuffs locked on Shanks's wiry wrists. Wearing the ubiquitous tracksuit of a Manchester street thug, he was a tall, slender man with close-cropped ginger hair above gaunt features. His face bore the marks of violence: a long, thick scar running from his right eye down to his jaw.

'Won't be a minute,' said Allinson, glancing at the big Italian.

'No rush,' replied Bov. 'This guy's not going anywhere.'

A minute later, with the paperwork completed, Allinson instructed one of the custody officers to take Melissa to cell 8.

Phillips watched on as the officer approached and asked Melissa to follow him. As she turned, she spotted Shanks.

'All right, Mel?' said Shanks enthusiastically.

Melissa stared back at him, but remained silent.

'That's right. You guys already know each other, don't you?' said Phillips.

'We go way back, hey Mel?' Shanks leered.

A look of fear flashed across Melissa's face.

It was fleeting, but Phillips had spotted it. She turned her attention to Shanks. 'Looks like Mrs Bradley doesn't want to talk to you, Shanks. Doesn't share your enthusiasm for jail-house banter.'

Melissa remained stoic.

'I think Mrs Bradley might be distancing herself from Mr Shanks. Don't you, DC Bovalino?'

'Looks that way to me, Guv.'

Phillips scoffed. 'Probably thinks she's above foot soldiers like *you,* mate.'

Melissa turned her back on Shanks and faced Allinson once more. 'I'd like you to call my lawyer now, please.'

'Of course,' replied Allinson as he pulled up the number on the screen.

The custody officer stepped closer again. 'This way, Melissa,' he said with an outstretched arm.

Melissa blanked Shanks as she stepped away from the desk and walked towards the custody suite.

'Not saying goodbye, Mrs Bradley?' Phillips shouted after her.

Melissa didn't respond. She just kept on walking.

Phillips turned back to Shanks. 'I don't think she likes you very much.'

Shanks's expression had changed. The leering cockiness had left him, replaced by rage. 'She needs to remember who I am and what I've done for her family,' he shouted, loud enough for her to hear. 'Show me some fucking respect!'

Melissa never faltered, and a moment later disappeared through the door to the cells.

Phillips glanced at Bovalino and winked.

He flashed a knowing smile, then marched Shanks up to the custody desk.

'Now, then. What's your name, son?' asked Allinson.

51

As Phillips waited for Melissa's lawyer to arrive, she headed to her office and pulled together her notes and questions for the impending interview. A knock at her door caused her to look up.

'You got a minute?' asked Carter.

'Of course, sir.'

Carter stepped into the office and closed the door behind him, then turned back to face Phillips. 'I understand you have Melissa Bradley downstairs in the cells.'

'News travels fast,' said Phillips, placing her pen down on the pad.

Carter's face was filled with concern. 'What have you got her in for?'

'Perverting the course of justice and possession of a firearm.'

'Really?' asked Carter. 'This is news to me.'

'News to all of us. We had to act fast or she'd have fled the country.'

'I heard you picked her up at the airport. Is it true she ran?'

'Yeah, she did, which doesn't exactly look good, does it?'

Carter folded his arms across his chest. 'You know how Fox feels about you going after Melissa Bradley. Are you sure you're doing the right thing, Jane?'

'We have CCTV that shows her giving instructions to her son Freddie to keep his mouth shut and do his time. It also shows Freddie admitting that Melissa gave him the unregistered gun that killed Tahir, and that Freddie ordered the knife attack on Adam.'

Carter's brow furrowed. 'Where the hell did you get that?'

Phillips had been trying to figure out how to explain the CCTV footage to her boss for the last few hours, but so far had struggled to come up with anything other than the truth. Now seemed like the appropriate time to come clean. 'Hawk Green visitors' centre, sir.'

'You what? Hawk Green? I don't understand.'

Phillips swallowed hard. There was no going back now. 'I requested a copy of the CCTV footage taken during Melissa's first visit to see Freddie this lunch time.'

Carter shook his head and said nothing as he dropped into the chair opposite Phillips. 'I knew your methods were unorthodox, Jane, but this is incredible, even for you.'

'I understand that. But at the same time, it wasn't a privileged conversation and I had reason to believe Melissa was connected to the murders of Archie Boothroyd, Paul Bradley and Mitchell Hodge.'

'Based on what?'

'New evidence. She lied to me about the fact she was never romantically involved with Boothroyd. This morning, we confirmed she was in fact his girlfriend at the time he was murdered – *and* that they had lived together Not only that, but we also believe Boothroyd is Freddie's father and not Paul.'

Carter recoiled. 'Really? And where did all this come from?'

'We found pictures of Melissa and Boothroyd together, taken just before he was killed. Inspector Hayley – who originally worked on the case – confirmed it was Melissa. As for the identity of Freddie's father, we compared photos of him and Boothroyd when they were about the same age. The resemblance between the two is uncanny.'

'So, it's just a hunch at the moment? You've no actual proof yet?'

'Not yet, sir, no, but it should be relatively easy to prove once we take blood samples and compare them to the original case files.'

Carter nodded silently.

'Anyway, acting on another hunch, I had a feeling Melissa and Freddie would do a debrief during her first visit, so I ordered a copy of the tape.'

Carter pursed his lips. 'None of this is ever likely to stand up in court. You know that, don't you?'

'I do. And that's why none of it will be put forward. It's merely a leverage tool to get Melissa talking.'

'Well, considering she's got Travis Tate in her corner, you're going to have your work cut out getting her to do that.'

'Maybe so, but I've got results before with far less.'

Carter said nothing for a long moment.

'I know I'm asking a lot, sir, but please trust me on this one. I won't let you down.'

Carter let out a loud sigh. 'All right. It's your call, Jane, but believe me when I say this: if all this goes south, Fox will want someone to hang. And I know where she'll be putting the noose.'

'Don't worry, sir. I know what I'm up against, and I'll take full responsibility.'

'And what about this lad, Shanks? I see on the charge

sheet he's been arrested for the attempted murder of Adam. Is that right?'

Phillips took a breath to steady her pulse as images of Adam lying in a pool of blood flashed into her mind's eye. 'Yes, sir. Freddie implicated him on the tape.'

'So, I take it you've informed DCI Cleverly and handed him over to SCU?'

'Not yet, no.'

Carter's frown reappeared. 'And why not? You know you *cannot* get involved in that case.'

'And I'm not. I need him to help me crack Melissa. He's up to his eyes in shit on behalf of the Bradleys, and with a bit of encouragement he could unlock the whole bloody organisation.'

'I feel very uneasy about this, Jane.'

Phillips nodded. 'I understand, but again. Trust me. I know what I'm doing.'

'Very well,' said Carter, 'But I want to be kept in the loop throughout. Ok?'

'I wouldn't have it any other way, sir,' replied Phillips with a smile.

Carter's face finally softened, and he chuckled. 'Remind me again why I left the comfort of the North East to come to Manchester.'

'Because it's *much* more fun down here.'

At that moment, Jones knocked on the door.

Phillips beckoned him in.

'They're ready for us, Guv.'

'Ok. I'll be right there.' Phillips began to gather her files.

Carter stepped up from the chair. 'Good luck, Jane.'

'Thank you, sir.'

'I have a feeling you're going to need it on this one.'

TEN MINUTES LATER, Phillips found herself opposite Melissa and her lawyer, Travis Tate. For this interview, she had decided to conduct the questions alone. It was cleaner that way should anything come back to bite her regarding the CCTV footage. Everything would be recorded, as usual, so there was no need for a second person in the chair.

Phillips activated the DIR and noted the date and time for the tape, as well as the subject of the interview. Then, with renewed determination, she got stuck into the questions. 'Melissa, why did you run when we found you at the airport?'

Melissa's arms had been folded across her chest since Phillips walked in. She unfolded them now and took a sip of water from a plastic cup. When she finished, she placed it back on the table and recrossed her arms before finally speaking. 'No comment.'

Phillips made a note in her pad and continued. 'Why were you going to Dubai?'

'No comment.'

'We spoke to your neighbour, who said you were moving out there permanently. Is that true?'

'No comment.'

'Were you in fact attempting to flee the country?'

Melissa crossed her leg over her knee before once again replying. 'No comment.'

So far, Phillips was not surprised with the way the interview was going, but she had a plan and needed to let it play out. As Carter had stated, her use of the CCTV footage was unorthodox, so everything else needed to be to the letter of the law. With that in mind, she continued to play the game the way Melissa was driving it.

'Were you leaving the UK because you were concerned that you would be implicated in the death of Tahir Bahmani during the shooting that took place at your home last week?'

Melissa glared at Phillips for a long moment. 'No comment.'

'You see, we believe the unregistered firearm used to kill him was given to Freddie by you.'

Melissa's left eye twitched ever so slightly. Phillips spotted it.

'When you visited Hawk Green prison this lunchtime, what did you and Freddie discuss?'

'Is that really any of your business?' Tate interjected.

'If they discussed criminal activity, yes it is,' Phillips said whilst keeping her eyes fixed on Melissa.

Melissa took another sip of water, then replied, 'No comment.'

Phillips opened her laptop and clicked on the all-important video footage. Placing it on the table so it was visible to Melissa and Tate, she pressed play and described what they were watching. 'This is CCTV footage taken from your visit this morning at Hawk Green.'

Melissa and Tate watched the screen in silence.

Phillips continued. 'Now, because there's no sound, we've had a lip-reading expert look at the footage. And because it's in colour and HD quality, she's been able to give us a transcript of what was said between you.'

Tate locked eyes with Phillips over the top of the laptop screen. 'This is nonsense. There's no way any of this would stand up in court.'

Phillips flashed a thin smile. 'Oh, *I'm* aware of that, but I wonder if Melissa's business associate, Dominic Shanks, is.' She pulled the transcript from her files. 'I'm sure he'll be more than interested in this bit regarding the knife attack on Adam Hudson a week ago: '"Don't worry, Mum. I didn't do it. Shanks did." Melissa, you then replied with: "It was a reckless move." Freddie responds to that by saying, "The bitch got what was coming to her." Doesn't look good for Mr Shanks, does it?'

'Really, DCI Phillips. This is ridiculous,' said Tate, his tone arrogant. 'We have no idea what is being said on that video and neither do you. If this is all you've got, then I must insist you release my client immediately.'

Phillips glared at Tate. 'As you well know, your client can legally be detained for up to twenty-four hours, which by my watch means she'll be with us for at least another twenty-one. She's not going anywhere.' As a prop, the CCTV footage had served its purpose, so she closed the laptop and turned her attention back to Melissa, who at last appeared to be paying attention. 'You see, Melissa, whilst Mr Tate may well be correct in his assumption regarding the use of this CCTV footage, it's highly unlikely your friend Shanks next door knows that. I'm also quietly confident that, unlike you, he cannot afford expensive legal representation. In fact, he may indeed wave his right to counsel. It's not unheard of with people like him: you know, cocksure, arrogant and hot-headed. If I'm not mistaken, I'd say he fancies himself as a bit of gang-staaaar!' She deliberately dragged out the word to imitate the street vernacular.

Melissa shifted in her seat and took another drink of water, only this time her hand appeared to shake slightly as she replaced the cup on the table.

Phillips was getting to her. 'And I'm sure he'll be less than impressed with your description of him here, when you're discussing getting rid of the knife used in the attack. "Shanks is an idiot and can't be trusted." How do you think he'll take that?'

Melissa swallowed hard. 'No comment.'

Phillips allowed the room to fall silent, then made a point of making detailed notes in her pad. The information she was writing down was nothing new. It was all part of the game, to unnerve Melissa in the hope she might want to tell her side of the story to counter whatever Shanks may share in his own interview. When she was finished, she looked up and stared at Melissa once more. 'In the video, you said Freddie should do his time like a man and keep his mouth shut. What were you referring to, exactly?'

Melissa closed her eyes momentarily before opening them again and replying, 'No comment.'

Phillips reached into her file now and pulled out the photo of the peroxide blonde girl from the Boothroyd file. She slid it across the table. 'Recognise her?'

Melissa gazed down at the image but didn't respond.

'That's Archie Boothroyd's girlfriend at the time he was murdered.' Phillips passed over the photo of a young Melissa taken from Freddie's Facebook page. 'You'd have to say this is the same person. Wouldn't you agree?'

Melissa's head remained bowed as her eyes moved between the two photos.

'You told us you'd never been involved with Archie. Yet we have the testimony of one of the officers who investigated his murder stating that you were lovers at the time he was killed. And that you lived together. Apparently, for all the womanising he did, once Archie met *you,* there was only ever one woman in his life.'

Melissa looked up, and Phillips could have sworn her eyes were wet at the corners.

'You see, we have three identical unsolved murders. Two of them are directly linked to you, Melissa, and the third man to be killed, Mitchell Hodge, also worked for your family business. Some would say that's a coincidence, but the thing is – as any of my team will tell you – I don't believe in coincidences. Never have, never will.'

Phillips pulled two more printed images from the file and placed them in front of Melissa. She tapped the first image.

'Archie Boothroyd a few months before he was killed.' Then the second. 'Your son, Freddie, on his eighteenth birthday. The resemblance is remarkable.'

Melissa visibly tightened in the chair.

'We know Archie was Freddie's dad, Melissa. So why don't you do yourself a favour and tell us what's really been going on here? You know the truth about what happened to Archie, Paul and Mitchell, don't you?'

Melissa glanced at Tate, who offered the slightest shake of his head before she turned back to Phillips. 'No comment.'

Phillips stared into Melissa's eyes for a long, uncomfortable moment, then sighed. 'Very well. Have it your way. I guess we'll just have to see what Mr Shanks has to say about all this.'

'I'd like some time with my client in a private room, please,' said Tate.

'As is your right,' replied Phillips. 'One of the custody team will arrange that for you.' She turned to face the DIR. 'DCI Phillips terminating this interview at 9.03 p.m.'

52

Phillips made her way to the observation suite, where she joined Entwistle watching Jones and Bovalino as they interviewed Shanks.

'Well, she was chatty,' said Entwistle, referring to Melissa.

Phillips took a seat next to him. 'Hardly surprising. Tate will have wanted to know what we have before he comes up with a counter strategy.' She gestured towards the screen. 'How long's this been going?'

'Just started, boss.'

'Who's the solicitor with him?'

Entwistle looked down at his notes. 'The name's Craig Lawton, Legal Aid through Mullens Solicitors.'

'Mullens? The ambulance chasers? God help him.' Phillips scrutinised the young lawyer as he fiddled with his collar and shifted in his seat. He appeared nervous, and had the unmistakable posture of a graduate in his first job out of college.

'Jones laughed when he found out it was Lawton. He's dealt with him before and says he's pretty shitty.'

Phillips shook her head, knowing Jones would take full

advantage of the situation. 'Might as well be two against one in there.'

'Yeah. I have a funny feeling we might get a little more out of this one,' said Entwistle.

Phillips remained silent for a long moment as she stared at the screen, then turned her attention back to Entwistle. 'That's just given me an idea.'

'What you thinking?'

Phillips stared at the screen once more. 'I need you to go in and interrupt the interview. Be really obvious about it and make a point about saying that *I* need to speak to Jones and Bov *urgently*, then casually – almost as an aside – say it's something about new evidence. Ok?'

'Got it.' Entwistle got up from the chair and made his way to Interview Room Six.

Phillips watched on the monitor as Entwistle stepped inside and played his part perfectly. Jones paused the interview and, a few moments later, he and Bovalino exited stage-left, leaving a clearly worried Shanks looking to his less-than-proactive lawyer for support; support that didn't appear to be very forthcoming.

When the team arrived back in the observation suite, Phillips explained her new strategy. 'Nothing against you, Bov, but I need you to step out so I can take your place.'

The big man looked puzzled.

'Based on how shit Lawton seems, I have an idea of how we can use the CCTV to really leverage our position here.'

'Whatever you say, Guv,' said Bovalino.

'Great,' said Phillips, picking up her laptop. 'Jonesy, just follow my lead.'

'Of course,' said Jones.

They made their way back to Interview Room Six. Once inside, Phillips explained the change in personnel to the room – without explaining why – before restarting the DIR and repeating the same information for the purposes of the recording. Next, and in total silence, she slowly and deliberately set up the laptop so she could access the CCTV footage. Then she laid out her notepad and files on the desk in front of her. When she was ready, she looked Shanks straight in the eye. 'Why don't you tell me everything you know about the murders of Archie Boothroyd, Paul Bradley and Mitchell Hodge.'

Shanks's mouth fell open slightly and he stuttered slightly, 'Er...er...no comment.'

Phillips flashed a wry grin. 'Really? You're going to waste the chance to tell us your side of the story by going no comment?'

Shanks looked at Lawton, who once again seemed incapable of asserting his clients' needs in the situation.

Phillips continued. 'Let me tell you how this works, shall I, Shanks? Or would you prefer I call you Dominic?'

'Nobody calls me Dominic apart from my mum.'

'Shanks it is, then,' Phillips said enthusiastically. The question had been a deliberate ploy to get him to drop his guard slightly, and it had worked. 'Right, so, as I was saying, every man and his dog comes in here these days and goes for a no comment interview, because they think it gives them time to figure out what we've got on them. Sometimes it works and other times it doesn't. In your case, I can honestly say I think it's a bad idea. Wanna know why?'

Shanks sniffed, then shrugged his shoulders.

'I'll tell you why. You see, as you already know, Melissa Bradley is also in custody, and it's thanks to her that you're sat where you are. Because her and Freddie are trying to stitch you right up.' Phillips cued up the CCTV footage and turned the laptop round so Shanks and Lawton could see it, then pressed play. 'This is video captured this lunchtime at Hawk Green. There's no sound on it, but we've had it transcribed by a lip-reading expert. In this bit, Freddie is telling Melissa that you're the one who stabbed Adam Hudson during a knife attack in Chorlton last week. She initially blamed him, but he was super quick to correct her and point the finger at you.'

'You're lying. Freddie's not a grass,' said Shanks.

'Oh, he is, mate. And we've already seen just how little Melissa thinks of you in the custody suite, haven't we? Looked at you like you were shit on her shoe.'

Shanks shuffled in his seat and appeared agitated.

'This footage is blatant invasion of privacy. I doubt very much if it would hold up in front of a jury.' Lawton finally joined the party.

Phillips shrugged. 'It's a legitimate piece of intelligence gathering. We had reason to believe Melissa Bradley and her son Freddie were connected to three murders, and seconded the tapes to monitor what was being said. As it happens, they implicated your client in an attempted murder plot, so it's more than justified. At this very minute, we're applying for a warrant to search your client's home and car for the knife used in the attack.'

Shanks's face fell as those words landed.

'All that blood at the scene, Shanks. That's bound to have left trace evidence in your car, on your clothes and probably in your flat. Where I'm sure we'll find the weapon, won't we?' Phillips scrutinised Shanks's face and noted that he swallowed nervously. 'Yeah, you strike me as a man who likes to keep mementos of his work – because up until now you've been untouchable, haven't you? Well, not anymore. Once we go through your stuff and match your DNA to that found at the crime scene, you're going down for the attempted murder of Adam Hudson.'

Shanks glanced at Lawton, who was scribbling his pad.

Phillips had her foot on his throat now, and she wasn't about to let go. 'You ever been to Hawk Green, Shanks?'

He didn't respond.

'I checked your record, and I can see you did a bit of time in a young offenders' institute when you were a teenager.' Phillips chuckled. 'A holiday camp compared to maximum security, and *you're* looking at fifteen years, give or take. Fifteen years watching your back in the showers, sharing a cell with proper gangsters as opposed to the clowns you've surrounded yourself with. Wasting away on your own while Melissa and Freddie skip off into the sunset without a mark on them.'

'I ain't no grass, right,' said Shanks.

Phillips turned the laptop back to face her. She quickly found what she was looking for and spun it back to face them.

Shanks's and Lawton's eyes were once again drawn to the screen.

Phillips narrated what they were watching. 'In this bit of the video, Melissa says, "Shanks is an idiot and can't be trusted." Not very nice, is it?'

Shanks's jaw clenched as he stared at the video.

'And as I said, based on her reaction in the custody suite, Melissa clearly wants nothing to do with you going forward.' Phillips pulled out the photo of a young Melissa from the Boothroyd case and tapped on the picture. 'This is Melissa when she was Archie Boothroyd's missus. Originally, she claimed not to know Archie when he was murdered, but as we now know, they were lovers. That means Melissa was connected to all three murder victims: Boothroyd, Bradley and Hodge. It's now my firm belief that she was involved in each of the murders as well.'

Shanks looked up from the picture and his eyes appeared to dance in his head.

'*You know* what happened to them all, don't you, Shanks?'

Shanks coughed. 'I need a cigarette.'

'And you can have one, but first I need you to tell me what really happened to those three men.'

'What's in it for my client?' asked Lawton.

Phillips sat back and folded her arms. 'The chance to tell the truth for once.'

Lawton finally appeared to be growing in confidence. 'You mentioned charges of attempted murder. Can we talk about those?'

Phillips had to dig deep to keep her raw anger in check. The reality was, she wanted to hang Shanks for what he'd done to Adam, but she knew he was just the lackey. Freddie had ordered the hit, and she knew full well he would say whatever was necessary to ensure he never served a day for the knife attack. 'Not my call, but I can certainly put in a word with the investigation team.'

Lawton looked at Shanks, then back a Phillips. 'I need a moment alone with my client.'

'Very well.' After pausing the DIR, Phillips locked eyes with Shanks. 'The thing you need to remember in all this is that blood is thicker than water. Melissa and Freddie have the money to buy the best lawyers in town, plus connections in all the right places. It's the two of them against just you. If you don't start working with *us*, then you're on your own. If that happens and I had to put money on who out of the three of you will be going to prison – it's only going to end one way. You, doing a fifteen-stretch while they walk free. It's your call, Dominic. Remember the old saying, "The first one in gets the deal."'

JONES SHOWED Lawton and Shanks to a nearby, unmonitored, room. He returned to Interview Room Six a few minutes later and took the seat next to Phillips once more. 'Do you really think he's gonna go for it?'

Phillips shrugged. 'Your guess is as good as mine. Depends on how many of my assumptions I've got right about him. If he does, then he must fear what we'll find once we search his flat and car. It also depends on how green Lawton actually is. If I was Shanks, I'd go no comment and take my chances, but then again, I know just how little we've actually got on him right now. Shanks, however, clearly doesn't, which could work in our favour.'

'Well, fingers crossed, hey?' said Jones.

'And toes, mate.'

Thirty long minutes later, Jones was notified by one of the custody team that Lawton and Shanks were ready to return. He headed off to fetch them. After everyone had taken their seats once again, Phillips restarted the interview and the DIR.

Lawton cleared his throat before speaking, and affected a more upright posture as he attempted to appear in control. 'My client is willing to cooperate, dependent on the deal on offer.'

Phillips's heart jumped in her chest. *We got him.* 'A wise decision,' she said.

Shanks folded his arms and sniffed loudly.

Phillips turned her attention to Lawton. 'As you know, the sentence in every case is down to the Crown Prosecution Service and the judge who presides over that particular trial. That said, the report that is put forward to the court on behalf of the investigation team can – and often does – have a large bearing on the length of the sentence. If Mr Shanks fully cooperates and tells us what he knows about the murders of Archie Boothroyd, Paul Bradley and Mitchell Hodge, then we'll ensure the Serious Crimes Unit – the team investigating the stabbing of Adam Hudson – are made aware of the help he has offered us in regards those three murders.

I'm sure that will have a very positive impact on the severity of his sentence.'

Lawton said nothing for a moment, then leaned in and whispered to Shanks, who nodded a second later. 'Mr Shanks is willing to tell you what he knows.'

Phillips did her best to appear stoic, while inside she felt like getting out of the chair and dancing a jig.

It was Shanks's turn to lean into his lawyer's ear and whisper.

'Before we get into the detail,' said Lawton, 'is there any chance my client could have a cup of tea and sandwich?'

As far as Phillips was concerned, if he spilled the beans, he could have a night on the town, so a cheese butty and a cuppa from the canteen was an easy win.

Once the interview was suspended, Jones offered to pick up the rations. He returned ten minutes later with a vending machine ham and cheese sandwich and a steaming hot cup of tea, which he placed in front of Shanks.

As Shanks took his first mouthful, Phillips restarted the DIR. 'Ok. So, why don't we start with who really killed Paul Bradley?'

Shanks chewed loudly and with his mouth open. Table manners were clearly not his forte. 'Freddie,' he finally replied after swallowing the large bite.

Phillips recoiled slightly. '*Freddie* shot Paul?'

'Yeah.' Shanks took another bite.

'How do you know this?'

'Cos I was there.'

'So, you took part in the murder?' asked Phillips.

Shanks shook his head. 'No way, man! That was never part of the plan. That was all Freddie.'

'So, what *was* the plan?'

'To rough him up a bit. Freddie said it was his mum's idea.'

'Melissa ordered the hit on Paul?'

'Yeah.'

'Why?'

'Freddie reckoned it was revenge for killing Archie Boothroyd back in '93.'

Phillips glanced at Jones, whose frown matched her confusion. 'Are you saying Paul Bradley killed Boothroyd?'

Shanks took a long gulp of tea. 'Yep.'

'So, hang on. Melissa knew Paul killed Boothroyd, but waited almost thirty years to exact her revenge?'

'No. Apparently she only found out recently. Came out when her and Paul were arguing.'

'That must have been some fight,' said Phillips.

Shanks nodded. 'Freddie said his mum and dad hadn't been getting on for years because of him shagging about. Slept in different bedrooms and lived separate lives.'

'So why didn't she just divorce him?'

'Dunno. Freddie never said and I didn't ask. Anyway, Paul wanted to retire and enjoy his millions, and she thought he was going soft. She said they needed to make *more* money. That if he retired now, she'd have to cut back on her spending big time and she wasn't having that. He'd mentioned the idea of selling the business, and she wasn't having that either. Anyway, Bahmani got wind of all this and started throwing his weight around, trying to get the business for a lot less than it was worth. Melissa said he needed to be sent a message that the Bradleys' empire wasn't for sale. Paul told her it was his business, that he'd built it and he'd do what the fuck he liked with it.'

'That must have angered Melissa,' said Phillips.

'Apparently, yeah. Freddie said she told him half of the business was hers, that she'd helped him build it, but he laughed in her face and told her to get fucked. That's when she got really mad.'

'And Freddie was witness to all this?'

Shanks swallowed his latest mouthful. 'Yeah, he was in the next room listening when it all kicked off.'

'So, what happened next?'

'Apparently she got right up his face and started telling him the only reason he wanted to sell was because he'd lost his bottle because he was getting old. Called him a pussy and said she'd married the wrong gangster. That she wished it was Paul who'd been shot all those years ago instead of Archie. Because Archie was a proper man. He would never have let Bahmani push him around.'

Phillips sat forward. 'So how did Paul take that?'

Shanks produced a wide grin. 'Freddie says he proper kicked off, like. Totally lost the plot. Started shouting about how Boothroyd was a worthless piece of shit and a coward, and that he begged for his life before Paul shot him.'

'Wow. That must have come as a shock,' said Phillips.

'Too right,' replied Shanks. 'Freddie said his mum didn't believe him at first, but then he showed her the tooth.'

Phillips felt her eyes narrow. 'What tooth?'

'Boothroyd's. Paul had kept it all these years. In the safe, apparently.'

'Do you know where that tooth is now?' asked Phillips.

Shanks shrugged. 'He never said.'

'So then what happened?'

'Freddie said Melissa left the house and stayed in a hotel for a couple of days. Then, without warning, she came back and acted like nothing had happened. She never mentioned the argument to Paul again, and he didn't speak to her about it either. Then about a month later, she pulls Freddie to one side and tells him that Paul's not his real dad. That Archie Boothroyd was, and Paul had murdered Archie when she was pregnant with him.'

'How did he take that?' asked Phillips.

'Ah man, he was all over the place. I remember him getting smashed on coke for three days straight after she told him. I didn't know what was going on at the time, but I knew he was angry as fuck about something. He only ever got that shit-faced when he was properly pissed off.'

'So, when did you find out Paul wasn't actually Freddie's father?'

'A couple of weeks ago, I think. Freddie finally told me one night when he was trashed.'

'So, aside from the drug binge, what happened after she told him Archie was his real dad?'

Shanks took another gulp of tea. 'Melissa started getting into Freddie's head big time. Telling him Paul had lost the plot, that he was planning to sell the business and cut them both out, and that he needed sorting.'

'Was that when you and Freddie came up with the plan to kill him?'

Shanks shook his head vigorously. 'No way, man. Freddie said we were gonna fake a break in and rough Paul up a bit. Put on fake accents and pretend to be Bahmani so that Paul would get mad and finally get rid of Bahmani for good. I had no idea he was gonna shoot him until he pulled the bloody trigger.'

Phillips took a moment to process the information. 'So, who removed Paul's tooth.'

'Freddie. I had nothing to do with that weird shit either.'

'And who's idea was it to plant the gun in Bahmani's yard?'

'Melissa. That stuff was *all* Melissa. Listen, everyone thinks Paul was the brains in that family. No fucking way, man. It was always Melissa pulling the strings on *everything*. She was just really clever about it. Even Paul thought he was in charge, but he wasn't.'

'So, what about Mitchell Hodge? Did you and Freddie do that one too?'

'No. That was just Freddie. I wasn't even there, but when he got back after topping him, he was boasting like he was a proper gangster. Kept waving the gun at me, saying he'd heard Hodgey suspected his mum and him were involved in Paul's murder because of something Paul had said after the big argument with Melissa. I don't know what exactly Hodgey knew, but Freddie said he had to be stopped. So that's what he did.'

'And the gun that he used? Where is it now?'

Shanks paused for a moment and looked at Lawton, who nodded. 'At my flat. Freddie asked me to keep it for him.'

Phillips sat back and folded her arms. 'What? Are you telling me you stored a murder weapon that you *claim* you had nothing to do with in your flat? Come on, Shanks. I wasn't born yesterday. The conditions of you getting a deal rely on you telling us the truth.'

'I am. I swear, I had nothing to do with Hodge's death.'

'So why get involved after the fact? Why hide the murder weapon when it could come back to you?'

'You've met Freddie. The guy's unhinged. If I didn't, who's to say I wouldn't be the next one you found with a bullet in my brain and my teeth pulled out?'

Phillips leaned forward on the desk now. 'That doesn't make sense. All the intel we have suggests you and Freddie were thick as thieves. You were his lieutenant, his right-hand man. Why would he want to kill *you*?'

Shanks swallowed the final piece of sandwich. 'We're business associates and we got on, but we're not really mates. The guy's a psycho, man. I wasn't gonna fuck with him. I mean, look what he did to Paul and Hodgey? That was some sick shit, man.'

Phillips watched him silently for a long moment, looking

for any signs that he was lying. He seemed genuine enough, but she'd been doing this a very long time and knew better than to truly trust a criminal. 'And you're willing to testify to all this in court?'

'Yeah,' said Shanks, without a hint of emotion.

'And front-up for your part in the attack on Adam Hudson?'

Shanks nodded.

'For the purpose of the tape, the suspect nodded,' said Phillips. 'Ok. In that case, I'm terminating this interview at 10.52 p.m.'

Phillips and Jones marched in silence back to the observation suite.

'Blood hell, Guv! You're a genius!' said Bovalino as she walked through the door.

Phillips allowed herself a satisfied smile, then blew her lips as she dropped heavily into one of the chairs.

Entwistle was shaking his head. 'Seriously, I've never seen anything like that. He gave up everything without even being charged.'

Phillips blew her lips. 'Right, well, let's not congratulate ourselves just yet. We've still got a lot of work to do to corroborate his testimony, but it's a start.' She checked her watch. 'Legally he's required to get some rest now, but we can get onto the CPS in the morning and get an extension to hold him for a further twenty-four hours. That will give Cleverly and SCU more time to pull together what they need forensically to bring charges against him for the attack on Adam.'

'Sounds good, boss,' said Jones, his face and posture oozing fatigue.

'Look, it's late and we're all knackered. Let's go home and get back on it in the morning.'

Each of the men nodded.

Phillips rubbed her face with both hands for a moment before standing. 'If you'll excuse me, I need to go to the toilet.'

A couple of minutes later, she found herself in the empty ladies' room staring, at her reflection in the mirror. Without warning, her hands began to tremble, and she suddenly burst into floods of tears.

The events of the last few weeks had finally caught up with her: Adam's attack, the impending IPCC investigation, the dangerous game she'd played. Now, with Shanks admitting his guilt, and Freddie and Melissa in the frame for multiple murders, it was as if the walls she'd put up to protect herself had tumbled down.

Moving into one of the stalls, she took a seat on the toilet lid and allowed the tears to flow unabated. Five minutes later, when she'd finally stopped crying, she headed back to the sink, turned on the cold tap, and bent forward to splash water on her face. She repeated the process over and over until her skin felt numb. Finally, she turned off the tap and dabbed her face dry with paper towels.

Gazing at her reflection once more, she hardly recognised the broken woman who stared back at her. 'What the hell have you been doing, Jane?' she whispered to the empty room.

Just then, her phone began to vibrate in her pocket. Fishing it out, she saw Carrie was calling. Her heart jumped into her throat. 'Carrie? What is it?' she asked, her voice saturated with panic.

'It's Adam. He's awake.'

53

By the time she arrived at the Manchester Royal Infirmary, Phillips had zero recollection of the journey to get there. It was only when she reached the secure outer doors to the ICU that it really hit her. Adam was actually awake! Until that moment, all she'd focused on was getting to his side as quickly as possible. Now, as the automatic door buzzed open and she stepped inside, reality rushed to greet her. The unique smells that hung in the air of the ward, which she'd become accustomed to over the last week, suddenly felt pervasive; every sound that echoed around her seemed louder and clearer than before. It was then that she realised, for the first time, just how much she'd blocked out during her previous visits; her self-preservation had clearly been working overtime.

As she approached the door to Adam's room, excitement and fear mingled. What if he'd woken up a different person? What if the damage to his body was still too much for him to survive? Was this going to be a joyful reunion or the beginning of a torturous goodbye? Her head spun with emotion, and her stomach churned as she stepped inside.

Adam lay motionless in bed as Carrie, sitting at his side, sobbed, her eyes locked shut.

Phillips stopped in her tracks. She was too late. He was gone.

Suddenly Carrie's eyes opened, and tears streaked down her cheeks as she locked eyes with Phillips. And then, without warning, a soft smile cracked across her face. 'Jane!' She shook Adam's hand. 'Adam, Jane's here.'

For a split second, Phillips felt as if her world had stopped spinning and she was hanging in space, staring at the scene. Then Adam opened his eyes and turned his head slightly to face her. His mouth turned up at the corners as he found her.

Phillips rushed to his side. 'Adam! Oh my God, I thought I'd lost you,' she said as she wrapped her arms around him.

'He can't speak because of the ventilator,' said Carrie, 'but hopefully they can take that out tomorrow.'

Phillips pulled back far enough so she could see his face, and smiled as tears of joy streamed from her eyes. 'Oh, babe, we were so worried about you.'

Adam grabbed her hand and squeezed it tightly as his eyes closed once more.

Phillips took a seat at his side, keeping his hand in a tight grip. 'I'm so sorry for all this, Adam. This was all down to me. If it wasn't for my job, none of this would have happened.'

Adam's eyes remained closed.

Carrie blew her nose in a tissue, then smiled as she stood. 'Why don't I give you both a minute, hey?' she said, then left the room.

Phillips pulled Adam's hand up to her cheek and leaned in closer. When she spoke, her voice was tender. 'I love you, Adam, more than anything in the world. Anything. And I'm done, babe. The job, MCU, all of it. It's over. I can't risk losing you again. Not ever. I'm handing in my resignation first thing tomorrow.'

Adam's eyes opened and his lips moved slightly as he tried to say something, but a moment later they fell shut again as he drifted into sleep.

Phillips gazed at his beautiful face as love for him made her body ache. It was like nothing she had ever known, and for the first time ever, she understood the double-edged sword of loving someone so much that it hurt. In that moment she made a promise to herself, to change the way she lived her life. She'd been given so many chances to be happy but had ignored them, choosing instead to focus all her energy on the job. Well, that part of her life was finished. Now was her time to start over, and she wasn't going to let anyone – or anything – stop her from doing just that.

54

FIVE MONTHS LATER - NOVEMBER 5TH

Phillips filled her travel cup from the coffee pot on the kitchen bench, then screwed the lid on tightly. Today was forecast to be the coldest day of the year so far, and she needed help to keep warm on her journey into the city. Sadly, as iconic as the classic Mini was, the ancient heating system left a lot to be desired during a cold British winter. After packing her bag and pulling it onto her shoulder, she moved across the kitchen to where Adam sat at the breakfast table, reading the paper. She kissed him on the cheek. 'What time do I need to be home?'

'The estate agent's coming at one.'

'And he's doing the photos today, is he?'

'Yep.'

'Ok. Well, I'll try and get back in time to tidy up the bedroom before he comes.'

'Don't worry. I can sort that.'

Phillips punched him playfully on his upper arm. 'Hey. You're supposed to be taking it easy. Doctor's orders, remember.'

'Stop fussing, babe. I'm more than capable of making the

bed without keeling over. And in case you forgot, *I'm* a doctor. I know what I can and can't do.'

Phillips smiled. 'This is really happening, isn't it?'

Adam stared at her with his big blue eyes. 'Are you absolutely sure you want to do this? We don't have to buy something else. We could just stay here. I wouldn't mind, you know.'

'You try and stop me. This will always be my house, and that's not fair on you. No. It's time to move on and get a place together.' Phillips flashed a smile. 'I'm a big girl now. I can cope.'

Adam returned her smile. 'Thanks, babe. That means a lot. So, what time are you meeting Carter?'

Phillips glanced at her watch. 'In forty-five minutes, so I'd better get a move on.'

'And he still hasn't told you what it's about?'

'No. And frankly, I don't care. I'm only going in as a courtesy.' Phillips grabbed her keys from the kitchen bench. 'I need to get going or I'm gonna be late. I'll see you later, ok?' She marched out of the kitchen.

Just as she pulled open the front door, Adam called, 'Drive safe, babe! Love you!'

Phillips stopped in her tracks and turned back. 'Love you too!' she called back, then stepped outside into the cold morning air.

Exactly forty-five minutes later, Phillips wandered across Albert Square and passed the Town Hall towards Caffè Corretto, where she was due to meet Superintendent Carter. As she approached, she spotted him sitting outside under one of the large gas heaters.

He spotted her and beckoned her over, and stood as she reached the table. 'Jane. You're looking well.'

'That's what getting enough sleep does for you,' she said playfully.

He motioned for her to sit. 'Thanks for coming. What can I get you?'

'I'll have a latte please.'

Carter placed the order with the nearest waiter, then turned his full attention back to her. 'So, how's the sabbatical going? We haven't heard from you in a while.'

'It's good. I'm enjoying it. I don't think I ever realised how burnt out I'd become. The pressure of the job, the weird hours, dealing with scum, Fox. Everything had taken its toll.'

Carter took a sip of what looked like an espresso. 'Yeah, this job can certainly eat you up if you're not careful.'

'Well, I wasn't, and it definitely did.'

'And how's Adam?'

Phillips felt a smile spread across her face. 'He's great.'

Carter smiled too. 'I can tell.'

'He's doing really well, actually. Especially with his physio. The doctors are really pleased with him.'

'That's wonderful.'

Still not massively comfortable with sharing the details of her personal life, Phillips decided to change the subject. 'So, I take it you're here for the big Task Force announcement this morning?'

'Indeed. Fox has invited the great and the good for the big reveal in the Town Hall at ten. She wants all her senior officers, as she put it, "suited and booted and standing tall."'

'Sounds very Fox.'

'Doesn't it?'

Just then, the waiter appeared and placed Phillips's latte on the table.

'Did you hear about Shanks's sentencing?' asked Carter.

Phillips took a sip the hot coffee. 'Yeah, Cleverly called me to let me know. Ten years was less than I was hoping for, but then again, the lighter sentence was part of his deal, I suppose.'

Carter nodded. 'He really came up trumps for us on Melissa.'

'Jones told me all about it. Fingered her for money laundering, racketeering, extortion. All committed under a veil of respectability as a Cheshire housewife.'

'Quite a woman,' said Carter.

'One hell of an actress, more like. In all my years, I've never met anyone who managed to play the grieving widow so convincingly, when all the time she'd plotted to kill him, and had been planning a secret life without him for years.'

'Did Jones tell you about her hidden investment portfolio?'

'Yeah,' replied Phillips. 'Over five million in different share options. She had us all fooled.'

'And Freddie? I'm still trying to figure out what on earth possessed him to keep Bradley's and Hodge's teeth. It was idiotic.'

'Arrogance,' said Phillips. 'Plain and simple arrogance. He thought he was untouchable.'

Carter drained his espresso and set the cup down. 'Well, thank God he did. Helped us get guilty verdicts on each of their murders, which was a result.'

Phillips smiled. 'Yeah. It's nice when their stupidity makes our job easy. Rare, but nice all the same.'

'And what about his mother, carrying Boothroyd's tooth around in her luggage?'

'I'm putting that one down to love,' said Phillips. 'Archie was a bad lad back in the day, but he was the father of her only child and she still loved him. Even after all these years.'

'Love makes people do strange things,' said Carter.

Phillips nodded. 'Yeah, it really does.'

'Speaking of strange things, did you see Bahmani's verdict last week?'

'Not personally, but again, Jonesy called me. Kidnap and murder, hey?'

'Yep. Again, why he used his own compactor to get rid of Shawn Harvey's body, we'll never know.'

Phillips frowned. 'I have to say, I thought that was a bit of an odd one as well. He'd always been so careful. But then, maybe his arrogance got the better of him too. I mean, kidnapping in broad daylight was certainly a new thing for him, and the shooting at the Bradleys' was a right cock-up from start to finish.'

'Like you say, he'd been getting away with it for so long, he probably thought he was untouchable too.'

Phillips took another mouthful of coffee. 'Yeah, maybe.'

They both fell silent for a moment.

'So why am I really here, Harry?'

Carter chuckled. 'Always the detective, hey Jane?'

'It's been in my blood for over twenty years, and it's going to take a while to work it out. Seriously, though, what's this about?'

'Well,' said Carter as he sat forward in his chair, 'I was wondering if you'd given any thought to coming back?'

Phillips blew her lips as she folded her arms across her chest. 'In all honesty, no.'

'*Could* you give it some thought?'

'I really don't know, Harry. I'm really enjoying being away from all the shit and spending more time with Adam. I finally feel like I have a life. And after what happened to him, I'm not sure I could risk putting him in danger again.'

'I get that, Jane,' replied Carter. 'But the attack on Adam was a complete one-off. We've never had a case of an officer's family being targeted before, and I very much doubt it would ever be allowed to happen again.'

'I know, but it's not just that.'

'So, what is it?'

'The truth is, we got lucky, Harry. On the Bradley and Hodge murders, I mean. As you said yourself at the time, I made a right mess of the investigations—'

'Look, about that,' Carter cut in. 'I really didn't cover myself in glory back then. I could have been more supportive, considering what was going on in your life. I made it all about me and my career, and that wasn't on.'

'But you were right. I *did* fuck it up, and I put the careers of each of my team in jeopardy – including yours.'

'And you also pulled a rabbit out of the hat when it mattered most.'

'But how long can I keep doing that, Harry? How long before I really screw up and the damage can't be fixed?'

Carter sat back and drummed his fingers on the table. 'Look. The reality is, Jones is doing a great job as acting DI, but he's not you. Don't get me wrong, he's a bloody brilliant copper, but you're *exceptional* and we miss you. Plus, Cleverly is trying to poach Entwistle to be part of his new Task Force team.'

'I heard Steve got the big gig. Rather him than me.'

Carter tilted his head. 'Why do you say that? It was a big promotion for Cleverly.'

'Because the Task Force is Fox's baby, and a very public baby, with *her* reputation attached to it. Which means she'll be all over that team for at least the next couple of years. You know what she's like to work closely with. Does that sound like a fun job to you?'

'Well, when you put it like...'

'Personally, I couldn't think of anything worse.'

Carter checked his watch. 'Well, speaking of she who must be obeyed, time's ticking on. I'd better be getting across to the Town Hall.' He stood, and Phillips did the same.

Stepping around the table, he leaned in and embraced

her. 'Will you at least think about what I said? We really do miss you.'

'I'll think about it, Harry, but like I say, don't hold your breath. I've finally realised there's more to life than Major Crimes.'

Carter produced a soft smile. 'Thanks, Jane. Well, whatever you decide, look after yourself. And please give Adam my love, won't you?'

'I will.'

Carter buttoned up his overcoat before picking up his briefcase and heading off.

'Oh. Harry?' Phillips called after him.

He stopped and turned back.

'Good luck with Fox.'

He smiled. 'Thanks. Take care, Jane.'

'And you, Harry. And you.'

ACKNOWLEDGMENTS

This book would not have been possible without the help of some amazing people.

My wife, Kim, who has never once told me to get a 'real job' and never falters in her support of me living my dream as a fulltime writer.

My amazing son, Vaughan, who inspires me to be the best I can, every day.

Zachary Eve, my seven-year-old nephew, who convinced me to call it *Deadly Night,*

Carole Lawford, ex-CPS Prosecutor and Lambo; once again your guidance on British Law was invaluable in navigating this complex story.

Senior Sister Angela Wilson who offered hands-on knowledge of all things medical.

Jo Robertson, the person I trust to read my manuscripts before anyone else.

My coaches, Donna Elliot and Cheryl Lee, from 'Now Is Your Time', and Fabio at 'Fabio Mazzieri Coaching'. I'm a better writer because of you.

Thanks to my publishing team of Brian, Jan, Garret,

Claire and Laurel. Your support and attention to detail is second to none.

Special mention must also go to my good friend, Stuart Barrie, who inadvertently inspired this story.

And finally, thank you to my readers for reading *Deadly Night*. If you could spend a moment to write an honest review, no matter how short, I would be extremely grateful. They really do help readers discover my books.

Best wishes,

Owen

www.omjryan.com

ALSO BY OMJ RYAN

DEADLY SECRETS

(A crime thriller introducing DCI Jane Phillips)

DEADLY SILENCE

(Book 1 in the DCI Jane Phillips series)

DEADLY WATERS

(Book 2 in the DCI Jane Phillips series)

DEADLY VENGEANCE

(Book 3 in the DCI Jane Phillips series)

DEADLY BETRAYAL

(Book 4 in the DCI Jane Phillips series)

DEADLY OBSESSION

(Book 5 in the DCI Jane Phillips series)

DEADLY CALLER

(Book 6 in the DCI Jane Phillips series)

DEADLY NIGHT

(Book 7 in the DCI Jane Phillips series)

DEADLY CRAVING

(Book 8 in the DCI Jane Phillips series)

DEADLY JUSTICE

(Book 9 in the DCI Jane Phillips series)

Printed in Great Britain
by Amazon

22433869R00199